Two Chances

Elite Escorts MM 2

Lynn Burke

Two Chances

I joined Elite Escorts MM as an eff you to my cheating ex-fiancé. My job offers me lucrative releases and also protects me from experiencing that kind of pain ever again.

Jaded AF, the last thing I need is another man prying his way into my life and mind...but Detective James Jenner—JJ—is relentless.

He's also hot as hell, a tall drink of water I thirst for.

Like a hurricane, he constantly batters against my weakening walls, but same as my ex, JJ will never put me first. His loyalties lie elsewhere.

I know better than to go outside EEMM when I need to clear my head, but old wounds rip open, leaving me vulnerable. Wanting validation and genuine affection, I cave to the magnetic pull between us.

But his faithfulness to another lays waste to the seed of hope pushing through the cracks of my defenses.

Will my reinforced barriers stand firm when JJ reveals his heart? Or will I find the strength to trust that a second chance at love is possible?

Chapter 1

Kellen

I couldn't sleep.

Big surprise.

An hour before the sun crested the eastern horizon, I quit trying and hopped onto Route 95, heading to my old stomping grounds for a few days. With it being a Sunday morning, traffic was a nonissue, and I made it out of Boston pretty damn quickly.

Mom's birthday breakfast wouldn't be for a few hours, but I'd been ready to disappear into the sticks of Maine to decompress like I did every couple of months.

My time as an escort for the gay branch of Elite was easy money and enjoyable so far, but I definitely missed my family and the solitude found outside the city. I'd signed on with the escort service as a blatant *fuck you* to my ex who'd cheated on me right before our wedding almost three years ago. He'd left me for a side dish I hadn't known about, and the debt we'd accrued in planning the exchanging of our vows had landed in my lap.

Fucking asshole.

Every night I got on my knees to suck dick for an

EEMM client, lubed up my cock to breach a needy hole, or offered up my ass for another man filled me with a sense of bitter righteousness and satisfaction.

Because fuck Xavier, fuck relationships, and fuck my broken heart.

That *time heals all wounds* saying? Bullshit. Two and a half years had passed since I'd walked into our bedroom to find my fiancé, who'd never bottomed for me, with a dick lodged up his ass, his legs wrapped around a back that wasn't mine.

"Fuck." I scrubbed a hand over my face, wishing yet again that I could erase the image of his infidelity burned into my memory. The damned sight was still vivid in color and sound, like a movie playing before my eyes. The side dish's waxed, twink ass flexing as he thrust. My fiancé begging him to give him more.

Harder, sweetheart. Deeper. Love having your dick in me.

"Jesus fucking Christ! Enough already!" I growled at myself and stretched my neck side to side since I didn't have anything nearby I could punch to drown out Xavier's echoing words. They continued to live in my head no matter how hard I fought to forget them.

Teeth clenched, I stared through the windshield, not getting the blessed peacefulness heading out of the city should have brought me.

Usually, escaping the constant reminders of my ex and the life we'd had there proved a great distraction. Xavier had never been about countryside living, and I'd gladly moved back to Boston to be with him after our long-distance relationship had begun to strain.

Never should have left Maine for a guy who'd seemed

too good to be true. It turned out he wasn't fucking good at all.

I'd lived in Boston years earlier for college. That was where I'd first met Micah, Elite's owner. We'd kept in touch somewhat once I'd returned home after graduation. He'd reached out to me just weeks after Xavier had broken my heart, and I'd hopped aboard the gay branch of Elite he'd wanted to test out.

I'd ended up staying in the city. Gladly. Happy in my vindictiveness to fuck as many men as often as possible.

The Welcome to Maine sign twitched my lips upward for the first time since I opened my eyes in the predawn darkness, and I released a slow exhale, imagining all the negativity of Xavier washing away as I drove over the bridge.

Family came to mind every time I saw that sign. Same as a warm, genuine hug given out of true affection I hadn't had in a while, my home state's greeting soothed the clenching in my guts.

Unlike my ex, my family loved me. Hard stop. No conditions. No secrets and no fucking lies.

I would be seeing all of the Roberts clan shortly, which was one hell of a reason to smile. As the third of four grown-ass children though, I should have been settled down like the rest of them with two-point-five kids trailing along after me and making me rip my hair out. I thought I'd found the love of my life—

Enough.

I inhaled until it hurt and slowly emptied my lungs again, determined to put aside the shitty memories in exchange for a little peace and quiet. Well, not exactly *quiet* with my nieces and nephews who would be running around Mom and Dad's. Four days of rest among people who loved me as-is would settle my insides so I could return to the work they didn't judge me for.

Elite paid well, and I felt hella satisfied fucking random clients to get back at Xavier even if he didn't know I did it. I had plenty of cash to do whatever the hell I wanted thanks to hiring my body out to bring others pleasure, but I also enjoyed my job.

And since I had zero plans of ever allowing my emotions to get tangled up in relationship-type bullshit again, Elite was the best way for me to hook up and keep my heart safe.

Once I exited the major highway, I turned off my AC and rolled down all the windows. Fresh, too-warm air whipped through my SUV, and I breathed in the scent of summer, contentment finally sneaking into my soul as it always did whenever I went back to my roots.

The old Maine farmhouse my family had been living in for three generations sat off a side road a couple of miles outside of Nodhead Falls, and a grin spread over my face the second it came into view. My older brother Jacob had helped Dad repaint the entire thing the summer before, the white clapboards blinding in the sun hitting it head-on.

We'd joked as kids about the sprawling additions that had been added over the generations to keep our ancestors from having to brave the cold in winter. The main house connected to a mud/laundry room, then another section had been taken over by the grandchildren and named *Play-Time*. That area attached directly to a garage. Another building spanned the distance from there to the barn and housed most of mom's gardening shit.

As young children when bored in wintertime, my siblings and I would race from the upstairs front corner of the house and through every part of the sprawling home until tagging the back wall of the barn, our breath fogging in front of our faces, the scent of cow and pig shit filling our noses.

Memories of those easier days when no responsibilities lay over any of us made an achy warmth spread through my chest. With five bedrooms and a finished basement, the house had plenty of space for the entire Roberts clan to crash and reminisce together.

As usual, I was the last man to arrive.

I hadn't called ahead to let my parents know what time I would show up because with how all of us rose earlier than the sun—nieces and nephews included—they would be fine with my getting there before the normal nine o'clock breakfast tradition we'd had for years.

The second I parked alongside my brother's minivan on our parents' driveway, the house's door pulled inward, and people began to spill out onto the porch. Kids jostled each other down the stairs, shrieking and laughing.

"Uncle!" voices hollered, filling me up with the kind of happiness I'd been needing.

Grinning like a fool, I hopped from my SUV and eyed the nine children headed my way. My oldest nephew, Brian, reached me first, a spitting image of me at fifteen with dark hair and hazel eyes.

He threw his arms around me and hugged me tight, and not for the first time, I thanked whatever God there might be that Brian had never gone through the hormonal *don't touch me* phase most teenage guys did.

Brian stood near my six-two height, and although he'd filled out a bit since shooting up the summer before, he still had a long way to reach my muscle mass.

"Still lifting?" I asked, slapping his back.

"You know it." He stepped away, grinning while the

younger kids swarmed around me, some hanging on my legs, others trying to hug whatever body part they could grasp hold of.

Chuckling, I ruffled Brian's hair. "Can't wait to see you on the field this fall."

His face flushed. "Unless some freshman shows up with a better arm, I'll be starting as quarterback this year."

"Damn right you will!"

I relented to the needy hands of those smaller than Brian and knelt to offer love all around to the rest of the Roberts grandkids.

A million questions shot out, the kids especially asking about goodies I usually gifted to everyone when I visited, mainly candy, and I promised I'd brought along the normal smorgasbord they could share—after breakfast.

Mom stood at the top of the stairs, Dad to her right. She'd gone fully gray but didn't look a year over sixty. Dad's shoulders had yet to stoop, his hazel-green eyes I'd inherited as sharp as ever.

Glancing at my siblings with their spouses, a strange pang shot through my chest. Xavier's cheating had emptied me to the point I merely existed with no one to call my own like they all had.

My oldest sister Sarah had Fred behind her, his arms wrapped around her waist. My brother Jacob and his wife Amy held hands, connected physically as always. My baby sister Suzi looked like a beached whale ready to pop for the third time in three years thanks to her husband Donnie and his determined swimmers. None of their kids had been planned, but they couldn't be happier as evidenced by the glow on both their faces.

Then there was me.

Single as fuck because the one person I'd finally found

and considered worthy of settling down with went out and sat on a dick that satisfied him more than the idea of mine.

I forced my faltering grin back into place and climbed the porch stairs.

"Happy birthday, Mom." I wrapped her up in my arms, my nose filling with the scent of vanilla and spices. "Tell me someone else made the cinnamon roll cake this year," I said before kissing her cheek.

She squeezed my hand, her eyes bright with happiness. "The day I let your father into my domain is the day I'm six feet under."

"Don't talk like that," I muttered and gave my dad a side hug.

"Welcome home, son." He patted my back, and I moved on to greet my siblings.

With how everyone loved on me, it was like I only got to the farm once a year.

It had only been two months since I'd last seen them all for Dad's birthday breakfast, but I wouldn't complain about the abundance of affection shown among us. There had never been a lack of physical touch, and while we were normal like every other family with bickering, misunderstandings, and grudges here and there, love was our foundation built by Mom and Dad.

I counted my blessings while we trampled inside and out of the July humidity, telling myself that I *wasn't* alone. That I was loved—and deserved every bit of it too. But sitting down at my parents' massive dining room table and listening to the younger kids crowded around the kitchen table through the archway made my chest ache for more.

Don't even go there. Just enjoy the free cock and balls, and live happily ever after without all the angst and bullshit relationships bring.

Man, woman, I hadn't ever been choosy when seeking out my forever person. Dick and pussy riled me up in equal measures, although I tended toward men back in my dating days. Since signing on as Elite Escort's first queer guy in their MM branch, I'd been perfectly content with dick alone.

I'd labeled myself bisexual back in high school, and thankfully, neither of my parents nor my siblings gave a shit how I identified when they were all straight. It had been a boy in a tux who'd accompanied me to the prom at the high school we'd had to bus to for four years. We'd gotten a lot of bull from the conservative rednecks that lived in our area, but I hadn't ever been one to care what others thought.

Until my wedding day approached and I was left on my own to notify every single person on the guest list that there would be no exchanging of vows.

I'd given a shit *that* day. Never had I felt such utter humiliation and a sense of insecure embarrassment. The topping on that cake of emotional turmoil was the barely beating heart inside my chest that still felt knifed even though it had long ago bled out.

Pushing aside thoughts of the past came easier when surrounded by my family, thank fuck. We got caught up on the latest gossip—all three of my siblings had settled in or near Nodhead Falls. I couldn't give a rat's ass about half the people they socialized with, more interested in my brother, Fred, and Donnie talking about their fishing trip the weekend before I hadn't been able to join in.

We had a camp farther east on the Androscoggin River —a fisherman's paradise. Loaded with trout and smallmouth bass, the rushing water supplied dinner damn near every night whenever we needed a respite from reality.

It had been a hot minute for me though.

Mom blew out the candles on her cinnamon bun "cake", a 13x9 pan of gooey deliciousness she'd baked herself same as every year. Another pan sat in the kitchen to feed the ravenous piranha grandchildren.

"So how's my little love?" Mom asked, and I shook my head, unable to help my smirk. She'd been calling me that for as long as I could remember, never mind that I'd grown to tower over her.

"Good, Mom."

"Don't you lie to me, Kellen Christopher Roberts."

I snorted and shoved a bite of her birthday cake between my lips.

"Have you seen that asshole lately?" my brother Jacob asked.

Mom elbowed him. "Language," she reminded him, tipping her head toward the kitchen and the little ears that picked up everything.

"Sorry," he muttered out of habit, his concerned focus still on me.

"No, I haven't," I answered. "His friends remained his when we split. Can't say I miss any of them—or him for that matter."

"Good riddance," my baby sister Suzi said, her eyes blazing with hormonal bitchiness.

She'd always been my champion even though she was a year younger than me. She had more spit and vinegar than any woman I knew, and I could admit to feeling downright thrilled when she'd gotten all riled up about Xavier being a lying, cheating whore and made everyone who'd been invited to our wedding aware of his actions.

"Take it easy, Suz," Donnie said, running his hand over her large belly.

She huffed and swatted at his fingers, shooing him

away. "I'm fine," she snipped. "I'll be even better when this third boy you planted inside me gets the hell out so I can breathe again."

I chuckled and filled my mouth with Mom's kickass cinnamon roll cake. Three kids in three years—I didn't know what the fuck Suzi and Donnie were thinking not using protection. Obviously the two of them were well on their way to having a football team of their own. Had they met earlier in life, they'd have had one already.

"How's business?" Sarah asked, and I snorted, kicking her foot beneath the table where she sat across from me.

"You mean my volunteering at the vet clinic?" I asked about how I spent most of my daytime hours when I wasn't in the gym or sitting by myself in my apartment when my few friends were busy.

She rolled her eyes. "No," she half-sang her reply. "I'm glad you're putting all those farm chores we were forced to do as kids to good use, but you know what I'm talking about."

My whole family was aware of what I did to make the money that had fixed up the cabin last year and had started nice little savings accounts for all my nieces and nephews, bun in the oven included.

"Can't complain," I finally answered her question.

"Aren't you tired of...well, the lack of intimacy?" Amy, my sister-in-law asked quietly. She was the romantic of the group, and when she wasn't connected at the hip with Jacob, she had her nose in a smut-filled book.

"I have zero interest in getting involved with anyone," I answered honestly. "Man or woman." Everyone at the table was aware of how deeply Xavier had wounded me. Ours wasn't a family who kept secrets or emotions to ourselves. Empathy ran deep, often to the point of weariness.

"So Brian's going to be the starting quarterback this year," I tossed out, needing a change of topic before my mind slid back into the dumps.

My nephew grinned down the table at me, and the guys started talking stats and college scholarships in a matter of seconds exactly as I'd expected they would.

Mom caught my eye, her sad smile hitting me hard. She was aware I still hurt—always had that sixth sense when her children suffered.

I forced my lips upward, attempting to put her mind at ease like I did whenever my thoughts overran with the asshole who'd torn apart my heart. *"I'm good,"* I mouthed her way.

Her steady gaze told me she didn't believe me.

I struggled to convince myself too.

Chapter 2

JJ

"**M**ove your hairy ass."

I burrowed my face into Alex's neck, hating that not a hint of intimacy lingered in his tone. "Just one more minute," I begged, every muscle in my naked body draped over his exhausted from our fucking.

"Seriously, JJ, you're squishing me," he added, tapping at my shoulder to get me to move off him. "Can't. Breathe."

I only had maybe twenty pounds on Alex, the fucking liar.

Heaving a sigh, I kissed his sweaty skin and tried to stay in the euphoric feeling from a moment before. My semi still lodged in his ass, his heels on the backs of my thighs, and his cum smeared between our abs. Heaven on fucking earth. My escape.

"You can have your freedom," I finally spoke, hiding the disappointment from my voice as usual. Alex hated to cuddle. He came over and got off. Nothing more, nothing less.

My best friend shifted a bit to kiss my forehead while ruffling my hair. "You're so good to me."

"I would do anything for you," I reminded him needlessly.

We'd had the same conversation countless times in our ten-plus years of being lovers, and while Alex filled a hole in my life, he wasn't aware of the full scope of my feelings for him.

We'd been friends since childhood when I'd had no family but a mother who worked around the clock to provide for us. I'd seen Alex through his drug addiction after college, helped him get clean, and soaked up his undying thankfulness. I'd also stood beside him on his wedding day, my heart breaking as he spoke vows to the person I'd dreamed of being.

I'd hinted at wanting more in the early days of hooking up when we were both single, but he'd laughed me off. Told me he would never settle down.

Then he'd met Teresa, and any hopes I'd held onto had been shattered like fine china against a brick wall.

But with him being the love of my life, what could I do but continue to support him? Alex claimed that were it not for me, he wouldn't have his wife and their two boys.

Unrequited feelings hurt like fuck, but I always put him first because that was what love did.

Lucky for both of us, his wife was also bisexual and had insisted on an open relationship prior to their marriage. She had a girlfriend, and Alex was free to fuck around with guys when the mood struck for a little rough sex. While his wife was aware of our hooking up, we didn't have an intimate connection outside sex—his wishes, definitely not mine.

And ever since our first drunken, sexual encounter, I'd been a goner. Lost in love and lust for the heart of the one man I could never have. Alex had a hold on me that bordered on obsession, and he oftentimes exploited my loyalty.

But I never complained. Having Alex all up in my space one night every weekend kept loneliness at bay since I had no other family to speak of. His presence filled up the silence in my house that welcomed me home every evening after slaving away for the city of Boston.

Thoughts of work trickled back into my satiated brain, and I shifted completely off Alex, holding onto the condom as I slid from his warm, wet hole.

He grimaced. "Fuck."

"Yeah, lover." I kissed his chest before settling onto my haunches. "I know."

Alex fingered his ass, soothing the gape I'd left behind after fucking him hard and deep, exactly as he'd begged for. "You weren't kidding about needing release," he muttered with a chuckle.

I rid my dick of the condom, tied it off, and nudged his thigh with more force than necessary. "Shower."

He grumbled and rolled, burying his face in my pillow. Fucker loved my bed but hated snuggling or anything that suggested intimacy outside physical release. "Don't wanna."

I slapped his ass cheek. "Then go home and crawl into your bed smelling like sweat and cum."

"Teresa won't care. She was meeting up with Janie tonight and will have pussy breath."

I didn't understand their marriage but wasn't about to complain since I got to reap the benefits of their being poly.

"I gotta get up in a few hours," I reminded Alex since his laziness would only hurt my heart even more, knowing I couldn't wrap my body around his and fall asleep holding onto the man I loved.

"Fuck." He grunted and rolled, his baby blues peering

up at me where I stood beside the bed, used condom between two fingers. "How's the case coming along?"

Exactly what I didn't want to think about, which was why the fucker had brought it up. Direct my focus on work so I would need him to help me forget again.

"Get dressed and lock the door behind you." I headed toward my bathroom, my mind starting to run.

While I loved my job as a detective, I needed to shut down my goddamn brain every night. Too many facts and questions raced through my head while sitting in my silent living room on the six out of seven nights a week I didn't have Alex to distract me.

Hot water pelted my back, and I leaned against the shower's tile wall, head hanging, eyes closed as the heat soaked into my exhausted muscles.

I loved seeing criminals go down and pay for their crimes. Nothing satisfied me like connecting dots and finding the evidence left behind like an obscure breadcrumb trail that led to an asshole's demise.

But my latest mind-fuck atop the trial I was ready to testify in the following week?

A case that wasn't yet something I could fully pursue because I still waited for the victim to decide on pressing charges.

I'd been up too damn long since the call had come in Saturday night about an assault in an alleyway right outside one of Boston's downtown luxury hotels. Then came the gunshots in the ballrooms moments later that had allowed me to continue my first investigation when I doubted the two events were even connected.

The man who had gotten the shit kicked out of him had named his attacker the afternoon before, and I'd slept all of three hours since. Joseph Delaney III. The young rich punk had issues with the law before—

My shower door snicked open, and I heaved a heavy exhale at seeing Alex's cock already hard and sheathed up. "I need some shut eye, Alex," I stated quietly.

He grasped my ass and knelt behind me. "I'm not done with you yet." Water rained down over his head, but he shoved his scruffy face between my cheeks and lapped over my hole.

"Fuck." I grunted as his tongue breached my ring, and my back arched on instinct, offering myself to him regardless of my need to pass the fuck out.

Alex could play me like a true maestro. He strummed strings I'd thought worn out, bringing life to my dick again when all I wanted to do was curl up and drop into dreamless sleep.

"Goddamn you, Alex," I hissed as he worked his cock into my ass.

"Mmm," he murmured against my ear, the heat of his body pressing against me as he gyrated and shoved, trying to get deeper with nothing more than spit and water to ease his way. "You like it when I make it hurt."

Normally.

But not when exhaustion weakened my knees, and I wanted rest more than a cock attempting to rearrange my guts. I grabbed the silicone-based lube from the shelf, shifted forward off his length, and shoved some up my hole.

"Fucking finish," I muttered, once more offering myself up for his use, back arched and all.

Alex chuckled and licked into my ear, making a wave of goose bumps crash over my arms. "You know the second time around is never quick." He slammed into me with one forceful stroke, pulling a grunt from my chest.

Biting my tongue, I allowed my curses to spill through my mind as he set a steady pace in finding release inside the condom we never went without. My dick perked up regardless of my preference to call it quits, and eventually I gave in to the need to empty my balls again.

Skin slapped, and breaths grew heavy as he clutched at my hips as though desperate to stay with me.

I loved Alex, but sometimes he took too much. It was my own damn fault for not setting boundaries with the only person I could somewhat call mine, but as usual, I kept quiet and allowed him to have me however he desired.

Masochist, much?

He came first, same as always, and I painted the tiles with a few spurts of spunk a moment later. My ass wouldn't like my office chair in the morning, but the soreness would give me something to focus on beyond my annoyance over a victim not wanting to bring his attacker to justice.

Silence settled over me twenty or so minutes later when I finally got Alex to leave and crawled into bed.

Alone.

I had no one to blame for my lonely situation but myself. I'd restricted my ability to live life to the fullest because of a one-sided love I couldn't help but wallow in.

Alex would never be anything more than a fuck buddy, but I couldn't control my feelings for him. He was all I had outside work, and short of death, nothing would ever make me turn away from him.

Chapter 3

Kellen

"Preston?" I addressed the slender ginger who opened the hotel door at my quiet knock.

Face flushed, he nodded and stepped back, allowing me entry. "Kellen, right?"

"Yes."

He shut the door, and I turned to find him running his hands down his jean-clad thighs.

"Nervous?" I asked, sure of that fact by his actions even though he'd been booking with Elite—my friend Mason—on a monthly basis since January.

"Yeah, a bit," he admitted, trying for a smile.

"I'm not quite a silver fox like your usual escort," I said, "but I promise I'll leave you satisfied."

Preston nodded again and motioned me farther into the suite. "Mr. Fox assured me of that fact."

Sean Fox, the manager of the gay branch of Elite, reminded us often that we were to please our clients as per the big man's instructions—EEMM's owner and Sean's older brother, Micah. Unless we felt unsafe or threatened, we were contracted to do that very thing. With men like

Preston, who tended toward being closeted and shy, I expected inexperience outside of Elite too. I settled in knowing I wouldn't have issues that night in earning my pay.

Thursday after coming back from Maine, I'd been with a vers guy, and I'd ended up giving and receiving before his eight a.m. time limit ran out. Friday, I'd bottomed exclusively, so I looked forward to topping with Preston who, according to his file, had no desire to stick his dick in any hole but a mouth.

Within a half hour, I had the younger man stripped and trembling while I knelt for him, his cock down my throat.

My *fuck you* to Xavier echoed in my ears, and Preston's soft groans offered me the usual sense of satisfaction of a job well done, but I could admit to being tired as fuck. Three nights, three different men, and weariness settled into my bones as I filled the condom while buried deep in Preston's tight ass.

Groaning, I tried to keep my weight off his smaller form, but he clung to me, encouraging me to relax.

"Heavy," I muttered.

"Love it," Preston argued with a sigh.

I allowed myself a moment to let go, resting fully on him with my face in his smooth neck. While Preston wasn't exactly a twink, I could have easily thrown his bubble butt around if he'd asked me to.

"Is Mason okay?"

It took a few seconds for Preston's question to register, and I nodded with a loud exhale while pulling from his warmth. "Yeah. Just taking a few sick days."

At least, that was what I'd been told. I wasn't sure I believed my friend's excuse for my loaded schedule due to his unavailability. He'd been attacked outside the hotel where we'd been celebrating Micah's birthday party the weekend before, and I expected he was still sore from the boots he'd taken to the ribs and the blow to his temple.

But I wasn't sure he'd be back once he healed. He'd seemed beyond troubled at the party. Unhappy, his smile disingenuous. And after the assault? I expected he might be done with the public for a while.

I went to the bathroom and cleaned up before taking a hot towel to do the same for my client. Pink fused Preston's cheeks while I cared for him even though I'd been balls deep inside his body minutes earlier. His shyness was cute —but the man was far from my type.

Xavier had ticked every box on my checklist. Close to my height, dark hair and eyes, broad shoulders, muscular enough to dominate me when the mood struck. Sturdy enough to take it should I feel the need to be in charge and release a little tension with a rough and tumble. But Xavier had never wanted my dick. That kind of guy would be a hard pass for me if I ever—

Nope. Not going there. I gritted my teeth.

"I really appreciate Elite."

I glanced up from where I wiped Preston's splattered cum off his lower abs, realizing I scowled while thinking about my ex. I needed to keep my head in the fucking game. "Elite appreciates loyal customers like you."

He huffed a soft laugh and looked away as though he felt guilty as fuck.

All of Elite's escorts signed NDA's, but sometimes things got shared at parties after too much booze. I'd been told Preston's stepbrother worked for Elite's gay branch but wasn't about to get nosy since Mason wasn't supposed to have told me that tidbit of information Preston had shared with him months earlier.

"Do you...know Drake?" Preston asked.

Well, shit. There it was.

I tossed the towel aside and crawled onto the bed, tugging Preston against my chest, spooning like his file had stated he enjoyed—same as me after sex. "Yeah," I answered. "I wouldn't call us best of friends or anything, but we talk on occasion. Why? You interested in booking with him?"

Preston stiffened, and I bit back a grin, rubbing my fingertips over one of his nipples until it hardened.

"Wh-What?" he gasped, arching into my touch.

"Drake." I played dumb. "Big dude with dark hair and bright blue eyes? Hot as hell muscular frame that could even toss *me* around?"

An audible gulp hit my ears, and I chuckled. "I've heard good reviews," I said, "but I can't say I've personally tasted the goods. Give him a try next time. I won't be offended with your desire for variety, and neither will Mason. Promise."

A full-body shudder rippled through Preston, and I squeezed him just a bit tighter, wondering how long my client had crushed on his stepbrother. While I wanted to open that can of worms, it wasn't my place—nor did I have the balls to cause possible legal issues from spouting off at the mouth.

But that didn't mean I couldn't give Preston more than he'd paid for. Climaxes weren't difficult to deliver...fantasies with a willing participant who didn't care about being called a different name in the heat of passion? I'd become a fucking pro at that shit—yet another *fuck you* to Xavier, who'd been careful enough to keep his lips shut while in our bed.

I slid my hand down Preston's taut belly with its hint of

abs, gathering his semi and soft balls in a light hold. Nuzzling his neck, I pressed my dick against his ass, chubbing up without effort from the feel of his soft, warm skin. Thank fuck for my voracious sexual appetite, or I'd be popping blue pills to give my customers satisfaction.

"Think Drake is hot?" I murmured against Preston's ear. "That's one hell of a picture Elite has of him on the website, huh? Those thick pecs. Fucking eight-pack. Cum gutters and a V any gay or bi man would love to lick free of cum."

Preston gulped again but nodded.

"Wanna pretend he's the one touching you right now?"

A literal whine rose from Preston's chest, and I chuckled again.

"Yeah, that's what I thought. Tell you what." I rubbed over his taint before hitching his leg back over my thigh. "How about you imagine that big boy is behind you. Feeling your hole."

I did exactly that, lust rising low in my groin as Preston's pucker twitched against my fingertip.

"Oh God."

My grin widened at Preston's whimper. "He's palming your balls...stroking your cock."

"Fuck yeah," Preston whispered, tilting his head to watch me play with his body.

"Tell me what you want, boy," I said, palming the wet head of his dick and smearing his pre-cum down his length.

"Shit—I'm going to come."

I grabbed hold of his balls and tugged them hard enough he flinched and cried out. "Nuh uh," I said, adding a tsking noise. "Drake wants to play."

"Drake," he groaned, thrusting into my hand that once more wrapped around his cock.

"That's right," I murmured and allowed him to feed off the fantasy in his mind. I stroked him to release, keeping up the dirty talk, even though I had no fucking clue if my co-worker was vocal between the sheets or not. Preston enjoyed the fuck out of our playtime, and he handed me a nice little bonus before I slipped through the hotel door at two in the morning once he finished with me for the night.

Temptation to shoot off a text to Drake tickled the back of my mind, but I knew better. I wanted to call up Mason and let him in on the secret I'd learned but expected his savior from the night of his attack shared his bed. I doubted they would appreciate being woken up for a mere bit of juicy gossip.

I had no doubt Mason was taken with Jasper, but I put aside thoughts of others' love lives and moving on from working as an Elite Escort. I had zero energy left inside me to consider my own future let alone someone else's.

Driving home to my small apartment in Everett, I struggled to keep my eyes open. After a three-nights-in-a-row fuck fest, I needed some goddamn sleep. Worry about friends and family could wait. As could the usual heavy thoughts about Xavier whenever I crawled into bed alone.

Balls drained dry, I passed out, satisfied yet again by a job well done.

Chapter 4

JJ

Thank fuck that's over with.

Blowing out a huge exhale to empty my lungs, I pushed open the Peabody Courthouse's door, happy to be rid of this case and ready to give my full focus to the next that had been tossed at me atop the one that had just been laid to rest.

We'd gotten a warrant for our latest suspect—that punk Joseph Delaney, and I couldn't wait to see cuffs locked around the fucker's wrists.

A man descended the stairs ahead of me, and even though I didn't get a glimpse of his face, I knew without doubt it was Joseph's original victim who had refused to press charges. Paperwork waited on my desk back at the station, thanks to a second man who'd come forward. At least the latest victim wanted to bring his rapist to justice.

"Mr. Thomson?" I called.

Mason halted at the bottom of the stairs and turned.

I hurried down the rest of the stairs, pushing out my hand, noting the man in front of him pulled up as well. "Mason." I greeted him with a firm shake. He appeared much more settled than when we'd last spoken down at the station.

"Detective," he replied, his brow slightly furrowing. "What are you doing here?"

"Court."

The guy he'd been following stepped close to Mason's side, ripping the air from my lungs as our gazes clashed. He was a fucking tall drink of water on a sweltering July day, and for the first time in a decade, I found myself thirsting for someone other than Alex. Unease at the very least should have rolled through me, considering my love for my best friend, but I couldn't help the quick once-over I gave the man I recognized from snooping online.

And I definitely couldn't stop my body's natural reaction to the magnetic draw of him in person. My pulse kicked up. My palms grew damp. My pants suddenly felt too tight.

Kellen Roberts covered his muscles in black from neck to boots regardless of the bright sun. He was pure fucking deliciousness, standing almost eye to eye with me and emanating a sense of confidence that turned me the fuck on.

I had the sudden urge to slam him against the nearest wall and devour his mouth when sex for me had always been on the tamer side.

Swallowing to ease my parched throat, I tore my focus off him for Mason. "Do you have a minute?"

"Sure."

I nodded toward the bushes off to the side of the court-house before glancing once more at his friend.

"He stays," Mason stated, his tone unrelenting.

I didn't have it in me to argue, so I focused on the task at hand. "I'm wondering if your thoughts on pressing charges has changed."

"It hasn't—I just filed a harassment order against him instead."

My brow furrowed, concern for Mason rising after all I'd learned about his attacker and what he'd recently done to another man. "Has he been in contact with you?"

"Texts—outright threats on my life," he replied with a slight nod. "Different number than the first time but the same shit."

Fucking hell.

I had information I wasn't allowed to share—but gray areas and all that jazz. The young punk who had attacked Mason and now a second man needed to be tossed behind bars, the key dropped into an abyss never to be found again. I didn't care if Joseph Delaney III had more money than I could imagine. Didn't give a flying fuck his dad had deep pockets and connections throughout our city. The boy was trouble, and it wouldn't be long before he took his sense of entitlement and knife play a little too far.

It was my job to stop such an event from happening again.

A quick glance around let me know no one would overhear what I was about to trust Mason with. "You aren't the only man he's attacked."

"What?"

"There was a similar incident...a couple of nights ago." My gaze slipped down to Mason's chest, the memory of the carving in his skin still fresh in my mind. "The man was around your age. Drugged, same means of binding but a different knife. That boy definitely has a type."

"Oh fuck."

"But unlike you, Joseph's latest victim wasn't employed by Elite." I glanced at Kellen, wanting to lay out all I'd learned onto the table to find out what else my honesty might gain me. The eye contact with Mason's friend once more seized my lungs, and I fought to stay still rather than encroaching on his personal space to see how he'd react.

Kellen didn't flinch beneath my stare like Mason did at mentioning I'd learned where he—*they*—worked thanks to a little digging. He also didn't reveal a goddamned thing about how the sexual tension snapping in the short distance between us affected him.

"Look—I don't give a shit what the two of you do to make a living," I said, deciding on a little vulnerability to hear what I wanted. "My mom turned tricks to keep food on our table when I was little. People do what they have to in order to survive. You'll get no judgment from me."

"H-How did you find out?" Mason asked, his voice unsteady.

Kellen stood unmoved, arms crossed over prominent pecs, his hazel-green eyes void of emotion while I explained how I'd simply done my job as a detective. The man appeared like a brick wall, and fuck if he didn't make me want to break him down. Put him on his knees. Listen to him gag on my cock and moan for me to wreck his ass before he did the same to mine.

My cock attempted to buck inside my tight briefs it wanted to spring free from.

Jesus, what was he doing to me?

"So are you going to be able to get him for attempted murder or something with the other guy's case?" Mason asked.

Fuck.

I needed to focus on what the night ahead would bring rather than salivating over a gorgeous man whose mere presence made every bone in my body ache in ways I didn't understand. Especially considering I was in love with someone else.

"I can't discuss the charges at this time, but if you agreed to come forward with your story..." I trailed off, hoping the fact another had suffered at the hand of Joseph would entice Mason to do what needed to be done.

Mason refused to relent, and I gave my attention to his friend, ready to see what else I could stir. While I'd found Kellen's image on Elite's website hot as fuck, naked from the waist up, the truth of him in the flesh made me happy I'd looked into his background—without crossing too many ethical boundaries. I planned on doing a hell of a lot more now that I'd been close enough to inhale the slight scent of bergamot and citrus wafting off him.

"You're a good friend, Kellen Roberts." I named him, making him aware I knew exactly who he was.

Kellen's passive eyes glanced down over me, pausing on my obvious bulge, and even though he gave nothing away with his face, the electrical draw crackling between us seemed to intensify. I could sense Mason's gaze pinging between the two of us as though he felt the palpable connection between me and his friend.

"It seems like you're decent at your job, Detective..." Kellen arched an eyebrow, waiting for me to fill in the blank.

And fuck, I was going to give him everything he asked for, my best friend and unrequited love be damned. Even though I'd been faithful for ten years, Alex and I had no understanding. He was open to fucking whatever man he wanted, and I wasn't so stupid as to think I was the only dick he enjoyed riding when the mood struck him.

"James Jenner." I stuck out my hand, my trustworthy intuition making me aware shit was about to change. But for the better or not, I had no fucking clue. "My friends call me JJ," I tacked on, obvious in opening a door I wouldn't mind Kellen walking through.

A shot of adrenaline and lust burst through my body at the feel of his calloused palm sliding along mine. Our fingers grasped tight with just a hint of challenge. My dick perked up fully, ready for a good rough and tumble that ended up with a dick in a hole. I was good being on either end. A slow smirk curled my lip, widening into a full grin as he pulled away first at Mason's elbow to his side.

Good enough for now since my time had run out.

"Mr. Thomson," I said, turning toward Mason. "Reconsider," I begged, thinking about that warrant for Joseph Delaney waiting for me on my desk. "Two against one, double the evidence, will put that blond punk where he belongs. Behind bars for a long fucking time."

A minute later, after assuring Mason in a roundabout way he wouldn't have to deal with text messages from his stalker after that evening, I strode off. Kellen's gaze seared my backside until I turned the corner, leaving the front of the courthouse behind.

In over a decade, I hadn't considered fucking another man. Hadn't wondered outside of Alex what life could be like with an actual partner sharing my space.

Kellen Roberts had come in like a tornado, ripping the roof off of my stagnant yet calm existence. While no one would ever hold my heart in their hands the way Alex did, I couldn't help but wonder about having another man in my bed.

On top of me.

Beneath me.

Inside me.

My groin burned with need I hadn't felt since my early

twenties. The desire to fuck all night long, empty my balls countless times in twelve hours, and collapse in exhaustion covered in sweat and cum slammed into me.

"Goddamn." I groaned and clenched my steering wheel tighter as the traffic on Route 1 barreled past my car creeping in the far right lane.

Thoughts flooding with and warring over lust and responsibilities, I focused on arriving at my office in one piece. All things Alex and fucking around with an escort who definitely knew how to please a man got put on the back burner.

I had a young man to track down, lock up, and help build a case against.

Chapter 5

Kellen

Micah, Elite's owner, had the guys over for the ballgame on Sunday afternoon like he did once a month. At the invite, I'd gotten a little homesick thinking about the farm up north—because Elite had become my family away from home when I'd joined the ranks of professional escorts.

I was surprised at the number of men sprawled over his massive living room area. It was double the normal, and some of them had actually retired from Elite into the land of partners and children.

The straight boys intermingled with the bent—I gave myself a chuckle at the thought, slapping backs and bumping fists while making my rounds. I'd met a few of them at the holiday party when Micah first announced the EEMM branch, and most had been in attendance at his birthday party a couple of weeks earlier too.

Retirees Blake Harper, Reid Sullivan, Jarod Zimmerman, and Daniel Cooney stood bullshitting by the bar area in a huddled group, but the newer straight Elites lounged on the couches with Sean and the infamous Drake our client Preston secretly lusted after.

It fucking killed me to zip my lips on the whole stepbrother pining, but I knew how to be professional. The last thing Micah needed was private information to be leaked, Drake to confront Preston, and then have the business get sued for breaking an NDA.

Nope. I kept that shit to myself.

Mason was absent, but I wasn't surprised seeing as how that Joseph asshole had broken into his lover's place on the night the police had gotten the warrant for his arrest. Mason had been pretty shaken up when I'd spoken to him over the phone, and he and Jasper were laying low for a while.

"Kellen!" Sean called out, patting the empty couch cushion beside him. "Grab yourself—and me—a beer and sit your fine ass down!" His blue eyes twinkled with mischief as usual, and smirking, I simply shook my head at his harmless flirting and headed to the bar.

"What'll it be?" Blake asked, slipping behind the counter to act as the bartender.

"Sam Adams," I replied, not in the mood for anything stronger since it wasn't yet five o'clock. "Go ahead and give me two—one for the brat over there."

Reid snickered along with Jarod, but Daniel's calm face didn't so much as twitch.

"How's it going, boys?" I asked as Blake handed me my beer. He didn't bother getting a second for Sean.

"Hey! Where's mine?" Sean called with laughter in his voice. At least my boss wasn't yet slurring his words.

"Kellen isn't your daddy, and neither am I!" Blake hollered back. "Come and get your own, you little shit!"

Sean grumbled, causing more laughter, but he didn't

look embarrassed or put out. I swore he didn't know the meaning of the word self-conscious. Or tact for that matter.

"I'll grab you another," Drake said from his other side, clasping his best friend's shoulder real quick before pushing up from the couch.

I eyed Drake as he rounded the bar, only paying half-attention as Reid told us about his oldest daughter's antics the day before. Something about getting a box of ice cream from the freezer and trying to feed her baby sister, who they'd found out was lactose intolerant.

"How's it going, Drake?" I asked quietly, and he dipped his head while twisting caps off two beers.

"Good."

"Elite keeping you busy?" I sipped.

"Couple of nights a week," he said with a shrug. "Enough that my dick's satisfied, and there's a nice little pile of money in the bank."

I wanted to push for info about his personal life. Hint around that he had a stepbrother salivating over fantasies of him. Instead, I kept quiet and allowed him to return to his seat since I wasn't one to pry or stir up shit. Fuck knew I couldn't stand anyone getting nosy about my business.

"Kellen," Blake said, pulling my attention back to the men around me, "Micah said something went down with Mason after his birthday party but hasn't shared the details. Any idea what the fuck is going on?"

It was no secret that I was aware of, so I told them what had happened. The attack. How he'd met Jasper. How he'd texted his official resignation from EEMM the week before. That same night, I'd broken down a little and admitted to Mason in a rare moment that getting and giving dick for a living was starting to become...boring was the word I'd used. Even if my job soothed my bitterness and emptied my balls without entanglement of any sort, it had less enjoyable moments that sometimes left me feeling restless.

I was sure I wasn't the only one.

Well, Sean probably never had those thoughts. If ever a fuck boy existed, he was it.

"My uncle said that kid who got arrested—Joseph Delaney—got nabbed at Mason's boyfriend's house," Reid said, studying my face as though waiting for me to spill more beans.

"You some big detective now?" Jarod asked, elbowing Reid.

Detective James Jenner.

JJ.

Heat surged through my blood at the memory of the man. Perfect size. Perfect coloring with his dark hair and eyes. Perfect enticing energy had crackled between us at our meeting outside the courthouse too.

Mason had all but named the obvious connection I'd felt, that instantaneous draw toward the detective when our eyes had met for the first time, but I didn't believe in soulmates like Mason did. I wasn't interested in trying for a second chance at love either.

My heart couldn't handle it. I still hadn't gotten over my first failed attempt.

Micah joined us, and he confirmed Mason's moving on from Elite as well as the facts that Joseph, a former Elite client, had indeed been stalking Mason and had abused him. He didn't share too many details but enough to satisfy those who had befriended our favorite silver fox.

I sipped my beer, glancing around the room. Mason was my closest friend, but the men in Micah's living room, most of whom ignored the Sox on the massive flatscreen on the wall, were brothers of a sort. Just not Jacob-like brothers.

The Elites welcomed me with open arms, but would they have my back if shit hit the fan? If I decided to one day take off for the hills, would they miss me? Even care?

Some might. Mason for sure.

Sudden longing for the farm, my parents, and siblings rolled through me. Attempting to push away the homesickness, I glanced around the room.

I noticed a guy I didn't recognize sitting in a recliner sans beer, his focus on the game. He didn't look uncomfortable, but he wasn't exactly chatting it up with the Elites sitting close by either.

"Who's that?" I asked, elbowing Micah lightly since he'd fallen silent, and the other former Elites had started chatting about Jarod's wedding next summer we'd all been invited to.

"Zack Briggs," Micah answered. "Newest Elite, hired by Sean last week."

"Not super outgoing, huh?"

Micah shrugged, eyeing the guy. "I gave Sean full control over EEMM, so I didn't personally interview Zack. He measured up on paper though, and even as a straight guy, I can admit he's hot."

"Sean did alright," I stated. "Looks-wise at least."

"Time will tell. He's booked for next weekend, asked for by name, so I'm keeping my fingers crossed."

Even though he sat and I could only guess at his height, Zack appeared to be my type. Tall, dark, and handsome—but he couldn't hold a candle to JJ.

Fuck.

I scrubbed a hand down over my face, letting a slow exhale leak from my lungs. That man entered my brain too damn often for comfort.

"You okay?" Daniel asked, and I turned my focus on the

non-jolly red giant on my right. He was a soft-spoken Dom, a lover of shibari and his wife. He studied me with an intense gaze that made me shift on my feet.

"Just...bored," I admitted, surprising myself with a candid answer when I usually didn't share personal shit.

"It can get old after a while," he said quietly as the guys around us continued their storytelling and laughter. "Maybe you ought to come down to Chantelle's some night you have free."

Chantelle's was a kinky person's dream, an exclusive BDSM club Micah and his wife also frequented.

But getting freaky wasn't my jam.

"Appreciate the invite, but I'm vanilla as they come." Not exactly a lie, but I didn't consider enjoying a little roughness in the sack enough to be a part of the lifestyle Cooney lived.

"Say the word, and I'll get you an actual invitation," he said before clasping my shoulder with his beefy paw and moving off toward the food table Micah had set up against the far wall.

"Oh, Kellen!" Sean called, and I rolled my eyes. "Be a sweetie and get me and my boy Drake another beer?"

Huffing a snort, I rounded the bar.

"Don't let him near your dick," Micah said, shaking his head at me while I did as asked. "The brat hasn't had a client in a week."

I chuckled and twisted the caps off. Elite Escorts weren't allowed to hook up outside of work—at least, that was what Micah had told Sean to keep his brother from partying too much. "You're a sadist."

Micah winked and sipped his beer, and laughing, I moved across the room to hand his little brother and best friend their drinks.

"Sit," Sean said again, patting the cushion beside him. "I need a broody, sexy man to tell me how cute I am."

Laughter burst from me, and I ruffled his blond hair, completely unmoved by the twinkle in his baby blues. "You aren't my type, boss kid."

"I'm not a kid."

He wasn't, not really at twenty-seven or thereabouts with decent scruff, but he sure as fuck acted like one.

JJ, however, was all man.

I sat where Sean had indicated and allowed his antics to keep my mind from returning to the temptation of maybe— just *maybe*—exploring that shift I'd felt between me and the detective. It would be explosive between us, no fucking doubt, but no matter my stance against relationships, I wasn't sure I could trust myself from being sucked in by his tractor beam.

Fuck knew the man had a hell of a magnetic draw. He'd been on my mind too much. Flashing before my eyes while I pleased Elite's clients, making me empty my balls prematurely more than once.

I needed to get my thoughts in order and figure shit out before I did something stupid like lower my walls and allow myself to be vulnerable again.

Chapter 6

JJ

The Delaney punk sat in jail awaiting trial, and I was finally able to breathe and buckle down on the investigation to hopefully keep him there for the rest of his miserable life.

Court was set for November, and I looked forward to watching his face fall when he was found guilty. The shit we had on him...

One victim coming forward *could* be enough to land him behind bars, but I still pushed Mason regardless of the pickle he was in as a former escort and Joseph being a client. Elite Escorts, both branches, were aboveboard legally, but barely. I expected Mason wanted to protect not just himself but his former employer as well from the wrath of Joseph's father.

Not everyone had the balls to lean forward into a storm and face it headfirst, determination staying their stance.

I'd done my homework, checking a bit into Mason's past to see if I could find some way to talk him into pressing charges but hadn't dug up anything enticing. Underhandedly, I'd also learned a little more about his friend too.

Kellen hailed from Nodhead Falls, Maine which was known for its apple orchards. He was the third of four children, the lucky fucker. I'd been an only child. He'd never married while his parents were still together forty-plus years later. Kellen had an impeccable record and envious credit score. With an MBA, he'd worked as an operations manager after moving to Boston a few years earlier. He volunteered at a veterinary clinic and had a gym membership right down the road from his Everett apartment.

He'd also been engaged to be married, but the wedding had gotten called off a couple of days prior to the exchanging of vows.

After the breakup, he'd signed on with EEMM and had been escorting men around in the two and a half years since. With his looks and build, I doubted he went a single weekend without being booked with clients. I wondered over his reasons for the career change, since he'd done well for himself prior to selling his gorgeous body.

Having looked into his ex-fiancé, Xavier Riviera, as well and seeing the current wild lifestyle Kellen's ex lived according to his social media, I expected he was the catalyst for their ended engagement. Had he done so due to a need to sow more wild oats? Had Kellen? Or had it been something worse...infidelity?

I could imagine that latter would make a heartbroken man lash out and become an escort.

But what did I know other than the fact I wanted to see Kellen Roberts again? Lusted for interaction of any sort.

Alex hadn't scratched the itch I'd felt deep inside me since meeting Kellen, nor was he the distraction he used to be. Sinking into my lover's body or presenting my ass no longer gave me a sense of rightness.

I pulled into my driveway Saturday morning after grabbing groceries, my mind conflicted over my personal life. Or rather, a true lack of one. Outside Alex and his family, I had no one. No siblings. No mother still around to love me, nor the stepdad she'd married who had claimed me as his own. They rested side by side in Riverside Cemetery, no longer filling my existence with real family, laughter, and the unconditional love I longed to experience with a partner.

Forty years old, and I usually spent birthdays and holidays alone and unhappy, wishing for things I would never have all thanks to a heart that was hung up on a married man. Not that I had much time for a social life outside what I already crammed into my free hours. Between work, Alex's neediness, and his boys who called me uncle, I didn't have the energy for much else.

Except for my elderly neighbor, that is.

Upon opening my car's door, the scent of his freshly mowed grass greeted me.

Mr. Rogers—no fucking lie—knelt on a thick pad alongside the flowerbed separating his lawn from mine. His smile, crooked from a stroke a couple of years earlier, met mine.

"JJ, my boy."

I nodded since my hands were loaded down with grocery bags. "How are you, Mr. Rogers?"

"Knees aren't happy with me right now, and it's a good thing you just got home because I can't get up."

Goddamnit, not again.

Lips in a thin line, I set my bags onto my front porch and hurried over to my neighbor. Widowed long before I'd bought my split-level in Saugus, he'd been living alone.

While I hadn't lost a husband, the rest of our lives aligned. He'd been a police officer prior to retirement. Had no family to speak of. His best friend had been his lover— but also his partner.

Lucky old fart.

Mr. Rogers groaned a bit as I helped him to his feet, and I grasped his elbow until he steadied himself. We'd celebrated his ninetieth birthday earlier in the spring over cold beers and a Boston cream pie I'd grabbed from the local bakery.

"I think you need to hire a lawn service that does more than just cut your grass," I told him, my tone firm.

"Bah," he grumbled, pulling from my hold, stubborn as always. "I'm fine."

I grinned and bent over to pick up his foam pad before he attempted to. "Where's your cell phone?"

"On the kitchen table," he muttered as I handed him the pad.

"I thought we agreed you would keep it on you in case something like this happened again."

It hadn't been the first time I'd come home to find Mr. Rogers unable to get up from wherever he'd settled on the ground for one reason or another. He loved his flowers and the spiral herb garden I'd built for him a couple of years earlier, but perhaps I needed to set aside a few hours every week to do more for him.

Mr. Rogers brushed soil from his pants. "I forgot the damn thing, but I knew you'd be back from the store soon."

Nosey and observant, same as me, he'd learned the few parts of my schedule that didn't change week to week. He'd also grilled me about my buddy he'd seen hanging out at my house late into the night at least once every weekend.

"How about we take an hour together tomorrow afternoon to tackle the weeding together?" I suggested.

"If it's not too much trouble..."

"You know it's not," I assured him. "Now come on, let's get you out of this heat."

"That boyfriend of yours coming over tonight?"

Chuckling, I turned him toward the ramp leading to his house. Mr. Rogers couldn't handle stairs very well, so I'd helped him put in an easier way of getting onto the front porch. "Not tonight," I answered.

"I don't understand why you don't dump his ass and find the man who will love you as you deserve."

My smile faded. Perhaps I'd shared a bit too much with my elderly neighbor, but loneliness and too many beers loosened my tongue once or twice when hanging out on his back patio. "Alex is my everything."

"Bah," he repeated, sounding like Scrooge. "That boy already has a spouse of his own. His heart isn't available, so why waste your time? Life is too short, son. I speak from experience."

Mr. Roger's words rang in my ears long after I deposited him in his favorite recliner with a glass of ice water and went on to the task of putting my groceries away. Alex had cancelled for the night earlier that morning via text without an excuse.

But I rarely asked him to explain himself. The man was married. Had the two cutest little boys ever. His family came first, something I had to remind myself of on a daily basis.

I got the refrigerated items put away, and my cell rang.

Seeing Alex's wife's name on the screen, I frowned.

"Hey, Teresa."

"Sorry to bug you, JJ, but have you heard from Alex?" Her voice shook slightly, halting my steps toward my pantry.

"He texted me this morning that he had to work today," I said, "but that was around eight. Everything okay?"

"No." Teresa choked on a sob, and I set the jar of peanut

butter down on the counter and grabbed my keys from the table.

"What's wrong?"

"Wesley fell off the jungle gym at the p-park by Janie's and b-broke his arm."

"Shit. You're at Melrose-Wakefield?" I asked and headed out my front door.

"Yeah—the ER." She sniffled as I climbed back into my car. "Alex isn't answering his phone. He always calls me back, and I've been trying to get in touch with him for two hours!" A hint of panic laced her tone.

"Is Janie there," I said, naming her longtime girlfriend who would give her the support she needed.

"Right beside me as usual."

"Is Aaron with you?" I asked about their other young son.

"Yeah, and he's really upset."

I could imagine at the age of six that he fed off her emotions. "I'll be there in about fifteen and can take him for some ice cream. You just focus on Wesley. Alex is probably in a meeting and will call you back soon," I assured her even though it might be a lie.

"Thank you," she whispered.

I rang Alex as soon as I hung up with his wife—his cell went straight to voicemail. I tried the main number to the company he worked for but got the answering service stating they were closed until Monday morning. His direct office line rang a few times before his voicemail kicked in.

"Alex—fucking call your wife," I snipped the message, my forehead deeply lined with a frown while turning into the hospital's parking lot. Hanging up without another word, I cursed my friend under my breath.

He was a workaholic to the max, never satisfied with the money in his portfolio.

I tried his cell again. Shot him a text.

Then headed into the ER to help his wife along with Janie pick up the pieces as we'd done so many times I'd lost count.

I loved the man, but his lack of availability for the people who needed him the most pissed me off. Having no family of my own made me envious of what he'd found and want to wring his neck to remind him of all his blessings. He ought to cling to that shit. Remember what ought to come first.

Fuck knew I would have my priorities set if I had his life.

But I never would.

Chapter 7

Kellen

My client for the night rubbed all over my front like a cat in heat, his flirty smirk a permanent fixture on his face since EEMM's limo driver and I had picked him up a couple of hours earlier.

Eighteen years my junior, he had major bratty daddy issues. Reminded me of Sean to be honest. I allowed him to explore his sexuality, humored his desire to play games where he was the naughty boy and I was his protective care-taker. While the dynamic didn't do shit for me, the young-ster was cute as fuck, and it'd been almost a week since I'd gotten off.

He had my dick hard with how he rubbed his ass all up in my junk, his arms lifted so he could wrap his hands behind my neck. I grasped his hips as we gyrated to the thumping bass at his favorite club. I wasn't one for dancing or the wild gay nightlife he preferred, but I would please the client without voicing a complaint out loud since it meant I would get paid afterward.

My head began to pound after two hours of tolerating

the atmosphere—I was ready to move onto the good shit and find some relief for the eruption brewing in my balls.

I bent to whisper in his ear to see if he was ready to head out, and my gaze snagged on a couple dancing a few feet to our left.

JJ.

Sudden lust jolted my dick in the confines of my jeans. I released a groan at how his hips rolled—against a blond man an inch or two shorter and more slender than his build. Leg between the blond's thigh, JJ ground his pelvis in slow, sensual movements that mimicked fucking. Their foreheads pressed together, and they swayed with effortless grace as though they'd been doing so for years on end.

Erection aching, I stared, trying to work out what I was feeling. Annoyance? Jealousy? No fucking way either were true since I hardly knew the man and wasn't interested in him beyond this ridiculous sexual attraction. Somehow, I managed to continue dancing with my client, but my heart was no longer in the moment with him. Nor was my shaft aching like a motherfucker due to his warmth pressing against my front.

As though JJ felt my stare on his profile, he turned his partner slightly to face me head-on and met my gaze.

Same as when our eyes clashed outside the courthouse, my insides incinerated and twisted up tight. Desire beyond lust lit in my guts and groin, bucking my cock inside my jeans.

"Fuck," I groaned the word, and JJ's gaze dropped. I licked my lower lip he stared at.

A muscle jumped in his jaw.

The blond caressed JJ's cheek, turning his attention back on his face, and claimed his mouth in a move so damn possessive there was no questioning they were together.

My heartbeat thrummed, fighting the song's bass for dominance in my ears. While JJ gave his dance partner his full focus, I found myself slowly manipulating my client closer to them. We dry humped to the music within touching distance when JJ once more looked our way.

Pupils dilated in the flashing strobe lights, he stared at me for a few seconds before glancing at the young man who'd turned and clung to my shoulders like a needly little bitch. I palmed his pert ass cheeks and clutched him closer, grinding my hard dick against his stomach.

JJ spun in the blond's arms, leaving his front vulnerable.

As though of the same mind, we both stepped closer to one another, and the heat of the detective pressed against my backside. Goose bumps shivered over my skin, waking my senses.

Holy fucking shit.

Eyes clenched shut, I focused on the warmth of his palm settling on my hips, searing my skin through my jeans. His rigid length pressed against the crack of my ass. The same cologne I remembered from that day in front of the courthouse swarmed my nose with sandalwood. As a single unit, the four of us moved in an erotic dance, caught up in a consuming energy that attempted to drown me in pure bliss.

Had I been on a real date rather than attending to business for Elite, I'd have talked the cutie in my arms into a night of debauchery with the men behind me. I hadn't been involved in an orgy since college...going on twenty years.

That granite-like length ground through my crack, the swivel of JJ's hips making my eyes roll back. Headache? Gone. The desire to leave and escape the too-loud music? Demolished.

I wanted to linger in the moment. Hell, my hole was

desperate to be bared and fucked raw by the addictive man singeing my backside with his hard heat.

JJ's fingers crept along the waistband of my jeans, closer to my zipper—and my client must have felt the brush of JJ's on his stomach.

"Dude!" My client slapped at JJ's hand while hollering to be heard over the music. "He's mine for the night!"

Shit.

JJ's touch skimmed from my waist, and a few seconds later, something slipped into my back pocket. "Sorry, kid," JJ yelled, his presence fading away.

I wanted to turn. Yank JJ against me. Tell my client to take a goddamned hike.

But I did nothing of the sort...I had a job to do, money to make, and a boss to keep happy.

Forcing a smirk down at the young man climbing my body, I grabbed his ass cheeks as he wrapped his legs around my waist. "Feisty little shit," I stated against his ear before biting on his lobe, fighting off the disappointment of JJ's addictive energy having left my backside.

"Damn right! I paid a lot of money to lose my virginity tonight."

Ah, fuck. That tidbit of information had been missing from his file. With how sexually he danced, with the flirting he'd been doing since the minute we'd picked him up, I'd expected his experience rivaled mine regardless of his age.

My mind wanted to replay those brief moments of JJ fucking my ass through clothing, but I had a smile to return to my client's baby face. I shifted him a bit lower in my arms until our granite-like cocks pressed together.

"Ready for me?" I asked at his ear, thrusting against him.

"Oh fuck." He shuddered, and I wondered if he came in his pants.

"Let's go, sweet boy. I'm gonna take care of you and give you the best damn night of your life."

"Yes—yes, please."

Less than a half hour later, I had my client on all fours atop his bed, two fingers stretching his unused hole.

All I could see, all I could think about was JJ. The feel of his firm hold on my hip, his length grinding against my crack. The life-giving sparks between us that had awarded me a buzz without ingesting a hint of drugs or alcohol. The alluring draw that made my dick like an iron spike yet scared the shit out of me.

Detective James Jenner had become my muse.

A delicious fantasy to escape into when I was paid to perform.

"Please," my client gasped the word, his back arching deeply. "I'm ready."

I wasn't sure he spoke truth, but my balls ached and cock throbbed with the need to bury deep in tight heat.

Imagining JJ's ass in front of me, the thought of filling him up and listening to his groan, sent desire rushing through me.

"Fuck," I whispered, pressing the tip of my sheathed dick to the pink hole smeared with lube. Flexing my glutes popped me through the first ring, and I moaned, eyelids fluttering shut as my head tipped back in ecstasy.

He was vise-like.

Intensely hot.

Fucking luscious around my cock.

Groaning, I shoved in, hearing JJ beg for every inch deep inside him. My hips moved in time with the memory of how he'd danced, a slow, sensual gyration. With shallow, short thrusts, I worked my way into the slick hole.

By the time my balls met skin, I panted, my hands bruising soft skin.

Still, I stayed in the image behind my eyelids.

Fucking JJ.

Stroking over his prostate.

Drinking in his whimpers, tattooing them in my mind.

"You're so fucking hot inside," I groaned the words, dragging my length from his body and shoving in with a snap of my hips.

"Oh fuck." The voice was too high...didn't have the natural low rasp of JJ.

I opened my eyes and watched my slick, condom-covered cock pull on the pink ring of flesh while backing out. My balls tightened regardless of the reality brought to life in front of my eyes.

But I kept the image of JJ in my mind while fucking the client into a whimpering, shuddering mess who begged me to help him.

I reached around and palmed his leaking dick.

Stroked him until he cried while releasing all over the sheets.

Then I allowed myself to fill the condom...breeding JJ's ass. Stuffing my seed deep inside his body. Marking him as mine.

"Jesus," I gasped as a final shudder ripped through me.

Soft whimpers broke through the ringing in my ears, and I blinked the client beneath me into view once more.

Shit.

I slowly backed out, rubbing his red, swollen rim until it winked closed. "Okay?" I murmured, sinking onto my haunches as he collapsed onto the mattress into the puddle of his cum beneath him.

"Mmm," he hummed, but I couldn't tell if it was a positive or negative response.

Had I gone too hard on him? He'd told me I didn't have to be careful when we'd first started. I could have sworn he'd begged me to fuck him harder. Or had that been part of my lust-fevered state fantasizing about having JJ on my dick?

Cursing myself, I went into the bathroom, rid myself of the condom, and wet a towel to take care of the kid.

He sprawled, still face-down, unmoving, and didn't so much as flinch when I gently touched his hip where my fingertips had bruised his pale skin. The young man would be sore for days.

My jaw clenched, and I turned him over.

A smirk curled his lips, and he gazed up at me with sleepy wonder in his sapphire eyes.

Insides settling over the blissed-out state of his face, I set to work cleaning him up. We still had hours left on his contract, so I sprawled on the king-sized bed and tugged him against me.

He sighed and snuggled in close. "Thank you," he murmured, his breath hot on my chest.

"My pleasure." I spoke the truth, having thoroughly enjoyed my job, no trace of boredom to be found.

But only because of a fantasy. It was for the best daydreams about having JJ beneath me, in me, remain buried in my head for when I needed a little inspiration.

I had no whole piece of my shattered heart left to give, and with JJ, there would be no holding back.

He would take everything, I had no doubt.

Chapter 8

JJ

I hated the nightlife scene. There were too many bodies. Too much noise. But for the first time, I was thankful as fuck that my lover had dragged my ass out to his favorite club and that I'd allowed myself to enjoy more than my usual two-beer limit.

It had been two weeks since Alex's son Wesley had broken his arm. Fourteen days since I'd been livid at the man for disappearing without his electronic leash. He'd forgotten his cell at home that Saturday morning. His all-day meeting had supposedly been on a golf course then the clubhouse afterward, both of which he'd not bothered telling his wife about in advance.

Two nights after settling things between him and Teresa, he'd come to my house an hour before my bedtime and dropped to his knees to make up for how he'd upset me.

I'd forgiven him as usual—but something nagged at the back of my mind, keeping me on alert. It wasn't the first time Alex had "forgotten" his cell phone. Years earlier before his marriage, he had exhibited similar behavior in his downward spiral with drugs, but he'd showed no signs of using when he'd finally arrived at the hospital.

Or when I'd picked him up for our date at his favorite club.

Seeing Kellen on the dance floor with a man much too young for him had stolen my attention thoroughly, setting aside all thoughts of what my best friend might be up to.

Alex had become nothing but a body, a nuisance...a ball and chain, in the moment my eyes had met Kellen's. Sudden longing for more of Kellen had swayed me toward him and his partner, where they moved together in an erotic display of fully-clothed fucking. I wanted to rip the kid off Kellen and claim him.

I'd ached to touch him. Smell him. Fucking devour him.

And it definitely wasn't just the alcohol talking. That man did something to me...made me lust to behave like a damned animal.

The few minutes I'd been allowed to rub against his backside, clutch his hips in my hands, had been nothing short of perfection. I allowed myself to dream of a different life in those brief moments. One where Alex didn't have a hold over my soul. One where Kellen would be open to exploring the palatable connection between us. One where I wouldn't feel guilt for fucking someone other than the man I loved.

A hand grasping my hard length pulled me back to the present, to the man who had his claws so deeply embedded in me I would never be free.

Somedays, I really hated the engrained loyalty I'd been taught as a young teen by the man who'd taken over as the father figure in my life.

Alex plastered to my backside, fondling my dick as we moved together with the bass. Music thumped in my ears in time with my heartbeat. The sense of Kellen and his dance partner no longer sent shivering currents over my skin.

I had led us away intentionally after hearing Kellen's partner.

Nothing more than a client.

I had managed to slip my card in Kellen's back pocket. I hoped he found it, called, or at least texted because I needed...*more* of him regardless of how my integrity told me to stay away.

"I wanna fuck." Alex's whiskey-laced breath wafted over my cheek from where he'd propped his chin on my shoulder, his hand giving my bulge a squeeze.

My dick bucked in his hold.

I needed release too, but for the first time, it wasn't my long-time lover's body I wanted spread out for me to feast upon. It had been Kellen's firm ass against my groin that had gotten me worked up, but my hole was desperate to be filled too.

My best friend was ready and willing—for once at *my* disposal.

Fuck it. I would gladly take advantage of his availability like he always did to me.

I grasped Alex's hand and led him toward the back hallway and darkness beyond, a little more buzzed than I usually allowed myself when out in public. The bathroom's stalls had been renovated with enough space for what half of the men gyrating on the dance floor hoped to acquire before night's end.

A hole to fuck or a dick to suck.

The music muffled in my ears as the bathroom door shut behind us. Thank Christ a stall remained available because I couldn't wait any longer. Sounds of slapping skin and groaning filled the air, letting me know we weren't alone, tightening my balls even further.

Without a word, I shut us in what little privacy we could have in that moment, dropped my jeans to my thighs, and bent forward over the toilet, my hands on the wall.

"Hurry up," I muttered, dick already leaking as I shook my ass at Alex.

Cool, slick fingers slid through my crack, and I groaned, pushing back to impale myself.

Alex snickered. "So needy for me—fucking love it."

"Quit talking and give me your cock," I muttered, not in the mood for games that would only end up with me aching for more and left disappointed.

Curses rang from someone in the stall beside us, another wave of lust pulsing through me at the knowledge someone found release.

"Goddamnit, Alex!" I growled as he slowly worked in a third finger. While I appreciated him taking his time and making sure he wouldn't hurt me, I wanted it rough. Lusted to feel him stretching my hole with just enough pain to set my blood on fire and incinerate thoughts of Kellen from my mind.

My heart belonged to Alex, and my head—and body— needed to be reminded of that fact.

Finally, the bluntness of his dick pressed against me, and I relaxed, releasing a slow exhale as I shoved backward, filling myself full of his cock with one thrust.

"Fuck!" I bit my lower lip and lost myself to the feel of Alex's long strokes deep inside me.

The familiar connection, the sense of emotion I always experienced when we fucked didn't swell inside my chest. I fought to keep the image of Kellen from my mind, but he crept along the edges of my reality.

Losing the battle, I stomped down the guilt that tried to rise and make me feel like a piece of shit.

Alex had a wife. We had no understanding, no agreement to not fuck other guys on the side even though I couldn't imagine doing so. But while with him, I *should* give him my undivided attention—be in the moment regardless of intimacy in public.

The draw of Kellen didn't allow my self-control to dictate my thoughts and actions.

I imagined the scent of bergamot and citrus in my nose, remembering the warmth of his backside cradling my hard shaft. The heat of his skin radiating through our shirts, the ripple of his back muscles as he moved between me and his young client.

Had he been hard for the kid?

Me?

Would he lead the small blond back to a hotel room and destroy his ass? Would he kiss and lick into his pouty mouth? Would he see *me* while doing so rather than the guy he'd been paid to please?

Fantasize it was me willingly taking his dick?

My climax rushed like a swell through my body, crashing into me and making me spurt all over the toilet without a single touch to my cock.

"Jesus Christ," I gasped, head thrown back, spine arching, reveling in the release of the goddamned century— hands-free for the first time in my life.

"Fuck yeah," Alex groaned, reminding me who fucked my ass, but I was too far gone in rapture to give the hint of disappointment that flitted through my mind another thought.

He buried himself deep, stilling as my hole contracted

around his girth. His cock pulsed as he filled the condom, and all too soon, we finished and panted, the sounds of others getting off echoing in the bathroom around us.

Alex didn't speak, just backed out and handed me some toilet paper.

I cleaned up the best I could, tucked my spent dick away, then considerately wiped down the toilet as well. There was no hand holding, no sweet kisses shared in the aftermath of our lust.

We exited the stall, washed our hands, and exited the bathroom without touching.

But our actions weren't new. Occasionally, I peppered his sweat-slickened skin with kisses, but we never made out just to taste one another's mouths. That along with cuddling were Alex's hard limits. Too intimate and everything I longed for.

It wasn't for my lack of trying. In the beginning, Alex and I had a deeper connection of sorts, but as the years passed, the vulnerability we'd shared became less and less. I assumed because he'd found Teresa and she'd given him two sons. Perhaps it was Alex's creeping up the ladder at the finance company he worked for that reduced the mental space he had available for his faithful side dish.

While he was still my best friend, sex between us had become a mere means of finding release.

For him, anyway.

Up until a few weeks earlier, I'd been troubled by that fact and had tried to find ways to reconnect with my lover outside of fucking.

But now?

I studied the back of his head while following him from the club into the humid summer night. He swayed slightly, definitely more buzzed than I was. He'd called and begged for a night out, claiming to be overwhelmed with stress at work. I'd given in as usual, wishing I could sever the ties that bound me to him.

But they weren't visible. Or tangible enough I could cut them with a blade.

There was nothing to do but survive on the scraps he offered me.

The Uber he'd contacted before leaving the bathroom waited for us at the curb. He gave the driver his address, which meant he wasn't coming back to my place.

Guess our date is over.

Strangely, disappointment didn't wash over me as it would have a mere month earlier. We rode in silence, but I'd had enough alcohol that the lack of interaction didn't make me feel uncomfortable. I watched Alex stumble up his house's front stairs and fumble with his keys before he managed to unlock the front door and let himself in.

He hadn't turned. Hadn't waved goodbye.

Yet another reminder that I'd dived deeper into our relationship than he had. Could I even consider friends with benefits an actual relationship? What we had together no longer fulfilled me in any emotional way as it had in the beginning.

Sighing, I faced forward and gave the Uber driver my address.

"Ever been in love?" I murmured, tipping my head back and closing my eyes, hating the spins wracking my brain.

"Can't say I have."

"Don't bother—it's nothing but a heartache."

Rather than responding, the driver started to hum an old Bonnie Tyler song.

"Nothing but a heartache," I joined in, so damn out of tune it wasn't even funny.

We sang together, and all I could do was laugh until I cried.

Chapter 9

Kellen

om called me Sunday morning, waking me from a deep sleep. I'd gotten home from work the night before a little after three instead of eight since my client's hole was wrecked after a single use. He'd asked me to swallow a second load before leaving, and I'd given him the blow job of his life.

His words, not mine.

Easy to do with his shorter, slender dick though. Deep throating hadn't been a problem, and I swallowed down every drop since his file showed his bloodwork to be spotless.

Blinking the sleep from my eyes, I tried to pay attention as my mom prattled on about the latest family gossip, but I couldn't stop the memories from the night before replaying in my mind.

JJ's muscles against my backside.

Imagining his ass while thrusting into my client.

Finding release with JJ's name echoing in my mind but thankfully not on my tongue.

"Are you listening to me?"

"Huh?" I rubbed a hand over my face, noting the laughter in Mom's voice.

"I gave you enough time to wake your sleepy butt—are you ready to hear the real reason I called?"

"Yeah, Mom." I rolled to sit on the edge of my bed, running my fingers through my hair. "I'm up."

"Good. Suzi has been having contractions since five this morning, and they're bad enough she's heading to the hospital."

A grin split my face. "It's about time!"

My baby sister's third child was almost a week late. I couldn't even begin to imagine how miserable she was.

"I'm keeping Finn and Jackson until they come home."

I snorted a laugh. "Good luck with those two hellions."

"Dad will help."

I snorted again. Mom was dreaming. When those two tykes showed up, Dad tended to hide out. Finn was two, and Jackson just shy of a year, but they were up and moving, both having started walking at nine months.

"With how easy of deliveries she had with the other boys," Mom said, "I'm sure she'll be fine and ready to tackle the world in a couple of days."

I hoped so for everyone's sake.

After making a promise to get my ass north as soon as I could, I hung up and shuffled into my bathroom to empty my bladder and wash the tired off my face. A few more hours of rest would have been nice.

Once dressed in a pair of nylon shorts, I sat on my couch, sipping a cup of black coffee and toying with the business card JJ had slid into my back pocket the night before.

A blatant invitation if ever I'd seen or heard one.

I wondered over the blond he'd been with—who he was,

what they were to each other. I'd assumed a hookup since JJ wouldn't have given me his card otherwise. But how they'd kissed...

Regardless, he was interested, plain and simple. Same as me.

But I feared the draw of more than mere lust toward him, didn't trust my ability to keep my walls up well enough to protect my heart from a man who affected me as much as JJ did.

He was...too potent. Desirable in every physical way. My perfect type, and the magnetic pull between us was a force to be reckoned with.

And as a detective, he also probably had his shit together, unlike my ex.

"Fuck." I heaved a heavy exhale, shoving aside thoughts of Xavier.

Mom always told me there was no point in living in the past. I had to keep my eyes on the future and the bright possibilities of what might be for a "sweet soul" like me.

Why she still considered those words for me after learning I was a damned escort, I had no clue. That woman wore rainbow-colored glasses when it came to her kids.

"What should I do?" I muttered to myself, expecting Mom would grab me by both cheeks and demand I go for it. Call JJ. Ask him out on a date. Give love a second chance and fall hard.

You won't know if you don't try.

Yet another thing Mom often said to me.

Perhaps it would be best to just be honest with JJ. Fill him in on the sob story of my life, tell him how damaged I was, only good for a fuck or two to rid us of the obvious sexual desire we felt for one another.

But could I even handle that much?

Lips in a thin line over the fact I didn't trust myself, I set aside my empty mug, leaned forward, elbows on my knees, and dialed JJ's cell number.

"Detective Jenner," his deep voice greeted, sending a shiver down my spine and raising the hairs on my nape.

"JJ—it's Kellen."

"Mr. Roberts." His voice betrayed his grin and a hint of satisfaction. "Found my card?"

"Felt you slide it in." My eyelids slammed shut at the words that fell off my lips, and I waited for JJ to crack a joke.

He merely chuckled. "What a great opportunity, but I won't take it."

"Afraid I'll run off?"

"I know you would." He sounded confident as fuck—and he was right.

I was as skittish as a feral kitten like those back on the farm I'd attempted to tame when I'd been a kid. Same as the ones sometimes brought into the vet.

"What made you decide to call?" He spoke again before I thought of a response.

"You seem like a nice guy—"

"But?" he interjected, probably having already figured me out with being a detective. No doubt, the guy had psychology training and all that shit.

"I think you're hot as fuck—but I'm not interested." It fucking killed to lie like that, but I had no choice.

"I'm just looking for a good time, Kellen," JJ stated. "Hanging out and hooking up. My heart isn't available either."

Either.

I contemplated his declaration for a few seconds, realizing he knew someone had hurt mine past the point of being open. "Done your homework, I'm assuming?" I asked rather than focusing on the fact he must have had his heart broken too.

"I won't lie and say no," he admitted. "You intrigue me, so I took the opportunity to check you out before pursuing what I can't help but want."

His firm declaration lazed blood to my groin in a slow, sensual rising of need.

"Who was the blond?" I heard myself asking rather than letting him know what his voice and words did to me *or* giving him shit for doing a background check on me when nothing legal warranted such an act.

"He's the reason my heart isn't available, but before you ask, no, he's not my partner. We're not married—or engaged." He hadn't hesitated to answer his truth. I'd assumed by their possessive kiss that might be the case.

"I'm jaded as fuck," I gave him the same honesty. "My ex-fiancé cheated on me right before our wedding."

"Is that why you joined Elite?"

Nosey bastard. A muscle ticked in my jaw, but I answered anyway. "Yeah."

"A big *fuck you* to the asshole who crushed your heart." JJ sounded matter-of-fact as though he could understand my pain and grief.

"Got that right," I muttered. "But the guys I work with are great, even if my boss can be a brat sometimes."

"I want to explore the connection between us, that shot of lust whenever I lay eyes on your gorgeous ass, but it won't be anything more than fucking."

Oh, the temptation. It flirted with my better sense. Meeting up with JJ would be nothing but trouble—but I lusted for him, goddamnit.

"Feel free to hire me if you need my dick that badly," I suggested rather than simply giving in.

"Don't want your dick," JJ shot back. "I want your hole —but I suppose you *could* have mine after I've wrecked yours if you're up for it."

Oh, I would be, all right. No doubt. Nothing better than a man who enjoyed a little flip fucking.

"Just one night, Kellen." Pleading bled through his voice. "That's what I'm asking for. We can scratch this itch and both go on our merry way, get back to life as we know it."

"You're a pushy bastard."

"You have no idea," he purred the statement.

I toyed with the proposal for perhaps five seconds, but the memory of Xavier and how broken I'd been by his betrayal was fixed firmly in my mind. My stomach twisted to its usual gut-wrenching clench whenever he entered my thoughts.

"It's not a good idea," I stated. "I—I called to tell you I wasn't interested, not get talked into fucking the lust from our blood."

I had a feeling such a thing wouldn't be possible when it came to James Jenner. I'd experienced that kind of yearning before, the all-consuming desire for intimacy, and look where it had landed me.

"Kellen—"

"No," I cut off his sure attempts to sway me.

JJ's heavy exhale came through the cell loud and clear.

"I don't fuck outside of Elite for a reason," I stated firmly, "and that's not going to change anytime soon."

"Like I said, I'm not available," JJ assured me, his tone contemplative, "but don't you ever think about giving yourself another chance at something more than filling nameless holes?"

"Wouldn't be worth the possible pain," I stated bluntly.

"I beg to differ."

Deep down, I wanted him to *beg* for something differ-ent, but I squashed that thought as soon as it rose.

"I gotta go," I lied, needing to silence his sexy, raspy voice that made me want to fold and offer my ass up on a platter for him to devour.

"If you change your mind..."

"I won't," I stated firmly. "Hope you have a great rest of the weekend, Detective."

"You too, Kellen." At least he sounded resigned, thank fuck. The last thing I needed was him pushing my buttons to override my better sense.

I hung up, tossed my cell onto my coffee table, and buried my face in my hands. "Fucking Xavier!"

Chapter 10

JJ

Rain poured from the sky darkened by heavy clouds when I left the station on a Tuesday a few weeks into September. The heat of summer had finally relented, and a chill bit at me along with raindrops as I sprinted toward my car after a long day of work.

The case against Joseph Delaney III moved forward regardless of the fact Mason still refused to press charges. The rich, young punk would stand before a jury of his supposed peers in November for what he'd done to that second man, and I couldn't wait to sit and testify against him.

I'd been born with a strong sense of right and wrong, following in my stepfather's footsteps to become a cop. While he'd always dreamed of becoming a detective, he'd never gotten that far. So I'd accomplished his goal. Unfortunately, my detective's badge got pinned to my chest a few years after I'd lain him to rest alongside my mom.

My mom hadn't planned on getting pregnant with me at age forty, but when you fucked strangers without protection, shit happened. I hadn't lied to Mason and Kellen that day outside the Peabody courthouse, but my mom had only sold her body for a few months in order to feed the two of us before she'd met John.

He'd refused to let her return to the streets and insisted we move in with him. And she loved him for rescuing us from the ghettos. Their relationship had been a beautiful thing to witness, and their tender loyalty toward each other had made a deep impression on my teenage heart.

John had adopted me. Loved me as though his blood flowed through my veins. He'd been my hero, the man I'd looked up to most, the one who had instilled morals deep inside me.

I'd been without both of them for too damn long.

Loneliness hovered like a dark shroud in the evenings when I got home. It was why I tended to stay at the office, putting in more hours than necessary.

Rather than turning on music to empty my brain while heading back to my place, I replayed the conversation I'd had with Kellen yet again as I'd been doing more often than I should. His ex had done a number on him, and years later, he continued to hurt. His voice had also hinted he wasn't happy with his current life.

And I wanted to be there for him—

My cell rang, and I answered on speaker, surprisingly a little annoyed to have my quiet disrupted beyond rain hitting my windshield. Fucking guilt squashed the selfishness back down. "Hey, Alex."

"You off?"

"Yeah."

"Teresa is being an absolute bitch," he slurred, his voice indicating he'd self-medicated with alcohol, which he'd been doing a lot of lately. "Won't stop hounding me—I can't fucking sleep at night—she's driving me insane!"

"What did you do now?"

Alex swore. "What makes you think *I* did something?"

He was too damn defensive, but I'd been on edge with him myself since the whole "forgetting" his cell phone thing.

"Did you?" I asked, allowing him the chance to prove my thoughts otherwise.

"She's so damn needy all. The. Time! Keeps saying I'm not *emotionally available* to her anymore," he mocked. "What the fuck is that supposed to mean?"

Empathy for his wife for having the same feeling about Alex radiated through my chest. "When did you do something for her last?" I asked.

"Fucking...seriously, JJ?" He sounded incredulous along with being drunk. "I work my *ass* off to keep that roof over her head and put food on the table."

"You would be slaving away to pay your bills regardless of having a family, Alex," I stated not unkindly. "What have you done for her specifically? Flowers? Sent her to the bathroom with a glass of wine to soak in the tub while you put the boys to bed? Got her a gift certificate for a spa? Took her out to dinner, just the two of you?"

Alex didn't speak for a few seconds as he stewed over my words.

"You're busy," I said. "I get it, but you've got to invest in your relationship regardless of having an open marriage, Alex. Ignoring the problem isn't going to make it go away. Bitterness will eventually grow and fester, and one night you might come home to an empty house." My words, although the right thing to say, made my shoulders heavy, like a weight pushed me toward a silent, cold grave where I would be alone for eternity.

A part of me hated giving my lover counsel when my

selfish heart longed for that very thing to happen so I could have him all to myself.

But that would never be. I wouldn't allow it. His boys needed him in their life a hell of a lot more than I ever would.

"Alex?" I asked when the silence went on too long between us.

"Yeah." He sniffed.

My heart softened at the knowledge I'd gotten him to think beyond himself. "Just give her—her emotions and needs—space in your busy schedule. Trust me, if she has your attention in a positive way, she'll soak it up and treat you better too."

I knew that from past experience, but like Teresa, I'd become annoyed with Alex's behavior.

"Did you hear Ostroski got picked up by the Bruins?"

I blinked at the sudden change of topic, especially the one-eighty from the remorse it sounded as though he'd been feeling. "What?"

"Yeah—fucking landed a contract for eleven-point-three mil! Fuck, what I could do with that kind of cash," he spewed the words faster than he usually spoke when drunk.

Biting my tongue, I listened to Alex prattle on about hockey when minutes earlier he'd been pissed and supposedly broken up about his wife. Talk about a damned mood swing. He seemed way too upbeat...almost manic with excitement. He had a love for the ice and pucks, but something had gotten him riled up to a point he sounded...high.

Perhaps it wasn't alcohol he'd been downing.

Jesus fuck.

My heart rate kicked up in immediate concern. "You okay, Alex?" I asked as I pulled into my garage and shut off my car.

"Sure, sure." He rushed his breathless answer.

I wished he stood in front of me so I could see his eyes, but a question would have to do for the time being. "You popping pills again?"

"The fuck, man! Why are you asking me that?" His tone was harder than usual.

"You just...goddamnit." I scrubbed a hand over my face and shoved open my driver door. "Never mind. I'm fucking beat, soaked from the goddamned rain, and probably reading into shit. I know how much you love the Bruins. You just seemed really upset about Teresa one second then excited about their newest player the next."

Alex huffed a laugh. "All good. You gave me the answer I needed. Gonna take your advice and spoil the hell out of Teresa. That'll definitely shut her up."

Shut her up.

His words echoed in my head as I hung up a few seconds later and let myself into my quiet house. That shroud-like heaviness descended as it always did, and flicking on the kitchen lights didn't help to dispel the loneliness settling over me. Listening to Alex say that shit about his wife made me wonder what he thought of me. I'd been loyal when she wasn't—agreement for their open relationship notwithstanding—and I'd always been there for him. Every. Goddamned. Time.

He liked to shut me up with a cock lodged in my throat, but did I annoy him in the same way she'd been lately?

Alex tended toward selfish, but I'd never heard him behave...

The thought dissolved as memories of my best friend high on fentanyl resurfaced. He'd sounded drunk a lot. Couldn't sleep. Had trouble focusing and paying attention to conversations and everyday life.

Jaw clenched, I considered shooting off a text to Teresa to have her check in with her husband. See if his pupils were pinned. Obviously, he'd been pulling away from her enough that she'd confronted him with his treatment of her, but was his behavior truly a result from work or something more troubling?

Annoyance over the entire affair atop the aggravation I'd dealt with at the office earlier that day crowded the empty spaces in my chest. While I wanted answers from Alex, I knew from experience my hands were tied.

I'd paid for his rehab, had helped him get clean, but what if it had all been a waste? What if he once more strung me along, using me as he seemed to do with everyone else in his life?

A sense of hopelessness washed over me, heightening the feeling of wretched isolation.

Bottle of beer in hand, I settled on my couch and pulled up my cell's browser.

Elite Escorts.

I'd studied the website from home page to contact form countless times, admiring the sleek, professional design since Mason's attack had brought the company to my attention.

I clicked on the gay branch, same as whenever I felt abandoned by the man I loved. Scrolling through the images eventually filled my screen with Kellen's hotness.

"Goddamn," I muttered to myself.

Lust hoofed me in the balls, and I groaned, palming my thickening dick. The man was so damn fine, and I'd never physically ached so hard for someone before. What was it about him that did it for me? Why couldn't I set the thought of him aside? How had he burrowed into my consciousness, haunting me while dreaming and awake?

"Fuck it."

Lips in a thin line, I scrolled down to the bottom of the page again and clicked on the link to submit a request for a night with Kellen Roberts.

The man would be forced to face me, talk to me, *please* me if I booked an evening with him.

Then we could go on our merry way, sated from our mutual lust.

A part of me secretly wished being with someone other than Alex would help sever that tether my best friend had over me, the one that allowed him to take advantage of me.

But I didn't hold onto hope Kellen would be the one to set me free.

Chapter 11

Kellen

I opened the file sent over to me from EEMM's secretary and stalled out at the headshot of the man who had requested me for the night.

James Jenner.

"Oh fuck me," I groaned, sitting my half-dressed ass on the edge of my bed as adrenaline rushed through my limbs, making me weak. I'd just gotten out of the shower, but I wished I'd checked my assignment further in advance than a couple of hours.

It was too late for me to bail. Sean would give me shit. EEMM required at least a twelve-hour notice if they needed to reschedule with a different escort...unless there was an emergency—which I didn't have one, nor would I conjure up a lie.

Heart thrumming, I bit on the inside of my lip and flipped through JJ's information. Clean bill of health, on PrEP, vers, no limits other than scat play...

I rubbed along my jawline and the scruff I hadn't bothered shaving. While the idea of having the man all up in my space in a controlled, impersonal environment like the hotel he'd booked for the night turned me on, hairs still rose on my nape.

Everything about him screamed danger.

Keep up the walls.

Don't be vulnerable.

I could put my heart on lockdown and enjoy the fuck out of his fine ass though, I tried to tell myself. Swallow his cum as he thrust into my throat. My dick swelled at the image flashing through my head of him peering down at me while I brought him to climax. I lusted to hear his groans, curses spilling from his lips as he found release inside my body.

Slumping, I told myself I had no easy way out. He'd signed the papers and paid. I was his for the night.

And holy fucking shit did every inch of my skin come alive, pebbling and shivering with instinctive need.

Take what he offers, I told myself while blowing out a heavy exhale and pushing to my feet. *Enjoy the fuck out of him, ride the lust train of the first connection you've felt in years.*

It didn't have to be more than a transaction.

Wouldn't be.

Mind made up and set on protecting my heart throughout the hours of our sexual tryst, I took care in dressing in my usual black on black attire. We would meet at a swanky hotel in downtown Boston. No dinner. No bar for drinks. Just a room number and time to meet him was listed in the file.

I grabbed my assigned EEMM bag, which was outfitted with all the essentials: condoms, lube, various plugs, and a few different types of restraints. Since I wasn't showcased as a Dom on the Elite's website, my bag didn't include toys for impact play and other types of

BDSM kinky shit. While I wasn't exactly vanilla in my personal preferences, I tended toward tame with our clients.

Some parts of me I had no wish to share ever again because they required trust, a thing I couldn't give.

Adrenaline kept me antsy on the ride into Boston, and I worked my grip on the steering wheel like I would a stress ball. My protective instincts suggested I turn around, go back home, and hide from the man who made me feel shit I didn't want to experience again.

But the lure of Detective James Jenner...

Fucking hell, the man hadn't left my mind. I saw him in my dreams, those damn hips of his moving in a slow, sensual dance meant to make me mad with need. The rasp of his voice over the phone still echoed in my ears, and his chuckle, his firm tone caused my skin to prickle as though electricity rippled over my body.

My cock ached no matter how badly I tried to think of something else. *Anything* else.

The latest Roberts grandchild, while cute as hell and the perfect little angel, didn't even have space in my head. Nor did the fact that my oldest nephew had been named captain of his football team. He was the starting quarter-back at the game I'd caught the Friday night before while spending the weekend in Nodhead Falls.

All the good things in my life faded beyond the glamour of JJ, the sexiest fucking man on the planet.

"Jesus, I'm a mess." I found a spot in the parking garage and cut the engine—but didn't move. Silence settled over me, my heightened exhales the only sound keeping me company. "Just get in there and please the client. Make sure he comes first—"

I snorted at myself. My balls were going to erupt at a

mere touch of his hand or mouth. Hell, I was going to blow like a pubescent teenager the second I got a taste of him.

"Christ."

Teeth gritted, I climbed out of the car, locked up, and strode through the cavernous, echoing garage to the hotel's entrance across the streetlight-lit road. Coolness coated the evening, the temperature low enough my breath fogged in front of me. One foot in front of the other, I focused on keeping my inhales steady. I stretched my neck side to side as the elevator sped upward toward the sixth floor, but I still felt on edge, ready to combust.

More steps on nicer carpet than I had in my apartment took me to #613—a corner suite that had cost JJ a pretty penny. The man didn't hold back and had gone all out to finally get his hands on me, and I was thankful for the neutral location.

I released a steady exhale in an attempt to slow my rapidly beating heart and knocked.

The door swung inward before my arm dropped to my side.

The sight of a shirtless JJ in low-slung sweats pulled a grunt from my lungs, tightening my abs and groin.

Jesus fucking Christ, the man was gorgeous. Thick pecs with a smattering of dark hair caught my attention first. My gaze slid downward. Just a hint of padding lay atop a six-pack...and the goddamned V disappearing into his pants made my mouth water.

"You're drooling," JJ said with a chuckle, the rasp of his voice like a teasing caress over my balls.

"Can you blame me?" I asked in all seriousness, needing to adjust my aching cock at the sight of his bulge.

"Are you going to just stand there and stare or come in here so I can take care of that for you?"

"Fuck," I muttered, stepping forward and finally lifting my gaze to his face.

"That's the plan." Face slightly flushed, lips appearing freshly licked, he smirked at me, his dark eyes promising I was about to have the time of my life.

The door clicked shut on its own behind me, and JJ moved in without a word.

I didn't argue, didn't stop him—simply gave in to the moment I had no control over.

Our mouths met in a wicked clash of hunger, and fire erupted inside me as he grasped my face to hold me still. He plundered, and I responded just as greedily, licking between his lips and sucking on his tongue. Tasting mint, smelling it when he exhaled a deep groan.

My shoulders hit the door, and the heat of JJ pressed along my front. We stood eye to eye, a perfect match in every delicious way. His hard cock ground against mine, and I slid my hands up his smooth, hot back, needing to swallow the whimpers leaking from my lungs at the feel of rippling, tight muscles under my fingertips.

"Want you on your knees," he rumbled against my lips. "Need to hear you gag around my cock—moan for me to wreck your ass."

My abs contracted as he grabbed a handful of my backside, my dick bucking against his at his rough hold. His other hand landed on my shoulder and pushed downward.

I went willingly, rubbing my face all the fuck over his straining erection hidden behind cotton. A dark spot appeared on the material as I eyed the vivid outline of his cock, and I licked at the pre-cum stain while sliding my palms up to his waist.

"Take me out."

I moved to obey but not because I'd been paid to please

him. Lust for a taste of him, the feel of his hard shaft on my tongue prompted my hands to do as told.

His uncut length slapped upward against his belly, and I cursed beneath my breath. He was perfect in every way, damn him. His shaft had delicious girth and just the right length to drive me insane with deep strokes.

"Want it," I heard myself whisper.

"Suck me first," JJ rasped, making my balls tighten up against my body. "Then I'll fill you up and fuck the cum out of you."

Chapter 12

JJ

Wet heat surrounded the head of my cock, and I swore as Kellen licked inside my foreskin to tease my frenulum.

"Fuck yeah," I groaned, fisting his hair and soaking in the sight I'd fantasized about... Kellen Roberts on his knees for me. "Christ, the things you do to me."

Grasping my length around the middle, he pulled my foreskin downward, giving him access to the entire head of my dick. He took me deep.

"Yes," I hissed, unable to keep from rocking farther into his throat, nothing more than a creature of need.

He swallowed around me without issue, not offering me the gagging noises I'd dreamed of hearing. But in that moment, I didn't care. The warmth and suction of his mouth was a sensual delight, the sweetest foreplay I'd ever had lavished on me. Guilt didn't exist...physically connecting with Kellen felt too right for words.

Pupil-blown hazel eyes peered up at me, and I bit my lip, once more sliding my entire length into his mouth. His nose brushed over my trimmed pubes. I held him still. Choked him until he gave me what I wanted.

A ragged cough sounded around my cock, spittle leaking down my balls.

"Just like that," I stated through gritted teeth, backing out to allow him oxygen.

Kellen dug his fingers into my ass cheeks and forced me in deep again as though desperate for more.

"Oh shit." I muttered on a groan, my head tipping toward the ceiling, my eyes rolling back into my head. "So. Fucking. Good. Jesus, Kellen." Yanking him off me before I blew too early, I panted for breath. My balls ached, and my dick throbbed after mere minutes of having the man's mouth on me.

Still, he peered up at me, lazing a stroke up toward my cockhead and down to the base.

"What's it going to be, JJ?" he asked, his voice husky from lust and probably the throat fucking I'd given him.

"Want you bent over the back of the couch." I had fucking ideas. Things I'd never gotten to explore or enjoy before. And the sense of freedom I felt with Kellen? Fucking hell, I wanted to experience it all.

Kellen stood and moved farther into the suite, ridding his body of clothing as he went.

I kicked off my sweats and followed, drinking in the sight of him as he stripped. Gorgeously tanned...a few tattoos...rippling shoulders, and a broad back. He slipped off his shoes and shoved down his black jeans without pause.

Completely naked, he bent forward over the couch like I'd instructed, putting his ass on display.

"Jesus," I whispered, stepping in close to palm his cheeks and spread them wide. He didn't shave or wax, but I enjoyed the little bit of hair around his hole. "You clean yourself good for me, Kellen?"

"Yes."

"Thank fuck." I dropped to my knees and shoved my nose against his crack, inhaling a lungful of his natural musk and the hint of soap he'd used before coming to me. I hated that Alex entered my mind but couldn't help the excitement over finally being allowed to eat a man's ass. My best friend gagged at the mere thought, but Kellen? He moaned, spine arching as I licked upward from his taint to his tailbone.

"Tastes good," I murmured, my dick leaking between my spread knees.

"More," he demanded, the needy fucker.

Grinning, I went to town, making a sloppy mess of his hole, shoving my tongue in to taste as deep as I could go. He was fucking delicious.

"JJ," Kellen gasped, rocking against my face. "Goddamn—your tongue...want your cock though."

Shit, the lust in his tone tightened my balls right the fuck up. I sucked on his hole then licked over his taint once. Twice. Lapped at my spit, shoving it inside his pucker.

"Seriously, JJ," Kellen growled. "Get on with the fucking before I flip this shit around and shove my dick so far up your ass you won't be able to walk for days."

Chuckling, I stood and slapped his cheek hard enough it bounced. "On the bed."

Kellen glanced over his shoulder at me while stepping toward where I'd ordered him to go. Hazed with lust, those gorgeous eyes of his snagged my gaze, stealing the oxygen from my lungs.

I stalked after him on instinct, my entire body buzzing. "Need inside you so fucking bad."

He climbed onto the bed on his hands and knees then bent forward, forehead to the mattress, spine in a deeply bowed arch. His spit-slickened hole was a sight I couldn't look away from.

I fumbled with the lube and condoms I'd left on the nightstand. Trembled while kneeling between his spread thighs. My hand shook while I sheathed up. His ring had been softened by my tongue, but I wasn't about to take him hard without stretching him.

He groaned as I sank two lubed fingers inside his ass. His body sucked at them, drawing them in deeper without resistance.

"Oh fuck—right there." He shuddered as my fingertips grazed over his prostate.

I stroked into him a couple of times, a grin on my face as he grasped at the sheets and cursed up a storm. He thrust back to meet me with the same hunger driving me forward. Jesus, this man made me feel things I didn't know how to control. Didn't lust for anything but to lose myself in him and bring us both to exhausting completion.

"I'm ready. Give me your dick, JJ—don't want to come without you inside me."

"Christ." I clenched my jaw and slid my fingers free from his tight heat. A squirt of lube to my throbbing dick, and I crowded in close, eyeing his tight hole. "Let me in, baby," I murmured the endearment without thought, shifting forward to breach him.

Deep groans rose from both of us as I slipped past his tight muscle into decadent heat. I'd never fucked a man without a condom. Couldn't even begin to imagine how luscious Kellen's ass would clench at my girth. Fuck, did I burn for that. Desperately.

I slid in slowly, a slick glide until I buried deep. Even

with the rubber, he was deliciously warm, his hole a perfect, snug fit around my girth.

"Fucking hell, Kell." I gulped and pulled out, only keeping the head of my cock buried inside his body. "You feel so damn good—better than I imagined."

"Shut up and fuck me already. Want you to fill up that condom so I can have a go at your ass."

"Nuh uh," I disagreed with a low chuckle while slowly rocking back into him. "I've only got you until eight tomorrow morning, so I'm going to love on your sinful body all. Night. Long." Each word was accompanied a short stroke, pegging his prostate and making him mutter more curses.

I laughed again, enjoying myself entirely too much. Who knew sex could be fun?

Sitting on my haunches, I pulled Kellen upward until he sat on my lap. I wrapped my arms around him, clutching him close. My nose rubbed through his soft hair, and I breathed in the scent of bergamot and the underlying masculinity of Kellen. Heart pounding against his warm back, I basked in the still moment. Cuddling while buried deep was my new favorite. Goddamn addictive—

He shifted, and I sighed, planning on spooning the hell out of him between fucking. As a client, I could demand whatever I desired. And get it.

Kellen swiveled his hips and laid his head on my shoulder.

I licked up his neck. "Can I mark you?" I whispered what I wanted against his ear while thrusting upward into him.

"Fuck yeah," he agreed, his voice nothing but breath and need. "Do it."

I nosed down to his clavicle and sucked in the way no

man had allowed me to do before. Our lower bodies danced like we'd done at the club, but this time, no clothing hindered our touching. No thrumming bass pumped in our ears. We existed skin on skin. Panted breaths and whimpers were the only music accompanying our movements.

We were in our own little world where no one could interrupt or demand we stop—and it was fucking heaven.

"JJ," Kellen moaned and leaned forward.

I followed him down, planking over his prone form.

"Give it to me hard. Want to feel you for days." He swallowed audibly. "Need to remember…" He spoke those final words quietly as though sharing a secret.

Who was I to deny the one who'd stirred up my life in ways I'd never imagined possible? I hardly knew the man beyond what I'd learned from my online digging, but something inside me seemed to *recognize* him. Our bodies fed off each other. Flared the flames of intense desire that threatened my sanity.

I thrust in, snapping my hips in desperation to burrow so deep he wouldn't be rid of me.

Ever.

"Fucking hell," I muttered, watching as my dick tunneled into his hole with long strokes.

"M-more."

"Jesus, Kell." I swallowed hard and lay atop him, winding my arms beneath his torso to hug him tight. Sweat quickly slickened the glide between our bodies, his back hot as a furnace against my chest. I fucked into him with enough force the headboard slammed against the wall. "Need my hand on your dick?" I grunted against his ear.

"No—gonna get off just—like—this." His words ripped from his lips with my harsh thrusts, the slapping of skin rising above our labored breaths.

"You come first," I told him, ready for his ring to strangle my cock.

Two more thrusts, and his hole spasmed around me, his muscular back and thighs tightening beneath me.

"Yes, baby," I crooned against his ear—and promptly flooded the condom with cum.

That was the second time that word had slipped from my lips. What the hell was wrong with me? Why did I feel such a tangible bond to a man I hardly knew? Why did I yearn to do it all over again?

My heart ached even as it soared in euphoric bliss.

Our evening together was supposed to be a one and done night of fucking, not falling for someone else.

Chapter 13

Kellen

You come first.

I knew JJ meant climaxing, but seconds before my taint spasmed and cum shot all over the mattress rubbing against my aching dick, I dreamed he'd meant more. That he put me above his own desires, that my thoughts and feelings were valid and had merit to him.

Neither of which I'd ever had with a man before.

A swell of emotion rose up inside me as my balls erupted. I clung to JJ's arms wrapped around my chest, wanting to keep him close for-goddamned-ever.

I'd had hundreds of climaxes with Elite's clients.

But none of them had even hinted at plucking bricks from the wall I hid my vulnerability behind. No one had affected me like JJ. No one had ever eaten my ass, marked me, or fucked me like him—as though he wouldn't survive unless buried deep inside my body. My soul. With my taste on his tongue and evidence of his loving visible on my skin for all to see.

Fucking hell, this man...

I groaned and went limp beneath him, his heavy weight

still twitching atop mine. His hot exhales panted against my neck, and I shivered at his low moan.

"Goddamn, Kell," he murmured, squeezing me as he too relaxed in satiated contentment.

Without conscious effort, I slid my hand atop the back of his on my chest, threading our fingers together.

"Fuck." He kissed my damp skin, licking over my clavicle where he'd sucked on me.

We were wrapped up in a bubble of our own where nothing existed but a communion of satisfied pleasure. Addictive bliss I hadn't felt in... I couldn't remember how long. Had I ever experienced such a soul-deep connection? Especially after fucking, where all my puzzle pieces had found their place and no questions littered my thoughts?

The hairs rising on the back of my neck while JJ continued to rain kisses over my shoulders suggested I escape from beneath him. Gain some space from his overwhelming presence.

I couldn't move.

JJ hooked our ankles together and tried to bury his spent dick a little deeper inside me, the bulk of his hot muscles tightening briefly atop me. He felt too good tangled up with damn near every inch of my body.

"Could stay here all night," he murmured against my neck, stating the very thought I had.

The wetness of my cum beneath me wasn't exactly pleasant though.

"How uncomfortable is that puddle of spunk, hmm?" he asked and nipped my lobe.

I chuckled, enjoying how our minds aligned. "Very, but I'm too blissed out to give a shit."

JJ's huff of laughter against my ear caused goose bumps

to skitter down my arms. "Give me a second, and I'll clean you up."

He was the paying customer, but I didn't have it in me to argue he shouldn't be the one giving aftercare regardless of the fact I'd bottomed.

Backing out slowly left my ass gaping, and JJ slid down over sweat-damp skin until his chest rested on the backs of my thighs. He gripped my ass cheeks and spread me open.

"Look at that." He licked over my slack hole, and I grimaced over the thought of lube in his mouth, even though his tongue was sublime on my swollen, sensitive flesh.

JJ didn't seem to mind the taste, soothing my stretched ring until my dick attempted to twitch back to life.

"Goddamn." He sat back and slapped my right cheek. "Fuck, everything about you is hot."

The praise spilling from him swelled something inside my chest. Scary as fuck, a feeling I knew I should run from, but my body still refused to budge.

It was as if every muscle in me said a big *fuck you* to my brain stem, choosing instead to bask in the afterglow of the best lay of my life.

Because it had been that very thing. Mind-altering. Soul-filling.

Eyes clenched shut, I listened as JJ cleaned up in the bathroom, attempting to block the thoughts in my head. I succeeded easily by focusing on the tingles of pleasure lingering in my limbs. *So* relaxed. Sated. A heavy sigh rippled through me.

A minute later, the bed once more dipped, and I spread my legs when he tapped my thigh. He took his time wiping spit and lube from my ass, and when he murmured for me to roll over, he cleaned up the cum smeared all over my abs too.

He studied my flaccid cock while wiping the warm towel over me, and I stared at his face as he did. No lines furrowed his brow. A soft smile curved his lips, and when he tossed aside the towel and sat to gaze over the rest of me, I shivered again.

JJ trailed his fingertips from my hip to my chest, lingering a bit to tweak my tightening nipple.

He was an unselfish lover, something Xavier was not. Continuing to compare the two men would be like counting the differences between day and night, summer and winter. They were polar opposites...and I didn't even know JJ that well. His actions had proven his character though.

Why wasn't he married or with a partner? From what I'd seen, the man was a total catch.

"Who was the blond?" I heard myself ask for a second time as the memory of him flitted through my mind. They'd seemed cozy and comfortable dancing at the club. If I'd had to bet money they were more than acquaintances I would have, regardless of JJ claiming they weren't together.

"Alex Berset. My best friend," JJ answered, withdrawing his touch to rest his hand on his leg he'd pulled up onto the bed to angle toward me. "We've been lovers for over ten years."

Talk about brutal honesty. I fucking loved that JJ didn't hold back, but the questions that arose from his blunt statement cluttered my thoughts.

"Ten years, but you're not...more than friends with benefits?"

"No." His lips thinned for a second as he glanced around the suite that suddenly seemed too quiet. "He's married to a woman, but they have an open relationship."

Well, shit.

"So...fuck buddies for a decade? Are you averse to relationships or something?"

"No." JJ returned his focus to my face, carefully studying my eyes then mouth.

I licked my lower lip. "You love him."

"Yes," he stated bluntly.

"Oh, fuck, that must suck," I murmured as my own lingering sorrow sent a pang through my chest.

His smile had a hint of sadness to it. "It does. I've come to terms with the fact he'll never be more than my weekend lover, but it's been enough. Until now. You're the first man I've been with besides him in the years we've been...well, whatever you want to call us."

I blinked.

A huff of laughter rushed past JJ's lips, a delicious sound I wished I could hear over and over again. "Yeah, you can definitely let that bit of information swell up your ego."

Jesus.

His words didn't do jack shit for my pride...I was simply stunned. And smiling. "Why? I mean, why me...but yeah, why now? After ten fucking years?"

JJ studied me with his detective eagle eye long enough I squirmed. Without a word, he climbed fully onto the bed and stretched out on top of me. We touched from chest to toes, his fingers spearing into my hair as he cradled my head in his hands.

"There's something magnetic about you, a force I can't withstand," he stated without question. "Don't want to."

Fuck, he pulled the words from my mind.

"You feel it too, don't you?" he murmured, rubbing his thumbs over my cheekbones.

"Yeah," I admitted quietly, not realizing I gripped his waist until that moment. I spread my thighs wider, giving him space, but I pressed tight against the walls his presence alone attempted to topple inside me. He was in love with another man—

"I like it," he admitted. "This energy between us."

"I don't," I quickly refuted, although my groin argued with me.

The heat of his body seeped into me as he lay there staring into my eyes. I couldn't look away. He'd fucking ensnared me with those dark, fathomless orbs.

"You're scared," he murmured.

I didn't argue with his quiet assessment.

"It's been almost three years since your ex hurt you, but you're still grieving. Hiding yourself away."

Annoyance prickled up my spine over his nosiness, and I readied to shift his weight off me.

JJ lowered his head, his warm breath ghosting over my lips and freezing me in place. "My heart isn't available either, remember, Kellen? You have nothing to fear from me." He brushed his mouth against mine, and my lungs released a breath I hadn't realized I'd held. I went pliant, my lips parting and allowing him entrance.

Soft, shared kisses erased every thought from my mind, and when he rolled onto his back, allowing me to be on top, I settled in to enjoy every second I could with my new favorite Elite client.

I kissed, licked, and nibbled every inch of his body from mouth to belly button. Shoving his knees wide gave me access to his ass, and I ate him out until his dick dripped onto his stomach and he begged me to fuck him.

"Turn over," I ordered, grabbing another condom off the bed stand.

"No—want you just like this."

I rolled on the rubber while eyeing JJ's flushed face.

Lust dominated his black pupils, and I got caught up in a war of need and fear. My stomach clenched, that instinct in the back of my mind screaming at me to ignore JJ's wishes and demand he hide his face from me while I owned his ass.

Please the client.

Swallowing hard, I jerked my head in a nod, knowing I flirted with flames that had the power to burn me to ash.

I got lost in his eyes while stretching his hole to take me. Continued to study his satisfied expression as I slowly sank into his tight heat.

Without a word, he clasped my cheeks and pulled me down to claim my mouth, wrapping his heels around my ass and holding me close. We made love—there was no other explanation for how we moved together. Slow and tender strokes, caressing hands. Hungry yet unselfish mouths tasting whatever flesh we could reach without creating space between our heated bodies.

"You come first," I murmured against his mouth, once more covered in sweat and desperate for oxygen.

He gave me what I asked for, my name a gasped plea on his lips that I swallowed down to keep with me forever.

Chapter 14

JJ

sking Kellen to fuck me face-to-face wasn't the smartest thing I'd ever done. His agreeing and loving on me with complete openness left me sated but also broken. My emotions bleeding.

He'd stroked me so damn good, playing my body like a master. Bringing me to climax without effort.

But goddamn, did I ache deep inside where no one had touched me before—and not my ass, either.

Kellen lay atop me, spent and catching his breath while I continued to cling to him with arms and legs wrapped around his back. His thickness was delicious in my ass, still full even though he'd come moments after I had.

A heavy exhale expanded his ribcage inside my hold, and I expected only seconds remained until he once more got all up in his head.

But I would be right there with him.

What we'd shared...fucking hell, it was ten times the connection I'd ever felt with Alex. I loved my best friend, but was it possible I wasn't...*in* love with him? How did the emotions I experienced with both men differ so vastly? Why had I gotten so caught up in a man I barely knew?

Was it because he was something new? A fresh influx of experience I'd been missing for over a decade?

No. There was a tangible tether between us that couldn't be denied. I could fucking feel it in every cell that made up my body.

And it scared me enough I grew antsy.

As though on the same thought train leading to chaos and confusion, Kellen stiffened in my hold.

I loosened my limbs, hating the chill, the sense of loss from him pushing up off me. My ass didn't ache, was simply empty from the gentle way we'd found completion together.

"My turn," he muttered, stumbling toward the bathroom.

I stared after his fine backside, pushing aside all worries and focusing instead on the euphoria still coursing through my blood and tingling my skin. Reality could wait. I had until eight in the morning before Kellen would walk away— probably never wanting to see me again.

What we'd done had stirred up emotion inside him. I'd seen it before asking him to take me in that position. I'd done so deliberately too, selfishly needing all of him in that moment.

He returned, not making eye contact while wiping my cum off my stomach.

Since it was my night, my dollar, I took the cloth from him when he finished, tossed it aside, and tugged him down so he lay on his side in front of me, facing the wall.

"Cuddle time," I murmured against his hair. "Then a shower where you're going to fuck me again. Punish my ass for making both of us feel too much."

Kellen stiffened again as though I'd stated truth, but I

knew I did. I'd seen it in his eyes. Sensed his withdrawal emotionally when he'd slipped his semi from my sensitive hole.

"Shh," I murmured, wrapping my arm tight around his chest and sliding my leg between his. "Let me hold you."

He did, and I got to enjoy the peaceful quiet of snuggling with a man for the first time since...college, maybe?

I rubbed my thumb in circles over his thick pec, listening to his breaths, enjoying the thump of his heartbeat beneath my palm with a cadence that matched my own. Kellen was deliciously warm, all hard muscle but soft skin. Burrowing my face against the back of his neck, I breathed in the natural scent of him, my cock tempted to rouse for a third round.

Wasn't happening anytime soon though. The horny twenties were long gone, but I soaked up the affection he gifted me in lavishing on his body, something Alex always refused.

I allowed myself a few brief moments to consider my best friend but more specifically how he denied me my needs. How, except for that fuck in the club bathroom while I'd been thinking about Kellen, our love life had grown stale. Almost...boring, to the point sex with him had become a chore.

"Does it ever grow tiresome?" I asked.

"Escorting?"

"Pleasing other men. Not taking or having what *you* want."

"Not every client is satisfying," Kellen admitted after a few moments of reflection. "But I find my release. Sometimes I have to disappear somewhere else in my mind to get there, but I always do."

"Where do you go?" I asked, too damn curious.

He huffed a snort. "You're one nosey fucker."

"Can't help it." I pinched his nipple, and he hissed.

"You seriously want to hear about my fantasies?"

"Fuck yeah." I chuckled. "Want to know everything about you."

Kellen lay quiet, and I realized what we had done, *did*, and how the conversation I'd steered probably got his guard up.

"I'm intrigued by you, not gonna lie," I said, going back to soothing strokes over his chest so he wouldn't bolt from where I wanted him to stay. "But that doesn't mean I'm going to start stalking you and shit. I won't call you or text, begging for another go. This night is meant to ease the itch, remember?"

But would it really?

Less than four hours together, and I hated the thought of him walking out the door come morning.

"Do you have any family?" Kellen asked, and I smiled, closing my eyes and relaxing fully onto the mattress behind him.

I told him about my mom being older and single. Reminded him of how she'd put food on our table and paid the electric bill. I shared my joy over having a stepfather and how deeply he'd impacted my life.

Every question Kellen raised, I answered—but I noted his lack of interest in the topic of Alex.

I shared what I could about his friend Mason and the case against Joseph Delaney. We discussed the chances of the rich punk paying for his crimes without Mason's story.

He explained about Jasper, the younger man who'd come to Mason's rescue. How they'd attached themselves to each other as though they'd always been meant to be.

Longing hinted in Kellen's voice regardless of his strict

stance against relationships. And when our conversation came back around to family, and he spoke of his on the farm up in Maine, I recognized the yearning in his soul. I envied Kellen. Wanted what he had—a place to truly call home where loved ones welcomed him with open arms.

Kellen Roberts didn't belong in Boston, even though he loved all the hours spent volunteering at the vet clinic a few blocks from his apartment. It was obvious in how he spoke that his heart lay to the north, and I wondered why he lingered.

But I didn't ask.

Instead, I insisted on a shower, changing the topic off what would definitely make us both more melancholy than I was sure we both already felt.

Once more quiet, we took turns washing each other, and I cleaned his ass thoroughly, as I wanted one last taste of him. I waited until we were on the side of the bed that wasn't stiff from dried cum before holding his cheeks wide and feasting on his pucker.

But I was the one to get on my knees, and it was my hole that got speared a second time, and there was nothing soft or tender that go-round. I begged Kellen to wreck me.

And he did.

Thoroughly.

Once more spooning as though the world would end with the sunrise, we filled the silence. Talking. Whispering. I touched every inch of his skin I could reach, memorizing the dips and swells of the muscles spanning his torso. Fondled his soft sac. Held his dick in a comforting grip meant solely to keep us connected.

Simple acts of intimacy that filled me up to overflowing.

I would never have that with Alex.

But I couldn't have it with Kellen after our hours together ended either.

When eight in the morning arrived, we were both bleary-eyed, our voices scratchy. He moved away first, and I had no choice but to let him go.

Hand resting atop the warmth he'd left behind on the mattress, I watched him quietly, slowly, get dressed. Once he'd covered his gorgeous body and shoved his shoes back on, that ache from the night before lanced through my chest.

He faced me, a mere ten feet separating us, but it felt like the goddamned Nile. His focus flitted from my bare chest to the sheet draped over my waist.

Fucking clueless on what to say, I kept my mouth shut.

When his eyes once more connected with mine, I swallowed hard. "I'll be seeing you," I decided on, needing some sort of assurance that our paths would cross again at some point in our lives.

Kellen didn't speak, simply shared his presence with me for a few more moments, our gazes locked. Countless emotions swarmed through me, same as his eyes assured me he experienced. He severed the tether between us, turned, and walked away.

At least he hadn't said goodbye.

But strangely, my heart felt as though he had—taking a piece of it along with him when he'd left me alone.

Chapter 15

Kellen

I'd never felt so off-kilter in my entire life.

Even when I'd been stunned and speechless upon finding Xavier with his ass filled by another man's dick, my world hadn't exactly shifted enough to throw me off my feet.

One night of fucking, of talking myself hoarse with JJ, had impacted me to a greater degree than my ex's infidelity.

I was consumed by thoughts of JJ, but unlike the fallout of Xavier's cheating, I didn't suffer in actual pain. There was no grieving in my soul for something lost, rather... despairing over perhaps having missed out?

Vocalizing what I felt over the next couple of days proved impossible. Putting to words how JJ had moved me was beyond my abilities, same as explaining how gravity worked or how vast the solar system was.

Clueless, I went through the motions of life, lifting at the gym and volunteering at the local vet clinic, the days passing in a blur until the following weekend arrived.

As usual, I didn't look at the file EEMM sent me for my Thursday night booking. My breath left in a rush of what I realized was relief when I saw I would only have to be eye candy for the night at a charity event. JJ stood center in my mind the entire time, and I struggled to be present with the man I'd escorted to the party.

Saturday's client proved the same lack of sex-wise, thank fuck, but we attended an awards dinner for some rich asshole whose name I couldn't even remember the second I drove home. Again, JJ had haunted my thoughts, but at least I'd only been a pretty face who needed to smile and not much else.

Sunday, Micah invited the crew to his place for the Pats' game. Jarod and his fiery-haired fiancée hollered at the TV, high-fiving and whooping enough most would get caught up in their excitement.

But not me.

Can't move the fuck on...

"You okay?" Micah elbowed me where we sprawled on one of his couches.

Sean had stolen his brother's favorite recliner, forcing Micah to sit beside me. Like the others in our smaller group that week, he vocalized his thoughts on the game loudly and often.

"Yep," I answered on autopilot before taking a swig of my beer.

"You're full of shit."

I snorted and glanced over at my nosey friend. His blue eyes were shrewd as fuck, same as a certain detective's I couldn't get off my mind. "I'm good."

His pursed lips told me he still didn't believe me. "Need a break from escorting?"

"What?" I straightened, my brow furrowing. "Why'd you say that?"

"Because you haven't been happy for weeks. Much as I hate to say it, maybe it's time for another trip north."

If I went home to the farm, I might not return. After my night with JJ, the sting of Xavier had faded to almost nothing in my mind, and my reasons for originally sticking around didn't hold the same weight as when I'd been freshly heartbroken.

So why didn't I take all the money I'd saved up and just head back to the place that gave me a sense of rightness? Distance from Xavier, from the areas where memories cropped up would be healthiest, but would creating that same space away from JJ feel the same?

The idea of leaving, of truly never seeing the detective again didn't settle well in my gut. I feared it almost as much as I did pulling down more bricks from my walls than he had in the one night we'd spent together.

"Remember that new client I had last weekend?" I asked.

"Friday night?" Micah kept tabs on everyone under the EE umbrella even if he didn't directly manage them.

"Yeah—James Jenner. You know who he is?" I asked and swigged my beer to wet my suddenly parched throat. God, just the thought of the man made me thirsty as fuck.

"I'm not too involved in the gay branch these days," Micah said, "but I'm all ears if something's on your mind."

The memory of JJ's naked body stretched out beneath me flitted through my memory, tempting the blood to seep into my groin. "He's the detective on Mason's case."

"No shit."

"Yep. It wasn't the first time we met though. He...uh, asked for me by name." I wasn't sure what else to say. It was where I always stalled out whenever I'd considered talking to someone about where my head was.

"You like him." Micah didn't ask a question.

"I don't want to."

"We can't help instinctive attraction."

I exhaled a heavy sigh and picked at my beer's label. "Wish we could turn that shit off."

"Why not dial it up higher. Hotter? See where it leads?"

"Yeah, right," I said with a snort. "It worked for you with Jasmine, but you know my thoughts on relationships."

"You can't let your ex control your future, Kellen. You're what, thirty-eight? You've got a lot of years left to live. Are you planning on being an escort until you're past the silver fox stage? Not that I would mind you staying on forever. You're one of the best escorts Elite has. Honestly, I never wanted to be tied down either—until I met Jasmine. She changed my world."

He'd also fought like fuck to help her overcome some issues so they could be together.

That was what true love was. Sometimes choosing other's needs above your own. Putting your partner first. Thinking of them in all things.

None of which Xavier had done for me.

He'd never loved me, I admitted to myself—not in the way I had with him, self-sacrificing in order for his life to be easier. Better.

"Take some time off, Kellen," Micah ordered, his firm tone not allowing argument. "I know you aren't hard up for cash, so a couple of weeks without a paycheck isn't going to break you—nor will Elite suffer."

"Thanks for making me feel needed," I joked even though my chest was heavy.

"Figure out what your heart is trying to tell you," Micah went on, ignoring me. "If you stay with us for a few more months or years, we'll be happy to keep you onboard. If not, that's fine too. I just want you to find the place where you feel you belong. And, I'm always here if you need to talk."

"Thanks, man. I appreciate it."

Micah clasped my shoulder and pushed off the couch. "Hey, asshole!" he hollered at his little brother. "I've been patient enough—give me my chair back."

The two siblings tussled for a few seconds, making me think of how me and my brother Jacob had done the same as teenagers.

It had been months since I'd gotten home. Perhaps going to the farm would clear my head. I was scheduled at the vet clinic Wednesday and Thursday, so maybe I would head north for the weekend. The plan slid into place, and I made up my mind, happy to feel my insides settle somewhat.

On Tuesday, my plans were waylaid.

"Saturday?" I asked Mason, repeating what he'd said over the phone. I'd been sprawled on my couch staring blankly at the TV while replaying my evening with JJ when he'd called.

"Yeah," Mason said, his voice soft and a little uncertain. "I...made an appointment to get a tattoo and could really use the company."

"Jasper's busy?"

"Well, that's the thing." Mason's deep inhale sounded loud and clear over the line. "The tattoo is *for* him. I want it to be a surprise."

I grinned at the peacefulness in his voice I hadn't heard for a long time. "Someone's in love," I sang the words, imagining his face flushed.

"Will you go with me?" he asked, ignoring my statement.

"Not gonna need to hold your hand though, will I?"

He huffed a snorted laugh. "No. I'm not that much of a pansy. It's just...that scar on my chest?"

He'd finally told me the details of what had gone down that night with Joseph Delaney, and the knowledge had made me want to find the kid, slice his heart out with a dull knife, and bury him deep in the woods of Maine.

"What about it?" I asked, my protective nature causing my voice to tighten.

"I'm turning that jagged J into my boyfriend's name."

Mason was going to permanently etch *Jasper* on his skin. For some reason, my heart cracked open, making my eyes sting. "I'll be there, Mason. Hell," I chuckled through sudden threatening tears. "I'll proudly let you squeeze my hand the entire time if that's what you need."

"I knew I could count on you, Kellen. You're a true friend."

After hanging up with him, I lay on my bed, alone as always, staring at the ceiling. Silence rang in my ears as I admitted to myself I envied what Mason had found.

Thoughts of JJ crowded my mind, but I still couldn't come to a decision over how I felt about him or what I wanted. I could admit to fantasizing over being with him again, hell, even on a permanent basis, but the jaded part of me seized up tight at the thought.

And he's in love with Alex.

Groaning, I rolled over, shoved my face in my pillow, and hollered a few curses.

JJ was into me, no question about that fact.

But I couldn't allow myself to be vulnerable and get my hopes up. Especially over someone whose heart wasn't obtainable, whose name would never be available to tattoo on anyone else's body but Alex's.

Chapter 16

JJ

"**M**y God, Teresa, this is phenomenal," I moaned and spoke around a mouthful of her lasagna.

She smiled across the dinner table at me for the first time since I'd arrived. It was their son Aaron's sixth birthday, and when asked who he wanted to come over for his special night, he'd supposedly claimed me.

Not Nanna and Gramps, Teresa's parents who lived in Jersey.

Me. Uncle JJ. The man who'd been a staple in his life since the day he'd been born. While the thought warmed me and made me feel appreciated, for the first time sitting at Alex's dining room table, I wasn't sure I...fit in anymore.

Somehow, I'd become disjointed. Out of place. Like my presence sat on a different plane than the family I'd considered myself to be a part of. I hovered outside reality when I used to feel at home.

The shift had happened after spending the night with Kellen. I hadn't met with Alex since, claiming I'd been busy with work on the two times he'd texted asking if I was up for a quick fuck.

I felt like shit for lying, but sharing intimacy with Kellen had definitely done something to me on a molecular level.

Add in that Alex's behavior since I'd arrived was slightly...off, and my feet itched to take me back out their front door.

"I'm getting a dog for my birthday!" Aaron perked up from the end of the table where he sat in the "special" chair at the opposite end of his dad. He grinned at me, eyes alight with mischief as Alex's had often been when we were children.

"Is that so?" I asked.

"We said we would talk about it," Teresa reminded him gently, but I could tell by Aaron's face that his mind was set and wouldn't be swayed. I expected whatever hid inside the wrapped gift boxes atop the hutch behind him didn't include flesh and blood.

"Dad," Aaron whined, and I glanced over at my friend to find him on his cell, texting. He frowned, his face paler than normal.

"Hmm?" he questioned without looking up.

"You got me a dog, right? You promised!"

"Sure, sure," he replied on autopilot.

"Alex," Teresa hissed beneath her breath.

"It's all good." He set his cell face down on the table and picked back up his fork without looking at us.

I realized he hadn't eaten more than two bites. He'd also lost a little weight since I'd seen him last. His cheeks were hollow, his shoulders bonier.

Concern flickered to life inside me. "Alex," I stated his name, and he blinked toward me.

The lights in the dining room were on, but his pupils seemed too small. "You okay?" I asked quietly.

He flashed a fake assed grin. "Of course I am. Why wouldn't I be?"

A forkful of lasagna went into his mouth, giving him an out from conversation, and he diverted his gaze.

I glanced across the table at Teresa. She watched her husband with clear worry lining her face. Empathy for her—for Alex—welled in my chest.

But I wasn't about to let shit build and ruin Aaron's birthday.

"So your mom told me you're going to be Jack Skellington for Halloween next month," I said to the boy, needing to direct our attention elsewhere until the cake was inhaled and presents unwrapped.

The boys got all excited, their voices raising about the parade their school was having on Halloween morning that year, and I promised to be there. Even if work kept me busy, I would somehow make it happen.

Alex's phone pinged a few times, pulling his focus off his family time and again.

Aaron hadn't yet finished his cake when his dad pushed back from the table the second his cell rang. "Gotta take this," he muttered and shuffled away.

Teresa's gaze followed after him.

"Teresa."

She turned toward me, her brow deeply furrowed.

"What's going on?" I whispered.

Glancing at her sons, she held up her finger, asking me to wait a second. "Boys—go clean up the icing off your faces then we'll open presents when Dad's done, okay?"

They hopped up and scooted down the hallway, their

excited chatter about a dog fading a bit once they entered the half-bath.

"He's been acting really strange lately," Teresa murmured, her gaze flitting toward the stairs Alex had taken to the bedrooms. "If we didn't already have an open relationship, I would think he was cheating on me. He's dodging questions, lying about where he's been. Twice since Wesley broke his arm, Alex claims to have forgotten his cell when I couldn't reach him."

Fuck.

Teresa was aware he'd been addicted to drugs before they'd met, but I wasn't sure she knew what signs to watch out for that indicated he might be using again.

"His pupils look a little pinned."

Her head snapped my way at my statement, her face losing its color.

I leaned forward. "I'm not saying that's a sure sign he's popping pills, but it's possible. I can confront him if you want."

Teresa swallowed hard, wetness glazing her blue eyes and causing my own to sting. "N-no. I'll do it."

"How are your finances? Has money gone missing from the savings? Are the bills getting paid on time?" I pushed, going the detective route as usual.

"I don't have access to our bank accounts."

Jesus fuck.

I scrubbed a hand over my face, pushing my half-eaten cake aside.

The boys came tearing back into the dining room, and Teresa called up the stairs to Alex that Aaron was ready to open his gifts.

My best friend, the man I had loved without question or hesitancy for years, wouldn't meet my gaze when he came back downstairs. He was shifty as fuck. Antsy. He joked loudly, his words a little slurred when he hadn't drunk any alcohol since I'd arrived two hours earlier.

Unless that was why he'd escaped upstairs where no one would see him slam back a few shots.

Teresa and I made eye contact a few times, our shared worry tangible in the silent space between our hurting hearts.

Aaron didn't find a dog beneath wrapping paper, but Alex promised him they would go pick out a puppy at the shelter the following weekend. That was enough to placate the boy and deepen Teresa's frown.

Obviously, she wasn't too happy with him making a decision on the matter without discussing it with her first.

Alex brushed her off when she started in on him about it. "You worry too much," he told her after the boys had taken Aaron's new toys up to their bedroom. "Having a dog will be good for them. They'll learn responsibility. Have more stars they can earn on their chore chart."

"Alex."

He wouldn't lift his head from where he still sat at the end of the table, phone in hand.

"Alex!" I raised my voice, and he glanced up quickly before dropping his focus once more.

"Yeah?"

"What's going on with you?" Teresa hadn't given me permission to confront her husband, but I could poke a bit. Maybe peel back a layer and learn what I could so I could get answers for myself and stop stressing with worry.

Teresa sat silent—still, as though holding her breath.

"What do you mean?" he muttered, hands shaking a bit as he typed on his screen.

"Goddamnit, Alex, look at me!"

He gave me his focus unwillingly. Pupils pinned, he met my gaze.

Fucking hell, he *was* high.

"What are you doing?" I hissed, my frown deep and my heart heavy even though sudden pissiness replaced concern for his well-being.

He waved his hand, laughing my worry away. "No need to get your panties in a bunch. I twisted my back up playing racquetball at the gym a few days ago, and the doc gave me the good shit since anti-inflammatories weren't helping."

Shit.

I glanced over at Teresa.

She nodded, confirming his story.

"You can't take that stuff," I told him, my voice low and firm. "You *know* that."

"It's just a couple of pills, JJ—I'm gonna be fine."

His slurred voice didn't *sound* fine.

"If I find out you're abusing pain meds again—"

"I'm not," he snipped, eyes flashing as he met my stare head-on. "And I don't appreciate you bringing that shit up in front of my family."

I bit my tongue to keep from lashing out or fucking knocking him upside the head. His past was no secret, but I wasn't going to get into it with him while he wasn't in his right frame of mind.

"Just take it easy, yeah?" I softened my voice, glancing over his face I had memorized from the slight scar above his left eyebrow to the three freckles on the cheek below. Everything about him used to be beautiful to me, but a chasm had cracked open between us. Part of me longed to wrap him in my arms, to make everything better. The other wanted to let him reap what he'd sown. Walk away. Wash my hands of him and the trouble on his heels.

But his boys…

"I'm good. Really," he insisted.

I didn't believe him, but what choice did I have? Without further evidence he was using beyond what he'd been prescribed, my hands were tied, and I cared about his family too much to turn my back on them.

"Keep an eye on him," I whispered while hugging Teresa goodbye a short time later. "Call me if you need me."

She nodded, and I left their house, torn between the conflicting desires inside me. He wasn't the man I'd fallen in love with ten years earlier. I no longer trusted him—in his choices, or with my heart.

If there were more hours in the day, I would tail the jerk. Stalk him until I had evidence one way or another. Unfortunately, court loomed, and my plate was already full, my schedule packed.

Hell, I hadn't even had time to think much on my night with Elite's hottest escort. My evening with Kellen had been worth every goddamned penny—and I could admit to wanting more. Another taste. Another high like I'd never felt with a man before. Another night entangled with his body, talking until we lost our voices.

I'd gotten past some of his defenses and scared the shit out of him, no doubt. But I didn't have money to spare. And because of how I'd affected him, I knew he would never agree to fuck around with me outside Elite.

We had been a transaction, nothing more.

If only I could get my heart to agree.

Chapter 17

Kellen

On Saturday afternoon, I spent two hours at the tattoo parlor watching Mason get his tattoo. The artist turned the scar Mason had been marked with the night he'd been raped into something of beauty.

The J meant to claim him became the first letter in his lover's name gorgeously scripted over his chest.

Tears dripped down Mason's face as he looked at the finished product in a handheld mirror.

I got up from the chair I'd been waiting on—not holding his hand—and clasped his shoulder. "He's going to love it," I murmured, my voice thick.

Mason nodded, swiping at the wetness on his cheeks and whiskers, his timid smile a beautiful sight I hadn't seen in months.

Neither of us spoke as he put his shirt back on, and we walked out of the shop. We'd gone to a late lunch prior to his appointment and discussed the court case as well as his new job working for Silas Barlowe's company.

Mason was thriving, and while I was happy for my friend, that envy had grown substantially.

"How are you doing, Kellen?"

Fuck, what a loaded question.

"Surviving," I answered as honestly as I could.

Mason's gaze glued to my face as I drove him home. "Are you enjoying your break from Elite, at least?"

"Yes." That was easy to answer. "Just...bored. Spending a lot more afternoons at the vet. Heading north for a break from the city life soon too."

"That's good. You've been restless for a while."

"I have."

"Maybe it's time for a change. Speaking of...have you seen Detective Jenner lately?"

I'd never lied to Mason. Never withheld information from my closest friend in the Boston area, but for some reason, I didn't want to share. Didn't want to get into the details and relive the emotions JJ had stirred up inside me I'd been trying to set aside.

Instead of bullshitting, I shrugged. "Nothing serious."

Mason didn't push for more since he was well aware of my dislike for nosiness, and I pulled into Jasper's driveway.

I turned toward him when he didn't make a move to open the passenger door. Concern filled his eyes as his gaze flitted over my face. "You know I'm here if you need to talk."

A heavy sigh emptied my lungs. "Yeah—and thank you."

He held out his hand, and I shook it firmly. "I appreciate you."

"Same." I nodded toward Jasper's front door, slapping Mason's shoulder. "Now go show your man how much he means to you."

Another soft smile curved Mason's lips, and I chuckled at the look in his eyes. All dopey and shit. "You're so fucked."

"I'm about to be. I hope."

Laughing, I shook my head. "Definitely will be. Go on. Don't be nervous. Jasper is going to love it."

With a fortifying breath, Mason shoved open my SUV's door and climbed out. "Thanks again, Kellen."

I nodded. "Any time."

I drove toward my apartment, feeling as though gravity had doubled, attempting to pull me into the ground. While I was thrilled for my friend, jealousy chewed on my insides like a hungry bitch set on devouring the life from my soul.

My cell rang, interrupting my pity party.

A grin split my face when I saw my brother Jacob called. "What's up, bro?" I answered on speaker.

"Hey." He didn't sound happy, and my smile dissolved. "What's wrong?"

"Nothing—everyone is good. Promise. Dad's still a stubborn fucker, Mom is spoiling him rotten, Amy has her nose in a book, and the kids are all on electronics—so it's quiet for once, thank fuck."

I waited, the hair on my neck alert regardless of his assurances.

"I, uh, heard some news through the grapevine while down at the station this morning."

Jacob was a firefighter, and same as the rest of small-town USA, when there was downtime involved with a bunch of people sitting around, gossip filled the hours.

"Lay it on me," I muttered, already knowing I wasn't going to like whatever he had to say.

"Xavier's cousin said he got engaged."

I attempted to process what his co-worker had claimed but needed clarity. "His cousin got engaged?"

"No—Xavier did."

I waited for pain to smash me in the chest like a hammer

on an anvil. A slight sting raced through me but nothing like what I would have expected a few months earlier.

"You there?" Jacob asked, and I realized I'd been silent too long.

I cleared my throat. "Yeah."

"You okay?"

"Yeah," I repeated. "I actually am. I hope whoever he's fallen for cheats on him and leaves his life in ruination."

"It's Teddy."

I shook my head as that goddamned image of my fiancé on his back with a dick lodged up his ass flashed through my memory. "Seriously?"

"That's the rumor, according to Xavier's cousin."

It was through Jacob's co-worker that I'd met my ex when he'd been up in Nodhead Falls visiting five years earlier.

"Well, good luck to both of them," I muttered, that slight sting a little harsher than it had started out. At least it wasn't a goddamned knife to the chest like I'd experienced when I'd found them fucking.

"When are you coming home, Kellen?" Concern filled my big brother's tone, causing my throat to tighten. "There's nothing down there for you—you have to realize that."

"I'm taking a vacation soon," I stated quietly, hating that my voice shook from missing my family, who loved me without question. "Need to help at the clinic Monday through Wednesday next week, then I'll head up."

"Sweet. I'll let Mom know, and we'll get the whole family together, yeah?"

"Sounds good."

Fighting off sudden tears, I hung up a few seconds later, hating the storm brewing inside my chest.

I didn't care for Xavier anymore. He had no sway over

my life, my heart, or my mind, so why did the news twist my insides tighter with every passing minute? Why did I suddenly give a shit what he did let alone with whom?

Clutching my steering wheel, I spewed a few curses and pulled into my assigned parking spot a little too fast. My SUV's door slammed shut behind me, and I stalked toward my apartment building with heavy steps, my shoulders hunched against the coolness in the air.

Emotions crashed into me with every step, battering against me like a nor'easter bent on leaving destruction in its wake.

My hand trembled as I typed in the front entrance code.

Too shaken up to take the stairs like I usually would, I used the elevator to get to my floor.

"I don't care," I insisted to myself while letting myself into the loneliest place on earth. So why did I feel like I did? "Goddamnit!" I tossed my keys onto the counter, sat on a stool, and fumbled to unlace my boots. They dropped to the floor one by one, and I left them lying there, too caught up in my goddamn head.

I needed to do something to get my mind off Xavier and his happily-ever-after. A hard and rough fuck you in the form of an Elite client sounded perfect in that moment, but that wasn't an option as I was taking a break at Micah's insistence.

JJ.

My feet halted in the path I'd begun wearing from my kitchen to my living room window overlooking the parking lot and back again. I pulled my cell from my pocket without further thought beyond wanting to forget for a while...to feel something other than the shit Jacob's call had slowly stirred up inside me.

And who better than the one man whose mere presence tempted me to try for more?

I shot him a text rather than calling since I didn't trust my voice to not break. JJ was an intuitive fucker, and the last thing I needed was him being empathetic or wanting to get to the bottom of my emotional state. He was so damn nosey. Pushy. If he asked what was wrong, I would probably spill— and I needed an escape into someone who would shut down my mind, not a therapy session where he attempted to examine my thoughts.

Me: **Busy?**

Two laps later, he responded.

JJ: **Helping my neighbor put his garden beds to sleep for the winter. What's up?**

My fingers hovered over my screen as I tried to give an answer that wouldn't take five minutes to type. Even though it was exactly what I wanted, bluntly asking for a good, hard fuck didn't sit right since I didn't want him to think I was using him.

But that was the truth, wasn't it?

Me: **Any plans for after?**

Three dots appeared. Stopped. Appeared again.

"Come on," I muttered, stretching my neck side to side.

JJ: **What do you need, Kell?**

A shudder ripped through me as I replied with one word: **You.**

He would understand—I *knew* he would, same as I was sure he could take me outside my head and make me forget for a while. In that, at least, he'd proven himself trustworthy.

JJ: **I'll be done in a few minutes. I want you to go take a hot shower. Prep for me. Imagine about how I'm going to wreck your hole. But**

don't touch your dick—that belongs to my ass tonight.

"Oh fuck." I choked on the words, my mind instantly redirected to the lust brewing in my balls. Another flip fuck with the hottest man I'd ever seen.

Excitement curled in my belly, fluttering around like goddamned butterflies as I texted him my address. I ripped off my shirt while stalking toward the bathroom. JJ had told me he lived in Saugus, about fifteen minutes north of me. Add in time cleaning up from his gardening, and I had maybe a half hour to get ready for him.

My heart raced, but I slowed my movements, washing myself thoroughly inside and out. Even though I expected to be railed into tomorrow and to do the same for him, I couldn't help looking forward to the quiet moments after fucking. Cuddling. Snuggling into his warmth. Practically purring as he caressed those large hands of his over my skin.

I trimmed the scruff on my cheeks and shoved enough lube up my ass that all he would have to do was push in. Steal my breath with his hands on my throat, my thoughts stuffed full of nothing but him.

Jesus, I'd never known such need.

Every muscle in my body trembled for him, what he could give me, and the quiet moments in between. After wrapping a towel around my waist, I stood in the middle of the room considering clothing. Wearing something meant a few extra seconds of delay with getting his dick up my ass.

The intercom rang before I could make a decision, so I left things as-is.

Easy access.

Heart pounding, I grabbed a condom off my bed stand and hurried on weak knees into my entryway where I pressed the button to buzz JJ in.

I refused to second-guess or question myself over my impulsive action.

A knock sounded, jolting me thoroughly into the present. A slow exhale did absolutely nothing to calm my jacked pulse as I palmed the door handle and pulled inward.

Chapter 18

JJ

Mr. Roger's front flower bed was just about finished up when Kellen had texted. The fact he'd reached out to me had blown my mind. I'd never expected to hear from him after how he'd cut off eye contact without a word and left the hotel room as though I'd been nothing more than a paying customer never to be thought of again.

Obviously that assumption wasn't true.

His reaching out had shot insta-lust through my groin, and my grin had clued Mr. Rogers in that I'd gotten good news. He'd insisted we quit for the day after I'd admitted to him that I'd met someone.

"If he puts that kind of smile on your face, then he has my vote."

I hadn't taken the time to explain who or what Kellen could mean to me. Mr. Rogers had simply sent me on my way, wishing me luck.

I'd rushed through the fastest shower known to man, not showing my hard dick and tight balls any love other than a quick scrub. My hair still dripped as I jumped in my car and headed toward Kellen's.

While trying not to speed down Route 1, I'd worked through my mind all the reasons he would hit me up for a hookup. He wanted my dick—and hopefully my hole too—but he had access to other men a few nights a week with his job.

So why me?

I'd asked what he needed, and he didn't correct my choice of words. His contacting me wasn't from want. He'd answered my question simply.

You.

I lay at the front of his mind when desperation urged him to act for whatever reason. Further proof? He hadn't argued when I'd told him to get ready for me, simply dropped his address and nothing more as though suggesting I hurry.

When I pressed the intercom to be let into his building, he didn't speak but unlocked the door for his apartment.

"Fuck." I pressed down on my dick, grimacing at the ache while standing in front of his door, waiting for him to answer. I hoped like hell he wasn't planning on drinks or chatting first—

The door opened, and my breath ripped from my lungs with a grunt.

Kellen Roberts, still damp from a shower and towel around his waist, was nothing short of perfection. Dark, mussed hair. Borderline hopelessness in his hazel eyes. Slouching shoulders suggested he'd reached the end of his rope and needed a hug, but he was still utter beautiful masculinity.

I stepped in without a word, and he didn't do more than allow me enough room to slip into his entryway before kicking the door shut. His hands were in my hair, his lips on mine before I could speak.

Aching hunger radiated from him, and I trembled as he ate at my mouth, his hands grasping at my sweatshirt as though he hoped to find a hold for his emotions I could feel rolling off him like a storm. The heat of his chest reached straight through my hoodie, his shaft as hard as mine where they strained against each other.

"Tell me what you need, baby," I murmured against his mouth, pressing his back against the wall.

"Hurt me."

My dick bucked. "The fuck happened?" I asked on autopilot, my brain stuck in detective mode when it had no business being there between our overheated bodies.

"Can you do that for me?" he growled rather than answering.

I pulled back enough to see his eyes. Something heavy lay on his mind, troubled his soul. The openness he showed hit me low in the gut, and I swallowed hard.

"Tell me how you need it, Kell," I demanded, so I could give him whatever it was he searched for.

"Mark me. Choke me." He licked his lower lip, pressing a condom into my hand. "Bruises...hickies...make it so all I'll think about for the next weeks is your body on mine. *In mine.*"

Jesus fucking Christ.

I ripped the towel from his hips and spun him around. "Hands on the wall," I ordered, kicking his feet wide and shoving my sweats to my knees. "You prep for my cock?"

"Good enough."

I hesitated, grasping his chin to turn his face toward me. "Kell."

"Take me hard and fast, JJ." His voice cracked,

making me long to wrap him in my arms rather than pound his ass into next week. "Don't want to think anymore."

Teeth gritted, I squeezed the base of my leaking dick to calm the fuck down. It sounded like he ought to spill his guts rather than have his hole destroyed.

"JJ." Fucking hell, the ragged, pleading tone of my name from his trembling lips broke me.

"If it's too much, you tell me to stop, got it?" I stated, rolling on the lubed condom with grim determination.

His head jerked up and down.

While I would have rather started off by eating his ass, Kellen had a need he trusted *me* to fulfill. Fuck the ego and pride that truth should have bolstered. A sense of rightness settled over me, a recognition that what we had shared— what we would share again—was real. That tangible connection between us? Fucking iron rings forged together. Undeniable. Unbreakable.

Grabbing his hip in a tight grip that would definitely leave evidence of our fucking behind, I leaned in, my mouth against his ear. My other hand snaked up his torso to his neck, allowing me to feel his throbbing pulse against my palm as I lined up my sheathed cock against his hole. "Exhale and relax, baby," I crooned.

He shivered, doing exactly as I'd ordered—and I shoved into his tight heat with one forceful thrust.

"Fuck!" Kellen went up on his toes, but I wrapped an arm around his waist and used my other to put him in a half nelson. Holding him tight, I slammed him against the wall hard enough his arms folded beneath the force.

Jesus—fuck his hot insides squeezed me perfectly in a welcoming embrace. I never thought I would feel the rippling energy between us again. Never expected I would have the chance to be one with him. Share an intimacy so many parts of me craved.

I latched my lips onto his soft skin where his shoulder met his neck and sucked with steady pulls while giving him time to adjust to having a cock lodged up his ass. His tight ring strangled the base of my dick, and I groaned, releasing my mouth and the suction.

"Jesus, that's hot," I muttered, eyeing the purple mark I'd left behind.

"Told you to fuck me," Kellen groaned, and I bit his lobe.

"Ready?"

"Mmm," he murmured his agreement, trying to move on my cock.

I slid out until his ring stretched around my cockhead and slammed in once more, pulling grunts from both of us. Words screamed through my head—*so fucking tight—hot—goddamned perfect*—but I bit my tongue and set to tearing Kellen apart if that was what it would take to put him back together again.

He went pliant in my arms, allowing me to unleash deep-seated thrusts into him. I unwound my arm from his shoulder and neck to wrench his forearm between us. He sagged, chest and cheek resting on the wall, his free hand clasped atop my forearm across his lower stomach.

"Fuck," he moaned, arching slightly, which allowed me to stab deeper into his body.

I quickly grew overheated from fucking into him like an animal, half-crazed over how we fit together, but I needed to feel all of him.

Pulling out, I stepped away and ripped my sweatshirt and T-shirt off. My sneakers went flying free, and I rid myself of my sweats.

Kellen shuddered against the wall, panting.

I grasped his shoulder, spun him, and shoved him to the floor. The hardwood wouldn't cradle his back comfortably, but he'd asked for it. Pushing his knees upward toward his chest, I bared his glistening, swollen pucker.

He reached for me, the hazel of his eyes swallowed up by blown pupils.

Fucking hell, he was truly getting off on the roughness I'd never allowed myself to let loose with before.

But how far would he allow me to live out my fantasies?

I grabbed hold of his neck, squeezing with just enough force to leave fingerprints behind but not cut off his oxygen.

"Fuck yeah," he whispered—and I grinned, unleashing by shoving balls deep into his tight heat.

His spine bowed, a gasp ripping from his lips.

My hips became a steady piston, long, sharp strokes set on freeing his mind as I choked him out. Excessive lube he'd put up inside his hole made for one hell of a slick, messy glide but ensured I wouldn't truly hurt him. He took all I dished out, his ankles on my ass encouraging me to give him more.

Easing up my hold on his throat the slightest bit, I turned his face and went down onto my other elbow so I could mark the opposite side of his neck. He'd asked for it, didn't set limits on where he didn't want hickies, so I bit and suckled my way from beneath his ear to his shoulder, jack-hammering into his ass with relentless force.

Sweat covered my body, and my lungs struggled to fill with oxygen.

Kellen's groans, his hands grasping at my back, spurred me onward. Harder. As deep as I could go.

It wasn't enough.

Sitting on my heels, I wrapped my arms around his

thighs and set a punishing pace. The slap of our skin fought for dominance with our harsh breaths. Kellen's rigid dick bobbed against his lower stomach with every thrust of my hips, his pre-cum smearing over his skin.

My knees, glutes, and abs ached, and my balls began to tighten against my groin.

Kellen's ass was divine, every small noise and curse on his lips a symphony in my ears. His eyes hazed over with lust, the flush on his cheeks a gorgeous shade of pink.

I lusted to dump my cum in him. Shoot so deep inside his ass, mark his insides as vividly as I'd done his flesh where the world would see what he'd allowed me to do to his gorgeous body.

"Want to fucking breed you," I growled through gritted teeth, still relentless in my thorough owning of his ass.

"Oh fuck." He swallowed hard.

"Fill you up with my cum. Plug you so it can't escape."

"J-Jesus—"

I pulled out and flipped him onto his front, yanking his hips upward until he was on his knees. But I didn't thrust into his gaping hole. My fingertips once more dug into his hips, and I hesitated, allowing stillness to settle over us as I considered what I'd just told him. I longed to have him bare. As raw as his emotions.

I thumbed his slack hole, my chest swelling with feelings I couldn't make sense of. How could I want a man I hardly knew with so much damn desire I felt like I would die if I didn't join us together again? What about him caused passion, unrelenting hunger, to burn through me I couldn't withstand?

"Kell..." I whispered and trailed off, needy as fuck for something I'd never had before.

"Do it. Breed my ass." He arched his lower back in offering.

Curses and a shit ton of satisfaction coursed through my chest. Like a release of instinctive craving allowed freedom to partake—

"My bloodwork hasn't changed since I was with you," Kellen murmured, his voice tight. "Haven't been with anyone else."

Mind made up at his assurance, I yanked off the condom, suddenly shaking from more than muscular fatigue. "Me neither."

Kellen moaned as though pleased by my confession.

Rather than contemplating why Elite hadn't booked him since that night we'd shared, I rubbed the tip of my dick over his wet pucker. Slapped it a few times through the lube smeared all over his crack.

"Sure about this?" I asked quietly, the frantic push for release easing as what I was about to do settled fully on me. I'd never gone without a condom. Fucking *ever*.

"Give me what I never allowed him to." Kellen arched deeper, his request putting to rest my questions of why he'd reached out to me.

Xavier.

Something shitty had gone down. Hurt him again. Made him needy.

Kellen had told me he'd never granted full access of his body to his ex-fiancé, but he offered himself up on a platter to me.

Jesus, my heart raced, my mind blown at the vulnerability he showed after all he'd been through.

His actions were retaliation without a doubt, an even harsher *fuck you* for whatever Xavier had done now, but I focused on who Kellen had called.

Me.

And I was so here for it even if he was only using me to get back at his ex.

I slid my thumbs into Kellen's hole, stretching him wide. My dick bucked, leaking at the sight of his pink inner walls. My stomach tightened as a low groan rumbled from my chest.

Shifting on my knees, I poked the tip of my dick against the knuckles of my thumbs.

Kellen bore down, opening himself up to me.

I eased in, sliding my fingers from his ass as the head of my cock breached him.

"Fuck," I grunted at the heat of his clasp, my hands finding purchase on his waist to hold him steady.

We both stilled, connected in a way neither of us had been before. Barely inside his body, I stared, my pulse pounding in my ears and shaft.

Mine.

The word whispered through my consciousness—and I slid fully home in one slow, sensual glide forward.

Chapter 19

Kellen

James Jenner filled me completely, and nothing lay between us. My ass had welcomed him in as though he belonged regardless of the desperation and passion that had raged between us moments earlier.

My body had been made to take him. Lavish him with pleasure, same as he did for me. I submitted myself to his touch, the pain I'd begged him for. And fuck, how he'd given it. Like he'd reached into my head and read my need, JJ fulfilled me.

Bruises? Check.

Hickies? Dozens stung my upper back and shoulders.

Choking? Fuck yeah, he'd gone there exactly as I'd lusted for.

And the slow thrust of his bare cock into me?

I groaned a low curse, shaking involuntarily beneath him as his groin came to rest against my ass.

"Kell," he croaked the nickname I adored on his lips. "Baby..."

My throat tightened, and my eyes burned as I recognized the emotion in his tone. The frantic heat had gone—drained away at the seriousness of the line we'd crossed.

He fucking lived inside my head, offering me exactly what I craved. I bit the inside of my lip to keep from crying. Begging him to make love to me like his voice sounded like he wanted to do.

His grip on my hips loosened, hands gliding upward over my sweaty back. "Feel so fucking good on my dick. So hot." JJ pulled out halfway but groaned before sinking in again as though he couldn't bear the thought of leaving my body.

The heat of his length gliding against my stretched ring, the awareness of him being bare, made my balls constrict. Pre-cum dripped from my slit onto the floor beneath us. My knees ached from the hard surface of the wooden flooring, but I brushed aside the discomfort as he once more rocked in and out of me with an erotic gyration that allowed him to rub over my prostate.

"Oh fuck—right there." I gulped and writhed, my hands in my hair since I had nothing else to hold onto.

"Here?" JJ repeated the action, and I groaned.

"Shit, yeah." I gasped as he did it again.

A rumbled sound of satisfaction rolled from his lips, and he fixed his mind and body on driving me out of my goddamned mind. We moved together to silent music, the energy between our contracting muscles in perfect sync.

Pre-cum puddled beneath me, pulsing with every caress of his cockhead over my sweet spot. I wanted to wrap my fist around my dick and stroke to completion, but he'd told me it belonged to him.

And I would be patient because he would make good on his promise. Then hold me in the aftermath of whatever it was that thrived to life between us. There was no denying something potent had taken root, beyond temptation and mere lust. A deep longing, a yearning, to connect with the one who tugged on my soul. Enticed me to give in. Promised...

Shorter strokes made me pant, and I thrashed my head side to side, past experience telling me I should fight the draw and protect myself from possible heartache, but I couldn't.

"Need to come?" JJ asked, his voice low and ragged as I felt inside. Fucking raw and bleeding.

"Yes—fuck yes. Please."

He grabbed hold of my dick and pulled toward my base while filling my ass with his luscious cock.

"Oh fuck, yeah," I groaned, trying to bow my back even more so he could shove deeper, and I could lose myself to everything he was.

JJ hissed, setting a slow pace of jacking me in time with his longer strokes. He was going to fucking kill me.

"More," I gasped. "Harder."

"Nuh uh, baby." He growled low in his throat, making shivers ripple down my spine. "Just like this."

JJ was driving me out of my goddamned mind. My length was a slick mess in his hand, the sounds of wet fucking tightening my balls thoroughly to the point of pain.

"G-Gonna come," I stuttered, trying to move faster, to fuck myself on his dick, get my rocks off with his hand.

"Give it to me, baby. Tighten this sweet ass on my dick and milk the cum right out of me."

Fuck.

My nuts seized, and with a garbled shout, I shot ropes of spunk all over the floor.

JJ cursed and slammed into me with enough force my body slid forward. "Fuck yeah." Another stab into my ass, and his cock bucked hard past my pulsing ring. Wet heat shot deep inside my ass, and I drank in his continued curses as I groaned my own drawn out release.

My heart pounded, and I gasped for breath, every inch of my body on fire and convulsing. We had transcended to the stars. Shot across time and space where nothing existed but pure bliss in a bubble of euphoria.

"Jesus, Kell." JJ ran his cum-covered hand up my torso, his hold tightening to pull me upward with him into a seated position until I rested against his chest. His hot pants of breath on my ear made goose bumps skitter down my arms.

I clasped his hands, wrapping his arms tightly around me to keep him close and ground my shaking body that still soared.

His bare dick buried in me, we sat in silence, attempting to catch our breath. We were connected physically, but something deeper, potent as fuck, bound us together. I felt it as thoroughly as I did the droplet of sweat sliding down my temple.

Groaning, JJ latched his mouth onto the unmarked side of my neck, and I tilted my head, submitting to his suckling. He bruised my skin again, and I smiled, my eyes closed and head blessedly empty.

"So damn delicious," he murmured and licked over the sore purple splotch he'd left behind. "Salty yet sweet." He ran his tongue up to my ear then nuzzled his face in my damp hair. "Who *are* you, Kellen Roberts," he whispered, almost as if...he was as in awe of me as I was with him.

"I am who everyone needs me to be," I said even though I wasn't sure JJ had expected an answer.

"And when are you who *you* need to be?"

I considered his question before answering. "Tonight

was the first time in years." I allowed myself to admit to what I hadn't realized until he'd asked.

"You have to take care of yourself—you'll lose your identity if you don't, Kell." He kissed my neck and squeezed me a little tighter.

Maybe I already had.

Who was I?

What were my dreams? What made me happy? What did I actually do for myself that was fulfilling? I'd been so damn set on retaliation for so long. I had climbed onto a backseat with no destination in mind, leaving me aimlessly losing my sense of self to vindictive righteousness.

But I volunteered at the vet clinic. Spent a lot of time at the gym and exercising to keep myself healthy. Family made me happy.

I opened my mouth to tell him as much, but his lips found mine, quickly shutting all thoughts down and once more wrapping me up in everything he was. His touch, his scent, his heat that seared through clear to the core of me.

As though he branded me—

A cell rang, a tone I didn't recognize.

We both ignored it as JJ continued to hold and kiss me, the slow strokes of our tongues not meant to rekindle any fire but soothe and comfort. Share a newfound intimacy I suddenly craved.

His phone went off again.

"Want to get that?" I asked quietly since as a detective he might need to.

He groaned an exhale, shifting me in my arms, and I lifted off his dick, sliding forward to kneel onto my knees. A slow hiss escaped me as he left me empty.

A dinged notification let us both know he'd gotten a voicemail—or text.

"Ah, fucking hell. Look at that," JJ groaned, his fingers sliding through the mess dripping from my hole where I sat in front of him, legs wide, spent balls and soft dick an inch from the floor. I'd never felt so vulnerable in my goddamned life—but safe too. Contentment swelled inside me, a peacefulness I'd never experienced before, even with Xavier.

"Wish I had a plug to keep my seed inside you." Thick fingers shoved into my body, JJ doing what he wanted as his lips once more found my neck, the heat of his chest against my back.

Fuck, this man.

I would never get enough. Fucking ever. "Maybe we could—"

His goddamned cell notification ruined the moment for a fourth fucking time, ripping some seriously heavy thoughts from my head I'd been about to spill aloud.

"Fuck." JJ grabbed his sweats and pushed up to his feet, fishing his phone from a pocket with his clean hand to swipe the screen to life. He scowled at the message. "Jesus *fucking* Christ!"

Cum leaking from my ass, I peered up at him, wondering what the hell was going on. "Work?" I asked quietly, apprehension shifting along my heated skin like a cold breeze over how deeply his forehead furrowed.

"No." Glowering, he wiped his fingers clean on his sweats and quickly shot back a text to whoever had shattered the little bubble we'd been in. "Fuck!" he hollered again, yanking up his pants.

He was leaving when I'd lowered my defenses and had been about to ask him for more.

It was an easy guess who needed him since it hadn't been the city of Boston.

Alex.

Pain knifed through my chest, and I swallowed hard, fighting the urge to rub over my pecs. Curl up in a ball. Bite my tongue to keep from screaming.

"I-I have to go." JJ wouldn't look at me while swiping his other clothes off the floor.

Standing on weak, aching knees, I watched him dress, and with every piece of clothing he put on, I stoically replaced the bricks in my wall he'd torn down while loving on my body. Once he finished and turned, I was ready to face him.

Somewhat.

His dark eyes roamed over my face quickly, but I could see his mind had already gone elsewhere. He'd moved on from the intense intimacy we'd shared without struggle or hesitation. "I—"

His cum slid down my thigh as his voice cut off. Our gazes locked, and my breath left in a rush, leaving me feeling empty. Depleted of *life.*

Don't go. Don't do this...don't fucking leave *me for him...*

I swallowed hard, struggling to keep from begging, pleading for him to not break me like Xavier had.

Same as I'd done to JJ that morning in the hotel, he spun and walked away without another word.

No goodbye.

No see ya later.

No I'm sorry I can't put you first.

I sank back to the floor and buried my face in my hands while his seed leaked from my sore hole. My insides twisted tighter with every hard-earned inhale. I choked on a sob, rocking in an attempt to keep my stomach from erupting all over the floor around me.

What the fuck had I done allowing another man inside my head? My fucking heart? To be set aside so easily, so damn quickly, still coming down from the high of a lifetime...

My chest ached twice as much as my backside. He'd made me *feel* things. Question shit. Stirred my head up with too much indecision for comfort until I'd given in to the draw of him. I'd been escorting for over two years, and never had a man weaseled deep inside where I'd hidden all the pieces of me I feared to share again.

I'd been ready and willing to lay what was left of my soul at his feet—and he'd walked away.

Abandoned me to agonizing thoughts that had me wondering what the fuck I was doing, who I had become beyond a weapon of revenge, even if what I'd chosen to do wouldn't actually hurt the man who'd crushed my heart the first time.

Twice bitten.

I'd finally learned my fucking lesson for good.

Teeth gritted tight against the grief wanting to tear from my lungs, I wearily made my way into the bathroom. A hot shower would wash every trace of James Jenner from my abused body.

If only the rest of me could be as easily rid of him as his cum from my ass.

Chapter 20

JJ

Im beat up shit kicked me. need you.

Alex's garbled text was alarming as hell, but I was pissed he'd done something that warranted being someone's punching bag.

Of all the fucking ways he could have ruined the best night of my life.

I cursed up a storm while scampering down the stairwell in Kellen's building, filled with anger and annoyance when not even an hour earlier I'd been ecstatic with excitement. Concern for my friend had clogged my brain at seeing his worrying text, and I hadn't been able to find words to quickly explain the situation to the man whose hot hole I'd just filled with spunk.

And lost a piece of my soul to.

The deepest parts of me turned in on itself, a twisted knot, a slew of emotions I couldn't name atop the concern for my best friend. My attention attempted to go in polar opposite directions, but my brain couldn't focus outside one step at a time.

Kellen wasn't aware of Alex's past, his addiction, or the

times I'd helped him try to get clean and how I'd emptied my small savings to pay for his rehab when we were younger.

In that moment, I hated Alex as heartedly as I had ever loved him.

But I could never turn my back on him and leave him floundering on his own. He wouldn't survive, and I refused to allow those two boys of his to grow up without a father like I'd been forced to do for most of my childhood. Once I had him settled, I would get in touch with Kellen. I just prayed he would give me a chance to explain why I'd abandoned him.

I put through a call while shoving through the complex's front doors. "Where are you?" I shot out the second Alex muttered in my ear.

"Dunno."

Fucking drunk—or high. Maybe even concussed.

"Shit." I ran across the parking lot to my car. How the fuck did Alex not know where he was? He didn't sound like he was in any shape to answer all the questions wanting to spew from my lips. "At least tell me what city!"

"Lynn."

Fucking hell. There was only one reason he'd gone to that godforsaken place. "Closest street corner?"

"At...crossroads." He groaned, and I cursed again.

"Where?" I hollered, slamming my car door behind me and roaring the engine to life.

It took Alex a few seconds to answer, but he eventually managed to gasp out the name of the road sign a few feet away from him. That was all the information I needed. I knew exactly where he was.

I flipped on my unmarked car's siren and sped past vehicles slowing off to the side as I approached them.

Adrenaline raced through me as fast as I drove, but anger fueled the fire inside me rather than fear. Whatever state I found Alex in, I wanted to worsen his condition.

What the fuck was he *doing*?

I found him on the corner in a seedy part of Lynn where dozens of drug busts had gone down. Dealers and hookers scattered as I came roaring up the road, lights flashing and siren chirping.

He'd more than gotten the shit kicked out of him. I barely recognized the man curled on the cold ground covered in blood. His nose was broken, I noted before I even crouched beside him.

"JJ," he murmured, smiling through the blood coating his lips and teeth. "Knew you'd rescue me." His garbled words could have been from whatever drugs laced his blood or a concussion.

"What did you do, Alex?" I muttered, gently rolling him onto his back, glancing around to make sure no one crept in too close. The blue and red lights bouncing off the buildings around us were enough to keep bystanders at a safe distance.

Alex grimaced, eyes clenching shut.

No blood covered his torn winter coat, but he clutched at his side. Probably had taken some kicks to his torso.

"Open your eyes," I ordered, using my cell as a flashlight.

His pupils were fucking pinned, and I was thankful one hadn't blown out with how badly his head appeared from two bumps already forming.

"The fuck did you do?" I asked, shoving my cell back into my pocket, readying to get him to his feet.

"Nothin'...minding my own bus'ness."

"Bullshit."

Alex groaned when I pulled him to his feet.

"I'm taking you to the ER."

"No—I'm g-good. Just need bed," he slurred.

"Jesus fucking Christ, Alex!" I boomed, propping him against me while I opened my passenger door. "You're a fucking mess—might have internal injuries!"

"I'm *fine*. Reeeally." He coughed and grimaced again, clutching his side.

"Get in the fucking car."

He slumped on the seat, and I slammed the door, taking a good long look around us.

Darkness hovered over the corner thanks to a broken streetlight a few feet away, not that the few people still lingering allowed me to see their faces. A homeless man lay beneath a pile of blankets on an abandoned building's stoop across the street, his back to us as though the ruckus of my arrival had gone unnoticed.

Probably high out of his fucking mind.

"Thanks," Alex muttered when I climbed into the car and yanked on my seatbelt.

"Who did this to you?" I asked, my tone firm.

"Dunno."

"Why'd they do it?" I shut off my lights and pulled away from the curb.

He didn't answer.

"Alex!"

"Huh?" His head thumped against the passenger window, another groan leaking from his bloody mouth.

"What the fuck were you doing in this part of Lynn anyway? And where's your car?" I tacked on, suddenly realizing I hadn't seen it nearby where he'd been lying.

Alex tried to lift his head to look around, clearly dazed. "I...I dunno?"

"You don't know what you're doing in Lynn or where your car is?" I asked for clarity.

"Met...client," he muttered, his eyes closing once more.

Sure he did.

"And your car?"

He didn't answer.

"Alex!"

"Huh?'

"Where's your goddamned car?"

"Dunno."

Fucking hell.

Growling through my nose, I kept my lips in a thin line and my other questions to myself. It wasn't like he was going to be truthful anyway. My best friend, my *ex*-lover, was higher than a goddamned kite. No doubt, he'd been looking for more pills. A fix to ease the itching inside him.

I'd seen him desperate before and wouldn't have been surprised to hear he'd traded his BMW for a few thousand dollars' worth of opioids.

It was late enough that Alex's boys would be in bed, so I reluctantly decided to take him home. Through clenched teeth, I told Siri to text Teresa then gave her the simple facts. Her husband was high. Beaten to a bloody pulp. We would be there soon.

"Do you have any drugs on you?" I asked Alex after sending the message.

He didn't answer.

"You fucked up, Alex," I stated, my grip on the steering wheel when all I wanted to do was slap him across his bruised and bleeding face. "If you don't knock this shit off— get your head out of your ass—you're going to lose your family. Teresa and the boys. You hear me?"

He didn't reply or make any indication my words registered in his head.

Fucking asshole was ruining his life and didn't even care.

Goddamned drugs.

Teresa met us at the front door five minutes later, robe wrapped tight around her slender form, hair atop her head in a messy bun. Wetness coated her eyes, but she didn't speak as I fireman-carried her fuck-up of a husband into the house and up the stairs to their bedroom.

He groaned the entire time, but I didn't feel one goddamn ounce of pity for the fucker or how my hold on him might hurt his ribs. For Teresa, however? My damned heart broke at the thought of what lay in her and Alex's future.

While I laid him on the bed and removed his coat and shoes, she retrieved wet towels from the bathroom.

"Who did this to you?" she asked quietly, focusing on cleaning up his face while I stood back, hands on my hips. Scowling. My gut clenched.

He didn't answer her.

"I don't know, and he wouldn't say," I offered what information I had—absolutely nothing.

I'd walked out on Kellen for this fucking man, who didn't deserve the tender love his wife showed him or my cursed loyalty for that matter.

She hissed at finding the bumps on his head. "JJ..."

"I checked his eyes," I assured her.

"Would his pupils look messed up from a concussion if he was high?"

I wasn't sure, and his mutterings and slipping in and out of consciousness wasn't promising.

"He needs to go to the hospital," Teresa said, her voice shaking.

She was right—I should have taken him there immediately regardless of his insistence I not.

"Call Janie."

"She's already on her way," Teresa said, leaving her husband's side to toss the bloody towels onto their bathroom floor. A sob ripped from her, and I moved quickly to gather her up in my arms.

My throat thickened as Alex lay unmoving, his wife trembling in my arms.

"I—I can't do this anymore, JJ. He's...not right. Hasn't been for weeks."

"When Janie gets here, she can stay with the boys, and I'll drive you and Alex to the hospital. We're going to get him the help he needs, okay?"

Sniffling, she nodded against my chest.

I didn't have time to text an apology to Kellen for another five hours.

Alex had a small concussion, definite drugs in his system, but he was lucky to be alive, considering the cracked rib that had been centimeters away from puncturing his left lung.

That whole not giving shit about hefting him over my shoulder? It had been a stupid fucking move. I could have seriously injured him.

Teresa slept on a chair beside Alex's hospital bed while I slouched in one across from her, feeling like absolute shit. Guilt ate at my insides, and not just for my rough treatment of Alex.

Kellen would never forgive me for choosing my friend over him once he found out. He might get it—understand if I was allowed to explain—but from what he'd told me about

Xavier, I expected that sense of abandonment had hit him hard as fuck.

Especially after whatever had gone down that had prompted Kellen to call me in the first place.

I'm sorry for leaving like that. I'll explain as soon as I can, I texted him.

One step at a time.

Shoving my cell back in my pocket, I closed my eyes, telling myself I would help Alex get clean again and see him through to the other side so I could be completely free to pursue something with Kellen.

If I hadn't fucked up whatever chance he had been willing to give.

Chapter 21

Kellen

I didn't get JJ's text until I woke up around noon the next day. Pain and yearning, along with unanswered questions about myself, had made sleeping impossible. It had taken countless swigs of vodka to finally knock my ass out so I wouldn't remember Xavier's cheating or have to think about how perfectly JJ had filled me or put actual words to the question about who I was anymore or why he'd walked out on me.

My head pounded, and my mouth felt stuffed with cotton as I blinked his text into focus.

Snorting, I tossed my cell aside without replying. There was nothing to explain. I understood perfectly clear.

Fuck Alex for coming first, and fuck JJ's loyalty to the man who obviously still owned his heart.

He'd made that *very* clear in word and deed, and I'd been a fool to even begin to hope otherwise. The connection I would have sworn we'd shared had been nothing more than lust, plain and simple.

That little lie didn't stick, but I had no other choice other than to tell myself I believed it. Otherwise? I would drown again and probably worse than the first time I'd been beaten down by heartache.

I went to the gym. Sweated off the alcohol on the assault bike then lifted weights until I could barely move.

For the second night in a row, I drank myself into a stupor.

In a daze, I showed up the clinic the following afternoon and cleaned up after sick dogs and cats. An ugly as fuck iguana eyed me as I changed out his water. A big mother-fucking bird with a loud, foul mouth kept badgering me while I exchanged the old newspaper from the bottom of his cage out for new.

The staff found the damned bird amusing.

I wanted to wring his neck.

And the whole time, I questioned why I'd chosen to volunteer. Did I do it for my own sake? Sure, working around animals took me back to my childhood on the farm when Dad still had livestock, but did it really bring me any joy?

Or was I being a masochist, reminding myself of better times and what I was missing by continuing to live in Boston?

Nursing the mother of all headaches, I returned to my apartment without any answers to my questions. The quiet loneliness hit me like a wall when I unlocked my door and stepped inside the entryway.

I'd cleaned up the mess JJ and I had left on the floor, but the memory of how he'd made love to me, stroked into my body with tenderness, and marked my insides with his cum caused my chest to cave in on itself.

I'd broken down in those final moments and chosen him for myself, and the result had gifted me a brief, too-damn short happy moment in time. But that was all it could be. All it would *ever* be. He'd made his priorities clear.

Swallowing hard, I tore my gaze off the hardwood flooring and focused on moving deeper into the small place I'd called home for going on three years after I'd moved out of Xavier's condo.

Standing in my kitchen, I glanced around, hating everything about it. The sterility of white cabinets and lack of personal items to bring color to its starkness. The living room wasn't inviting except for two pictures I had of my nieces and nephews on the end tables. Hands on hips, I finally contemplated turning around and leaving.

Maine and family lay a few hours north. I could escape the shit of Boston once and for all. Try to find myself again and build a new life.

I wanted that—but I was hungover as fuck. Exhausted to the point I could barely keep my damned eyes open.

I couldn't take off without giving JJ the chance to explain what I felt sure I already knew, so I made up my mind to at least stay until the following day. I wouldn't be able to move on otherwise. Questions would continue to riddle my mind. Goddamn what-ifs wouldn't let me sleep.

There had been radio silence for two days, and I was growing antsy as fuck—couldn't get out of my own head.

Gnawing on my lower lip, I tried to talk myself into believing I was wrong about Alex and the hold he had over JJ's life. I honestly didn't know who'd tried calling JJ that night. It wasn't fair of me to assume it was the man who stood between me and JJ exploring the potent connection between us.

I'm so fucking tired.

Sinking onto the couch, I swiped my cell to life and pulled up his number. I was tired of waiting for answers.

Owed it to myself to find out for sure, so I could at least have closure even if it wasn't in the way I hoped for. Then I could figure out what and *where* I wanted to go.

Me: **We need to talk.**

I slouched back, closed my eyes, and sat in the heavy silence, not expecting him to answer anytime soon.

If at all.

The notification ding seconds later brought me upright.

JJ: **Can I stop by tonight?**

Hope wanted to spring to life inside my chest, but I knew better. A jaded soul took on wariness as a means of self-preservation for a reason.

Me: **What time?**

JJ: **Eight.**

A thumbs-up was all I had the energy to type. Dropping my cell to the couch, I once more slumped, hands rubbing my weary eyes. My stomach rumbled, but I couldn't be bothered to get up and take care of myself.

I passed the fuck out and woke to find the sun had completely disappeared, leaving my windows dark except for the peek of streetlight around the blinds. My neck also had a fucking crick from the pit of hell. I'd ended up tipping to the side while asleep, my head hanging off the arm of the couch at a weird angle.

"Fuuuck," I groaned, rubbing at my sore muscles. Grumbling, I stretched the best I could, patting around the couch cushion beside me for my cell.

What the fuck time was it?

I located my phone and swiped the screen to life.

It was a little after ten.

Ten.

I cursed again. There was no text from JJ. No voicemail to tell me he couldn't make it at eight. He couldn't even be bothered to let me know he was running late—by two fucking hours.

He'd stood me up.

Period.

Hard *fucking* stop.

I waited for emotions to erupt, but shock reigned.

Was I really so unimportant and irrelevant as men I'd allowed myself to fall for made me feel? I wasn't even a goddamned afterthought. A bump in the road, a passing moment of fun or release.

How emptiness could creep into a soul and fill it up, I had no fucking clue, but that was what happened.

An abundance of nothing. Thankfully, I'd been wiped out of fucks to give.

My insides were a dried out husk. Drained and simply... *done*.

Same as when Xavier had ghosted me, I blocked JJ's number and once more tossed my phone aside.

I took a long, hot shower, soaking in the heat and the numbness that had claimed my mind.

Knowing my brother Jacob worked the night shift at the fire station, I rang him while rifling through my closet for my duffel bag.

"What's up, baby bro?" he asked, but not as jolly as he would have been after telling me about Xavier's engagement to Teddy a couple of nights ago.

A muscle ticked in my jaw at the memory of walking in on my ex and his new fiancé. "Anyone at camp?"

"No. Dad and I winterized it last weekend."

"Good. I'm heading up there for a few weeks."

"You okay?"

"No, but I will be," I said, knowing that eventually I would get over having my heart stomped on for a second time. I hadn't realized it had healed enough to be broken—but JJ had somehow found a way, and trashed it, he had.

"Want any company?" Jacob asked.

"Maybe eventually." I tossed my bag onto my bed and made for my bureau. "But I need some time alone to decompress. Are those trees we cut down in the spring still there?"

"Yep, but you'll need to grab the chainsaw from the farm on your way up."

"Did you and dad finish building the back deck?"

"It's framed out, but that's as far as we got before he complained it was too cold to be working outdoors."

Dad and Mom enjoyed looking out the windows at winter but had grown tired of the freezing temperatures. They would never become snow birds though, nor would their family want them to leave New England.

I nodded, glad to have a second job to keep me busy. "And the new glass slider door?"

"Still packaged and sitting in the living room."

I would take care of that too, regardless of the temperature.

Plan set in place, I told Jacob I'd be seeing him, hung up, and packed enough warm clothes to get me through a couple of weeks. I even boxed most of the food in my apartment so that I wouldn't have to drag my ass into town for groceries and talk to anyone for a long time.

Feeling somewhat refreshed from my nap, I tossed my things into the back of my SUV, gassed up at a 24-hour station, and hopped on the highway. Boston faded in my rearview along with the suburbs. Darkness surrounded me on the lonely highway, as void of light as my chest felt of life.

I would be able to sneak into the barn to get the chainsaw without waking up Mom and Dad before escaping all hints of humanity and losing myself in the deep woods of Maine where no one and nothing could hurt me. I'd already suffered enough at the hands of men who didn't deserve my heart.

Maybe I would eventually figure out who I was again.

Find a reason for living beyond choosing and pleasing others.

Chapter 22

JJ

lex had signed himself out of the hospital against both my and Teresa's urging two days after his attack. He needed to be in rehab, but he refused. At least he'd remembered where he'd left his car—two blocks away from where I'd found him.

I'd had it towed to their place since I wasn't about to leave him alone. I'd been by both his and Teresa's sides since the attack, only going to my place once for a quick shower and change of clothes after Alex's wife assured me she wouldn't let him leave the hospital room.

When we got back to their house, both Wesley and Aaron came running out into the cold without coats.

"Dad!" They both shrieked, faces full of happiness.

Sadness pinged through my chest. My friend had no clue how blessed he was or how his choices would affect his loved ones if he didn't start thinking about more than just himself.

Alex climbed from the car with difficulty, the stubborn fuck, and both boys pulled up at the sight of his battered face. "I ran into a tree—and his branches got me good," he joked.

Giggles rang out, and I eventually shifted off the driver seat to follow him, Teresa, and the boys into the house.

Janie greeted us in the entryway but had no words and nothing but a glare for Alex. She stomped into the kitchen. "Boys!" she called out, motioning them to follow her. "Those cookies need to come out of the oven!"

Either she didn't want them to watch Alex's attempts to walk up the stairs, or the fact her brother had lost his life to drugs embittered her toward her girlfriend's husband.

Sulking and moving slow, Alex climbed the stairs to their bedroom, not allowing me or his wife to help him.

In silence, we watched him disappear down the second floor hallway.

"You had Janie sweep the house?" I asked quietly, double-checking she'd told her lover to find all the hiding spots Alex could have stashed drugs like I'd suggested. Fuck knew Janie was experienced having lived with her brother for three years while he'd battled his addiction.

"Yes. She didn't find anything," Teresa replied, shedding her coat and kicking off her shoes. "Coffee and cookies before you go?"

I only had an hour before Kellen expected me, and rather than running home only to turn around a half hour later and head back this way, I agreed to stay.

More giggles sounded as I followed Teresa into the kitchen that smelled of chocolate and sugar.

My stomach rumbled, and I realized I hadn't eaten since breakfast.

Janie used a spatula to transfer hot cookies from a pan onto a waiting cooling rack. "Not yet!" she barked kindly as Wesley reached for one. "The chocolate is too hot, and you'll burn your tongue. Aaron, why don't you get you and your brother a cup? Wesley, grab the milk out of the fridge."

Both boys obeyed without argument, and even though I still couldn't grasp the dynamic of the house, I was thankful that Teresa had Janie. While the boys' backs were turned, Alex's wife kissed her girlfriend's temple.

"Thank you," she murmured, lightly squeezing her hand.

"There's no need."

The women shared a heavy look, one of understanding, pain, and love.

Envy stirred inside me, and I turned away to help the boys.

"I got it, Uncle JJ," Aaron stated with assurance, so I retrieved three mugs for the adults and made for the coffeepot.

The steam of fresh joe filled my lungs once I sat with a cup. Bitter and black, the warmth slid down my throat, hitting the spot and perking me up. Add in the sugar from the cookies, and I felt revived after the drag and exhaustion of spending almost two full days in the hospital. I was running on near empty, but now that Alex was home, I had to make things right with Kellen. Then I could rest.

"You baked these?" I asked the boys, and they nodded, faces full of pride but both mouths too stuffed to reply. "Best cookies I've ever tasted—even more delicious than your mom's."

"Ooo!" Teresa exaggerated her disappointment while glancing at her sons. "Hear that? You're better bakers than me! And I'm the one who taught you!"

"*I* taught them, thank you very much," Janie said with the first smile I'd seen in a long while.

Teresa's arm moved beneath the table, probably

grasping the hand of the woman beside her out of sight where the boys wouldn't see.

The puppy for Aaron's birthday had been forgotten after Teresa had brought home a kitten. A pet, she'd stated, that wouldn't behave like another toddler for her to look after. Mr. Gibbles, aka Mr. Shithead according to Teresa, rubbed against my ankle, meowing and begging for food like any dog would do.

He was a cute little thing, a fluff ball who left long, black hairs on my gray sweats before he sauntered off toward another human who would give her what she wanted.

A loud thump sounded overhead, and I looked toward the front entryway and stairwell on instinct.

No other noise rose, no call for help, and I glanced over at Teresa.

"I'll go." She patted my hand. "Finish your cookies."

"So, your mom said Mr. Gibbles likes to climb the curtains," I said, biting back a smirk as the boys tried to not laugh.

"He's naughty," Wesley said.

"Yeah, Mom tried to put him in a time out, but cats don't listen," Aaron tacked on.

I chuckled, sharing a smile with Janie.

Teresa shrieked from upstairs, and I bolted from my chair.

"Stay put!" I ordered the boys. "Janie, keep them here."

Taking the stairs three at a time, I cursed.

No, no, no...

"Alex! Please, God. Alex!" Teresa's low voice sobbing told me what happened before I even rounded the corner into their bathroom.

Same as fifteen years earlier, I found my best friend

sprawled on a tile floor, eyes rolled back. But we weren't alone in his stupidity. Teresa cradled his head on her lap.

An empty pill bottle lay a foot away, a fact that didn't surprise me one fucking bit. My stomach turned to granite, same as the muscles in my jaw.

"Goddamn you, Alex." I dropped to my knees and felt for a pulse in his neck, wondering if his overdose had been accidental as it had been the first time.

His heart rate was too damn slow, and he wasn't responding to Teresa's gentle slapping of his face.

"Don't do this to us, Alex!" she cried, thankfully keeping her voice low so the boys wouldn't hear. "Damn you! Fucking *bastard!*"

I yanked my cell from my back pocket and swiped it to life. My hands shook as I dialed 911.

MM

Alex didn't get to sign his ass out of the hospital. He landed in detox, and I was once more left to pick up the pieces of his sorry existence atop the shit of my own.

I'd never made it to Kellen's, and he'd blocked my number. No big surprise there. I'd have done the same if I was in his shoes. Anger and hurt battled for dominance in my heart, neither of which I could control or had the time to work through.

Too overwhelmed with everything else, I had to put Kellen and I on the back burner and set Alex's shit straight for his family's sake. My brain had been wired to take a case, figure it out, finish it, then put it aside. Unfortunately, I wasn't able to treat my personal life any differently.

One step, one day at a time, I attempted to clear the

path for the next obstacle before I could move on in pursing the man who'd sunk his needy claws into my heart and wouldn't let go. Once Alex's home and personal issues settled, I would find Kellen and offer an explanation I hoped he would understand. But would he forgive me for how I'd stupidly left him? Would he hang on to that sense of abandonment? Even give me an opportunity to beg him for another chance?

Teresa clung to me as much as she did Janie, but when not down at headquarters working my ass off, I was hanging with her boys, bold-faced lying about why their dad wasn't around, all the while dying inside.

They didn't understand, and neither did I.

Why Alex chose drugs with all he had to lose, I had no fucking clue. At least his using hadn't been going on for very long. After detoxing for seven days, he was set to leave for rehab—on his own fucking dime rather than mine that time around.

But he chose not to go.

He came home, looking better than he had in a while, but I didn't trust his clear eyes or his apologies for fucking up.

Teresa and the boys welcomed him with open arms, but I held back, telling him we could get together the following day to work shit out.

He decided that was an invitation to show up unannounced at my office the next afternoon.

"Alex." I greeted him as he strode in, shutting the door behind him.

He looked good if not still a little thin. "Hey. I'm so fucking sorry."

I held up my hand, not wanting to hear it.

"Seriously, JJ." He rounded my desk and leaned down to kiss me.

I gave him my cheek, my stomach churning over him being in my personal space.

"Please, JJ—I wouldn't be here if it weren't for you," he said, straightening, his eyes full of remorse. "I can't thank you enough for taking care of my family while I was being an asshole."

"Asshole?"

"Okay." He laughed lightly, his eyes pained. "Perhaps something a little harsher would fit better, but I'm admitting I was wrong. I *chose* wrong. Almost lost everything I had." Alex leaned down again, putting his face in mine, his hands grasping my shoulders. "Forgive me—I fucking need you in my life, JJ. Can't do this shit without you. You've been my rock since what? Middle school? Without you..."

"Alex." I swallowed hard and closed my eyes since I couldn't stand to look into his blue eyes and let him suck me back into his toxicity. He'd easily manipulated my loyalty before, but—

His lips brushed over mine, a familiar feeling, one that used to comfort me and flood me with longing to have him all to myself until death parted us.

But his touch no longer felt right. Instead, unease crept through me like ghostly fingers, sending unpleasant shivers down my spine. Whatever desire I'd had for my best friend had quietly, slowly dissolved into nothing but a sense of caring and empathy.

Because of Kellen. He'd shown me something more... had given me his vulnerability without a hint of manipulation. We'd shared an honesty I never had with Alex—and my soul longed to expand on that connection. Seek out deeper emotions that would bind us together.

I put my hand on Alex's chest to keep him from tonguing into my mouth.

He blinked, his brow furrowing as I created space between us as I should have done years earlier regardless of Kellen opening my eyes to what a relationship could be.

"I'm busy," I stated, my tone firm. The office wasn't the place, nor did I have the time right then to get into everything I was feeling inside. Love for my friend, wanting his safety and health, but something *more* for another man I hungered to hold again.

Alex's face smoothed out, and he smiled, straightening once more. "We'll talk later?"

"Yeah."

I watched him walk away, not looking forward to the heavy conversation ahead of us.

But I hadn't lied—I was swamped with shit I needed to take care of for the city of Boston before settling things with Alex. Then I would hunt down Kellen and figure out a way to prove that I wanted him and no one else.

Chapter 23

Kellen

One week at the cabin up north on the Androscoggin River, and I finally got the to-do list finished up. A sense of satisfaction filled me over seeing the freshly split stack of wood out back beside the deck I'd completed the day before. The new sliding glass door leading from the living room to the outside space was also set in place.

I just needed to fix the drywall and trim work in the interior.

The sound of an engine reached through the cabin's walls, and I frowned, getting up from where I lounged in front of the fireplace to drink a much-deserved bottle of beer. Since hiding in the sticks of Maine, I'd stayed away from the hard shit, having no wish to drown my sorrows rather than figuring myself out.

Not that I'd done that yet.

I hadn't realized until the moment I laid eyes on Jacob's extended cab truck out the kitchen window how lonely I'd been. Grinning, I grabbed a flannel, slid on my boots, and went outside to greet him.

Dad sat in the passenger seat.

"I don't remember sending out an invite!" I teased as they climbed from the cab, both dressed in similar garb as me.

"Your mom said you'd been up here long enough sulking and hiding out," Dad said, giving me his usual side-hug squeeze, "and your brother has off the next two days."

Remembering JJ didn't have his hero, his stepdad anymore, I yanked Dad fully against my chest, slapping his back to remind myself of the family I'd been blessed with. My throat went tight with thankfulness to still have my father in my life, but I shoved against rising emotions as I'd been doing since I'd gotten to Maine.

Trying to work through my thoughts while numb hadn't been accomplished, but I couldn't imagine lowering my walls to *myself* and facing the bitter truth of my aimless existence.

Even though I knew that was exactly what I needed to do.

"Cold out here," Dad muttered, and I let him go.

"It's only October, you wuss. Thought you were a New Englander by birth?" I joked with him while heading for Jacob.

We hugged tight, and I slapped his shoulder. "Tell me you brought dinner."

"We brought dinner—Mom's pot roast."

"Fuck yeah." I helped them grab their bags off the back-seat, learning they'd planned on crashing my pity party even though I hadn't exactly told anyone why I hid away. Leave it up to Mom to figure shit out.

Besides, Jacob had told me about Xavier. I expected my whole family assumed I'd fallen into another depressive slump because of his engagement to the man he'd cheated with.

If only they knew that my heart ached for a different man, one who'd set me aside as easily as my ex had.

"Ah," Dad made his usual noise of appreciation over the crackling fireplace blazing and filling the cabin with the scent of woodsmoke. "Now *this* is heaven. Don't tell your mom I said that."

I snorted and took his bag to the main bedroom on the first floor.

I'd claimed the one at the top of the stairs where I usually slept whenever I had the place to myself.

Jacob tossed his bag on the stairs, and the three of us congregated in the kitchen for the dinner Mom had packed up for us. Everything was still warm in the crockpot after their half hour drive. I put the canned beef stew I'd planned for dinner back in the cabinet and settled in to feast on my first home-cooked meal in over a week.

Thankfully, both Jacob and Dad didn't ask how I was doing or what had brought me north. Over pot roast and a loaf of Mom's freshly baked sourdough, we discussed Brian's upcoming final football game, their 5-1 record, and how his coach dropped hints that a couple of colleges were already watching the sophomore star quarterback.

I'd only gotten to head home for two of his games since Friday nights had been booked with Elite throughout the beginning of the season. But I would catch that weekend's game and all the others while I hid out in the woods. Nothing would keep me away.

Once we cleaned up from dinner, Dad and Jacob got their shit settled in, then joined me by the fireplace. Jacob and I sipped on dark lagers while Dad enjoyed two fingers of scotch, his one guilty pleasure saved for nights at camp.

"Slider and deck look great," Dad said from where he sat on a recliner by the unfinished interior around said door. The outside lights illuminated the work I'd done.

"It was nice to contribute atop the money for a change."

"Maybe you should get your ass up here more often if it's going to make you feel this good."

I gave Jacob my full focus, studying his face that was void of teasing. He'd made it clear he thought I wasted time in the city and that my presence would be better appreciated back home.

"What brought you up here, boy?" Dad asked quietly, and I heaved a heavy breath.

Guess there wouldn't be any more hiding.

"You know why I joined Elite Escorts." I didn't ask a question, but both men nodded. "Someone brought it to my attention recently that I've been living for retaliation rather than myself. I've been putting my anger and need for revenge first for so damn long...and I don't even realize who I am. Who I used to be got set aside—for Xavier, a man who doesn't love me."

I'd done so since the day I'd met him, if I was being honest with myself.

"You're a giver—always have been," Jacob easily summed me up.

I nodded, not bothering with arguing.

"Same as your mom," Dad added.

A soft laugh rose inside me, the first in weeks, and I let it out. He spoke truth, and it wasn't anything to be ashamed of seeing as how most people loved Mom.

"I took a leave of absence with Elite last month," I said, staring into the fire. I honestly didn't miss the work or having to please Elite's customers. "My last client made me question everything I've been doing. What I want in life.

Who I wanted in my life." I sipped my beer, stewing on that final thought.

"Past tense," Jacob pointed out after a few seconds of silence while I'd been focused on the memory of JJ. "Who was it, and what happened?"

"James Jenner. JJ. He chose someone else over me. Same as Xavier." Fuck, it hurt to speak the truth. Pain radiated through my chest, and I rubbed over my pecs, hating the first bit of emotion I'd felt in days.

Neither Dad or Jacob spoke a word. What was there to say? We Roberts men tended to suffer in silence, but at least they both had partners to hold their hands and soothe whatever bothered them when they were in need.

"I'm proud of you." Dad eventually broke the heavy silence while I tried to squash my feelings back down so numbness would keep me company again rather than agony. "Rather than lashing out this time, you came home. Gave yourself a chance to work through it instead of losing yourself in men, booze, or drugs."

Eyeing the beer in my hand, I nodded, allowing Dad's encouragement to soothe over the brokenness inside me wanting to scream for attention even if I hadn't focused on what needed done inside my head. I'd been hiding. Period.

"Did you ever confront Xavier?"

I glanced over at Jacob. His brow was furrowed, eyes troubled. My guts clenched tight at the thought of laying eyes on my ex. "No. Never want to see that fucker ever again."

"Maybe it would help though. Unloading all that bitterness and anger. Keeping shit bottled up isn't healthy," he stated quietly.

I nodded, expecting he was probably right. Didn't make me want to do what he'd said though.

"What are your plans?" Dad asked.

Hide from reality until I die.

"I don't know," I answered since happiness would never be found in that kind of existence.

"S'mores?" Jacob suggested, and I breathed easier at the out. I guessed he'd figured I'd been poked at enough for one night.

"If you brought the goods," I replied.

"Ha!" He barked a laugh and stood. "As if I would come up here without the stuff to make the best dessert on the face of the earth."

We spent the next two hours hanging out by the fire, bullshitting about nothing, gossiping about everything, and downing way too many fucking calories in the form of chocolate and marshmallows.

For the first time in over a month, I climbed into bed feeling semi-peaceful, even if I was half-sick from having eaten too much sugar.

Maybe I did need to move back to Maine. It was an escape from the life I'd had with Xavier and the one I'd created after he'd broken me. And with JJ having made his preferences clear, there really wasn't anything left for me in the city.

Chapter 24

JJ

A second man came forward to press charges—Joseph Delaney's first victim. Same as the third and Mason, Terrance Hertz had a scar on his chest in the jagged shape of a J. He'd confronted Joseph's father after the attack and had accepted payment to keep quiet. But having learned Joseph was about to go on trial for doing the same to another man, he stepped in with his story, all but promising a win for the DA. The verdict would still be up to the jury, but the prosecution's evidence was irrefutable. Add in the videos found on Joseph's laptop that showed him in living color and had perfectly recorded every word spoken while assaulting all three men, and he'd nailed his own coffin shut.

That case settled in my head, I had attempted to move onto the next task, but Alex hadn't been available to meet with me, supposedly due to catching up at his office after being in detox. I didn't trust his excuses, but Teresa seemed sure he hadn't been getting high when I'd called her to check in.

He worked a lot though and oftentimes didn't answer his cell for either of us.

His behavior made me wary as fuck, but I no longer cared if he ruined his life. His wife and kids were another story, so I stayed in the loop for their sakes.

Kellen still had me blocked. No calls, no texts went through, tying my hands up tight. Five times I'd driven past his place to find his SUV missing from his parking spot. He'd ghosted me, but I couldn't blame him.

Since I'd been assigned another case, I poured myself into it, focusing on one thing at a time as always.

But at night?

I longed for Kellen—his presence, his warmth. The yearning went beyond my dick. Everything inside me ached for him. It felt like I'd ripped off a layer of skin, the pain stinging and constant.

I tried shutting down my personal life, and the resulting emotions while working weighed heavily on me. Constant tiredness rode my shoulders and began to make my brain fuzzy to the point I couldn't focus properly.

After a week, a mere couple of days before Joseph's trial began, I couldn't fucking handle any more silence between us. I *had* to take care of the Kellen issue before I could wrap up my current case. I called the one man who might be able to point me in the right direction. Fingers crossed he would prove helpful for the first time ever.

"Mason," I said when he answered, "it's Detective Jenner."

"I haven't changed my mind," he stated stubbornly.

I chuckled at his tone, his usual adamance. "I'm not calling about that," I said, shifting on my office chair and pushing my pencil side to side. "But I do need your help."

"With what, Detective?"

"I'm looking for your friend. Kellen Roberts."

He hesitated. "Can I ask why?" he questioned quietly, his tone cautious.

"Because I unintentionally hurt him, and I need to apologize. He never answered my last text, and he's blocked me. He's no longer listed on EEMM's website, or I would go so far as to book a night with him in order to see him face to face."

"He wouldn't get your calls even if he wanted them. He's up north in the middle of nowhere without service."

Well, that explained my inability to locate his fine ass, but it didn't make me feel any better.

"Can you tell me where he is exactly, or would that be going against the friendship code?" I questioned, hoping like hell it wasn't because I'd reached the end of my rope and needed to see Kellen as badly as my next breath.

"Kellen hasn't told me anything that's been going on between the two of you, but he's been hurt enough. If he's blocked you, it must be for a good reason."

"Look." I pinched the bridge of my nose, knowing I grasped at straws, but the sense of misery over the uncertainty of where we stood turned desperate. "We connected in a way I never have with someone before. There's a long story behind what happened that made me walk away from Kellen, which I can't get into, but it was an emergency, and I didn't have time to explain. I would really like to do so. I just need a second chance, Mason. Can you help me out? Please?"

"Yes."

I blinked my eyes open, surprised by his answer. Whenever I'd spoken with Mason in the past, asking him for something—to press charges—he'd denied me. "You will?"

"Yes," he repeated.

My breath left in a rush, elation sweeping through me. "Thank fuck—I'll owe you one. Seriously. You ever need anything, call me."

"Even if he won't listen to what you have to say and tells you to fuck off?"

"Even then," I swore, although the idea of him doing so turned my stomach. "I have to get on my knees and beg him to hear me out. If he won't, that's my problem, not yours."

"His family has a cabin on that big river up near Nodhead Falls, Maine where he's from."

I remembered Kellen mentioning it the one night we'd talked ourselves hoarse after fucking like rabbits, but he hadn't said exactly where the place was.

"Do you happen to have the address?"

"No, but I know who does—and I have her number. Kellen entrusted it to me in case of an emergency."

"Well, as far as I'm concerned, this *is* one."

Mason chuckled but didn't agree. Regardless, he gave me Kellen's mom's name and her cell without extra coercing. Both of us wished each other luck in the upcoming trial set to start at the beginning of the following month before hanging up.

I waited until I got home that night to call Mrs. Roberts. My palms sweated and heart raced like I was about to ask someone for their permission to pursue their son, something I'd never done before. Never had the opportunity to do so since I'd been stuck on Alex for so damn long.

"Hello?" Her kindly voice set me somewhat at ease.

"Mrs. Roberts?"

"Yes."

"My name is James Jenner, and I'm trying to get in touch with—"

"You're the second man to break my son's heart."

My eyelids slammed shut, and I swallowed hard. Her snipped words confirmed what I'd feared and intensified the feelings of guilt and remorse festering inside me. "I need to talk to him."

"Tell me why I should give you access to my son when I want nothing more than for him to heal and find himself again?"

"Because I desire the same," I stated with firm conviction.

"Do you?"

"Yes, ma'am. I don't know what all he told you, but he's offered me more than a man ever has."

"That's his problem," she said. "My baby boy always puts others first."

"Well, I plan to put *him* first, to give him everything—if he'll allow me that chance."

Mrs. Roberts didn't respond for long enough I checked the cell to make sure she hadn't hung up.

"Ma'am?"

"Hold on a second," she whispered, her voice wobbly.

My eyes stung with empathy. "I just need an address. I know there isn't service at the camp. I'm going to drive there so he has no choice but to hear me out about something I messed up without meaning to. Hopefully, he'll forgive me. Agree to be mine."

She released a heavy sigh. "If you hurt him again, I don't care that you're a detective. I'll shoot you dead, grab a shovel from the barn, and bury you so damn deep in the backwoods that no one will ever find a single hair from your head."

I burst into laughter, nothing but admiration for her motherly love toward Kellen on my mind. "You and my mom would have been best friends. She went to great lengths to provide for me." My smile dissolved, and my voice suddenly broke as longing for family of any sort rose up to choke me.

"Would have—she's no longer with us?"

"No," I whispered.

"I'm so sorry, love." Kellen's mom sounded like the type of woman who would wrap a hurting soul in their arms and soothe every ache away.

I knew where her son got it from. And fuck did I ache for him.

Throat tight, I had to clear it free so I could get words out. "How about that address, Mrs. Roberts?"

"Sharon—for now," she insisted. "If you make him sad again, feel free to call me Mrs. Roberts when I confront you with my husband's twelve-gauge. I'll give you a moment to beg for mercy, but don't hold onto hope."

Grinning but eyes still damp, I wrote down the information she gave and promised I would do my best to help heal the hurt I'd caused.

The next call I made was to my boss. Since I rarely took time off, he allowed me two days, reminding me I had a case on my desk and that I needed to be back in town for the trial since I would take the stand for the District Attorney's office against Joseph Delaney III.

Rather than waiting and wasting the few hours I had, I tossed some shit in a bag and got on the road. Kellen would probably already be in bed when I finally reached his family's camp which lay a little over three hours away, but I was done allowing him space.

It was time to go get my man.

Chapter 25

Kellen

The fire crackled, keeping me company and breaking the stillness of the cabin. Jacob and Dad had stayed back south when we'd gone down for Brian's game on Friday night. His team had crushed their opponents 42-7. I almost felt bad for the other team.

Almost.

I'd never experienced such pride as when my nephew got carried off the field, his fist pumping toward the stands where his entire family sat. He'd taken his team to a winning season with half the games officially over and was already talking about the following year.

While I'd enjoyed the time with my parents and siblings, I'd been ready to slip back up north to the cabin and enjoy the silence again. I didn't have an exact plan set in my head just yet, but I felt good about where I was both mentally and emotionally. I'd allowed myself to explore my thoughts on JJ, working through the sense of grief I'd experienced when he'd walked away then didn't bother to show up and explain himself.

I was sure he had excuses, but I wasn't interested in

hearing them. Hadn't even given him a chance with how quickly I'd blocked him. If I'd meant something to him—if that night of passion between us had moved his soul anywhere as deeply as it had mine—he wouldn't have left. He would have seen the importance of explaining *in that moment.*

But something or someone else had come before me.

Most nights, I reflected on my life since meeting Xavier, how unmatched we'd been according to who he'd cheated with, how I'd been dazzled by his good looks and body that first time I'd seen him with his cousin in a local Maine bar.

Sure, I'd been slapped in the face with initial lust in the same way with JJ, but the energy between him and I had been different. Talking to him had been easier. There was freedom in his presence I'd never experienced with my ex, who'd always had expectations I strove to meet.

I fucking missed JJ. Couldn't lie to myself, so I didn't. At least I didn't experience an urgent need to go out and do something stupid to get back at him. Hell, I wasn't even sure the guy had truly liked me beyond a fuck on the side. He'd claimed to though...that truth always resurfaced to make me question my negative thoughts.

And my action of blocking his number.

But there was nothing to do for it now. With the wilderness around me, only the silence to keep me company, and no cell tower for miles, I was truly cut off from humanity.

But I loved the deep woods of Maine, always had. It was where my family had gone for vacation when me and my siblings had been little. We'd made countless memories, some of my best ones on the property Dad had recently put into a trust under the four Roberts' kids' names.

Having read all of the old tattered paperbacks stacked haphazardly on the lone bookshelf against the far wall, I decided to head to bed early. I'd spent most of the day ripping out the upstairs bathroom that needed an upgrade. The next morning, I planned on heading back south into Nodhead Falls to pick up a new toilet, tub insert, and vanity. I was no plumbing expert, but we'd tinkered around on the farm enough that I knew how to get the job done.

And if I ran into trouble, I could always return to civilization until I had service and watch a couple of how-to videos to figure shit out.

The warmth of the fireplace and blower allowed the heat to rise, so the bedroom at the top of the stairs stayed toasty warm.

I stripped down to my boxers and lay beneath a sheet, my blankets at my feet for when I woke up during the night cold from the fire having burned down to embers.

Not for the first time, I allowed my mind to wander, revisiting my two nights with JJ. A small bottle of lube on the bed stand made jerking easier, so I lubed up and played, slowly bringing myself to completion like JJ, the sadist, had been fond of doing.

No one had edged me like he did while actually having sex. Dragging out the arousal, the need, until I came without effort.

But same as the other times I'd allowed myself some relief while thinking of him, I felt empty once done—and not in the good way. Release relaxed me into the mattress, but the sting of loneliness lingered where euphoria should have lightened my chest.

I cleaned up with a couple of tissues and rolled over, refusing to overthink. Focusing on the bathroom rehab, I eventually slipped into sleep.

A loud knock jolted me awake, making my heart race.

Scowling, I hopped out of bed, yanked on my sweats,

and hurried down the stairs. No way whoever banged on the door a second time was family. We all had keys.

I'd shut off the outside lights before going to bed but peeked through the kitchen window. Enough moonlight revealed a car I didn't recognize. The profile of the man on the porch, however, confirmed who'd gotten me out of bed.

The adrenaline from having been woken up intensified, and my mouth dried.

How had he found me?

There was no question as to why. He was either desperate for a good, hard fuck or had words he needed to say that I'd been denying him by taking off to where he couldn't get in touch with me.

My heart raced at the thought of both, my palms going clammy in a blink.

"Fuck." I scrubbed a hand over my face and blew out a heavy exhale before I flipped the locks. Pulling the door inward rushed cold air over my half-naked body, but it was the sandalwood scent of JJ, the sight of him in the flesh on the front porch, that stole my breath.

"Hey," he murmured, his face in shadow.

I didn't speak since I wasn't really sure what to think about him showing up in the middle of the night.

"Can I come in? It's kinda cold out here."

My nipples had pebbled, and goose bumps littered my arms. "Yeah." I cleared the frog from my throat, moving back so he could pass me and step into the kitchen.

He carried a small bag, which meant he'd assumed I would let him stay.

"What are you doing here?" I asked, not able to get a good read on him in the dark, but I didn't want to turn on the lights and have to face an even bigger temptation of seeing him fully. That close in proximity to him, I would probably drown in his gorgeous eyes that looked into my soul no matter how much I tried to stop him.

"I owe you an apology."

"More than *one*," I shot back, arms crossing, from nerves rather than coldness.

"Can we sit down?"

I huffed and motioned toward the living room, following him as he went to where I'd indicated. The banked fire gave off more than enough light through the glass doors of the fireplace, but I flicked on a lamp purely out of hospitality, planning to keep my distance.

He perched on the couch, leaving his bag alongside it.

I sat in Dad's recliner, settling back, draping my hands on the edge of the armrests, allowing myself to drink in the sight of JJ. His dark hair was mussed to hell as though he'd been dragging his fingers through it. Dark circles smudged beneath his eyes like he hadn't been sleeping.

Still hot as fuck.

JJ's gaze flitted down over my naked chest, and he cleared his throat, bringing his focus back to my face.

I raised an eyebrow and waited when I'd rather have dropped between his knees and begged to suck him off.

"Alex called that night."

My heart fell at hearing my assumption confirmed.

"I figured," I stated when he paused after that bit of unsurprising information.

"It's not what you think though," JJ insisted.

It's not what you think...

I'd heard those exact fucking words once upon a time before being ghosted. Blocked with zero communication, I'd been left to figure shit out on my own.

"I'm all ears." I didn't mean to sound snippy, but did. I told myself JJ deserved the attitude, so I didn't apologize for my tone even though the past influenced my stirred anger. At least JJ had made an effort, where Xavier had not. The least I could do was hear what the man had to say.

"He'd been beaten up and left for dead."

I refused to feel sorry for the jerk and kept my lips sealed.

"He had a bad concussion and was in the hospital for two days," JJ went on. "I also learned he'd been using."

JJ had told me his best friend used to be a drug addict, but again, I honestly didn't give a shit the guy had fallen back into it.

"And the reason you didn't show up at eight that night when you said you'd be over to talk?" I asked, still not ready to just up and forgive him because he'd asked me to. It was the no show, no call that had hurt more than his running off to help the man he loved when he'd been with me.

"The day we got him home from the hospital, he OD'd. With his wife and two kids in the house."

Shit.

That tugged on the empathy but not for him—his children.

"That was an hour before I said I would be over. I tried to call you the next morning but couldn't get in touch with you," JJ said, studying my face like a true detective, trying to figure out my thoughts and feelings. "I'm assuming you blocked me."

"I did. I don't have time for bullshit, JJ. I thought what we had going on was something more than getting off. Hell, you told me you felt it too, and yet you couldn't be bothered to shoot me a quick text. So, what the fuck?"

"Alex..."

I didn't speak. There was no point. He'd made it clear

where his heart belonged—where he would always go back to. The man who came first in his life.

"Look." JJ sat forward, elbows on his knees. "While a part of me will forever care deeply for Alex, I'm done being used by him. Done holding his hand. Done picking up his pieces. Yes, I'll look after Teresa and the boys as much as I can, but the relationship I thought I'd had with him is over."

Loving someone then deciding you're done isn't just a flip of a switch. It had taken two years—and another man—for me to recognize the fact I was no longer in love with Xavier.

"So you've broken things off with him?" I asked, wanting to hold my breath but not daring to.

"Not exactly." JJ's lips thinned, and he glanced around the living room. "He's blowing me off, making up excuses whenever I try to get a moment alone with him. I'm pretty sure he's back in the drugs even though his wife doesn't think so."

JJ sounded sincere. Appeared it for damn sure with those dark eyes returning to my face to stare with an intensity that had me ready to drop my pants and bend the fuck over. Wanted his slow lovemaking, his cum dripping out of my ass once he finished bringing us both to completion.

But a third time wasn't going to be the charm between JJ and I. I'd learned my lesson twice over.

"You're welcome the bedroom down here," I motioned toward the opened doorway back the hallway. "Maybe in the morning I'll be more open to further conversation, but I'm exhausted. You look like you are too, to be honest."

JJ rubbed a weary hand over his face.

"You need to sleep," I stated, standing and moving to grab his bag.

"Between Alex's bullshit, readying for court, and another case, I'm worn thin."

"Something about the mountain air always makes me pass out regardless of my mind," I told him, heading toward the bedroom, every inch of my body aware of his presence inside the cozy cabin.

I'd already replaced the sheets after Dad and Jacob's visit, so I tugged back the comforter and set JJ's bag on the foot of the bed, antsy to escape the energy of him wanting to pull me in.

Turning, I found him too close for comfort. Hands fisted at his sides, he stared at me, and I recognized the longing in his dark eyes.

"JJ," I whispered, my heart pounding again but more from wariness and a sense of self-preservation than lust.

"I know..." His gaze dipped to my mouth, and I fought to keep my tongue from flitting over my lower lip in invitation. He stepped closer, hesitant as though approaching a wild cat.

I didn't move—not away and not in response to his warm lips pressing against mine.

He sighed at the light contact, and I fought off that feeling of coming home. "Kell," he whispered over my mouth, and my walls cracked enough that I kissed him.

Soft swipes. Gentle flicks of our tongues together. Heat simmered but remained on the back burner. He didn't push, but I wouldn't have let him anyway.

I wouldn't be able to deny my emotions if we got too intimate.

It took every ounce of willpower I had to step away and release my hold on his hoodie I hadn't realized I'd been clutching.

"We'll talk more in the morning?" he asked, desperation leaking into his tone.

"Yes."

His chest shuddered with his next inhale. "Okay."

I left him standing there, calling a soft goodnight before disappearing down the hallway.

What I told him about easily crashing in the mountain air? Bullshit. I stared in the dark for hours, straining to listen as he washed up in the bathroom then settled on the queen-sized bed a floor below me.

Obviously, JJ had good intentions if he'd traveled three-plus hours in dark in order to talk to me.

How had he found me?

The sudden question made my mind race even more, but because I'd been anxious to escape his addictive presence while half-dressed and standing beside a goddamned bed, I would have to wait until morning for answers.

Sleep was long in coming.

Chapter 26

JJ

The scent of frying bacon and coffee made me crack my eyelids open.

Kellen hadn't been lying. I'd slept like the dead, but like a moron, I'd closed the bedroom door, which had kept the fireplace's heat out. There were vents in the hardwood floors, I'd noticed the night before. I was sure the cabin had a heating system, but it seemed Kellen enjoyed using wood to take the chill off rather than the press of a button.

I scurried to throw my clothes on, shivering yet oddly invigorated by the cold air on my skin. I found Kellen in the kitchen dressed the same as me—sweats, a hoodie, and socks.

While I would have preferred to press up against his back where he stood in front of the stove and bury my face in his neck, I decided on getting myself a cup of coffee from the pot across the kitchen from him.

"Good morning," I offered, not wishing to startle him.

"Morning," he muttered without turning.

Talk about stifling discomfort. I fucking hated it. He'd

allowed me to have my say the night before, but I shouldn't have gotten my hopes up that he'd fall right into my arms and kiss me senseless then invite me into his bed to make up for lost time. With what he'd asked about my speaking with Alex, I expected he would hold me at arm's length until I proved myself in his eyes.

"When do you have to head south?" he asked.

"Tomorrow afternoon." I poured hot joe into the mug Kellen had left beside the pot for me. "I'm only allowed two days because of court."

I sipped my coffee as he nodded—still not looking at me.

"Do you want me to leave sooner?" I outright asked, needing to get the show on the road, even though the thought of heading south again without settling things between us didn't sit right in my gut.

Kellen hesitated long enough my stomach twisted even tighter. "No," he finally murmured. Setting aside the tongs he had in hand, he turned and leaned against the counter beside the stove. He watched me warily, same as he'd done the night before, his eyes more green than brown in the morning sunlight coming through the window behind me.

There was no question I made him uncomfortable but not fully in a bad way. He looked good in his black sweats, and he sported a semi he couldn't blame on morning wood, considering breakfast was half made and the bacon was almost done frying in the pan atop the stove.

"What's it going to take for me to set things right between us, Kell?" I asked, placing my coffee aside and slowly moving in to lessen the distance separating us.

He stiffened, so I paused just beyond his reach.

"I'm sorry," I repeated, my voice low. "I wish I could make you believe me when I say that I want to explore this connection with you. What we have isn't something I've ever felt before. Even with Alex."

Kellen blinked and swallowed hard.

"I hurt you—I totally get it. Abandoned is probably the word you've got in your mind. Set you aside for another man, even like your ex did. I *hate* that I caused you to feel that way. It wasn't my intent. There's no excuse for my poor behavior, but those boys of his...I'm caught up in empathy, considering the dad I never had, and my own desires get put on the back burner. Please believe me, Kell."

His gaze flitted from one of my eyes to the other and back again, and I kept still. Open. Hoping he could read the truth on my face.

"I want to try," he finally stated quietly, his shoulders slumping. "But it's going to take a lot for me to trust again, JJ. I—I've been hurt."

"I know, and I'm so fucking sorry." I stepped closer, and he didn't stop me. Moving right into his personal space, I lightly clasped his hips and pressed my forehead to his, taking care to keep my thickening dick away from his body. I couldn't give in to lust. Not when I was attempting to prove myself and the truth of what I wanted with him.

His hands found my shoulders, but he didn't push me away.

Warmth radiated between us along with shared want. Hope rose inside me, and I soaked in the moment, breathing in the scent of bergamot and citrus atop the smoky bacon to my right.

We shared breaths, their heightened quickness as obvious as the desire zapping the small space between us. He was so damn delicious. Addictive.

I needed just a small hit—

"Breakfast," he whispered as I made up my mind to press my lips to his.

I sighed and peeled my hands off him. "Yeah—okay." I stepped back, giving him the space he'd asked for rather than physical affection, which might cloud his mind. I had to put his needs first, show him that I wasn't just there for his dick or the luscious hole I couldn't wait to taste again.

We finished getting the scrambled eggs and toast together before sitting down to eat in silence. Halfway finished, Kellen finally broke the more comfortable quiet that had settled between us since our semi-hug.

"How did you find me?"

"Mason first—then your mom." I explained about his friend helping me out, then how Sharon had threatened my life.

He chuckled, the sound like warm sunshine on my face. "She *would* too," he assured me when I told him what she promised to do if I hurt her baby boy. "And yet you still came."

I held his stare, both of us with soft smiles on our faces. "Wild horses couldn't keep me away, baby."

Kellen squirmed and went back to his food, his lips flatlining once more.

Grinning at how his ass shifted on the chair, I did the same thanks to the sudden tightness in my pants. He might not *want* to want me, but he did. I could work with that. "Tell me what you've been doing up here the past couple of weeks without internet or TV. Aren't you bored to death?"

He recounted all the projects he'd completed, true contentment settling on his face, the likes of which I'd never seen. Part of me was happy for him, that he might have found where he felt he belonged, but the bigger part of me hated he was over three hours away from where I needed him.

By my side. In my bed every damned night.

"Plan on heading back to Boston anytime soon?" I had to ask.

"Not sure," he said with a shrug. "Obviously, I took a break from Elite. I have enough money saved up that I could live here without having to worry about expenses for quite a while. I've been thinking about it, honestly. But the cabin isn't a permanent home any more than the farm. I'm still waiting for an epiphany or something to help me make up my mind."

Kellen sat back in the kitchen chair, toying with the handle of his empty coffee mug. "I moved to Boston for Xavier, not because I enjoy living near the city. Then I stayed to get back at him by dropping to my knees and allowing men to fuck me like he'd given himself to that jack-ass, Teddy."

I wanted to reach over the table, grab him, and drag him into my arms. Show him that *I* cared. That I would never make him feel like a second choice.

But that was exactly what I'd done, and I hated myself for it.

"There's no rush," I stated rather than trying to talk him into going back to Boston for me. That was the last thing I wanted. He needed to decide that for himself—not another man even if I did have his best intentions at heart.

We cleaned up and headed south into town to pick up supplies to finish his current project. He'd gutted the second floor bathroom to the studs the previous couple of days, and although I didn't have any experience in construction, I offered myself to be his slave helper.

After hauling the purchases up the stairs, we made

sandwiches and set to work. I kept conversation light, and it flowed, same as that first night we'd lain in bed and talked for hours.

Until dinnertime rolled around, Kellen seemed comfortable with me. We both showered in the downstairs bathroom—separately, unfortunately—but after dinner in front of the fire, quiet once more crept in along with familiar yearning.

Our eyes caught, and he sipped his beer to give himself something to do. I stared, drinking in the sight of him until he shifted.

"Don't look at me like that," he muttered.

"Like what?" I asked, excitement sizzling in my bloodstream.

"Like you want to strip me down and love on every inch of my body." A flush rose on his cheeks.

"Fuck." I adjusted my thickening dick intentionally, getting off on how his gaze dropped to my groin.

"I...I can't do that. Touching you, being touched by you, messes with my head," he murmured. "Can't fucking think straight. It's hard enough being in the same goddamned room as you."

His confession caused my lips to curl upward, and the sight of his tented sweats made my mouth water. "Why don't you take care of that," I suggested, my tone low as I nodded at his dick. "I'll stay over here and watch. You can find release, and I get to enjoy seeing you come."

"Jesus, JJ." Kellen pressed on his cock.

"Pull it out—show me," I pushed, watching his eyes darken at my bossiness. Alex had never appreciated that side of me, and I'd allowed it to go dormant. But Kellen? Fuck, he made me want to explore it all.

Kellen cursed but did as told, stroking down to the base and holding his hard shaft straight upward.

"So fucking hot," I murmured, squeezing my own cock inside my sweats. "Stroke yourself."

He did, his lips parting. Pre-cum welled on his slit, and he smeared it over his palm and fingers, making for a smoother glide to his base.

"Fuck yeah." I swallowed hard and filled my ears with the sounds of his low grunts and eventually the slick noises of fist fucking. My man leaked like a faucet. "Faster."

"Oh fuck," Kellen breathed the words, dropping his focus to his hand working himself over. "I'm gonna come."

"Pull up your shirt," I demanded, my mind made up on my next move once he was too blissed out to care what I did. "Shoot all over your chest."

With a low groan, Kellen did exactly as I asked, cum erupting clear up to his chin and the shirt he'd bunched beneath.

"Fuck yes," I hissed, squeezing the base of my dick to keep from blowing in my pants as shorter spurts painted his skin.

One last clench of his abs and Kellen went limp, sagging back against the recliner.

I stood, tucking my stiff dick in my waistband. "Can I clean you up?" I asked, slowly crossing the living room.

"Mmm," he hummed as his eyelids fluttered shut, his face a gorgeous shade of pink.

"Gonna use my tongue, baby." I dropped to my knees between his feet, and his eyes popped open as I gently laid my hands on his knees where his shoved down sweats kept me from getting any closer.

Pupils still swallowing his hazel orbs, he stared at me.

"That okay?" I asked, stroking my thumbs over his pants, wishing it was his warm skin I touched.

He swallowed. Licked his lower lip.

And fucking nodded.

My dick bucked. "Give me your hand."

Kellen's breath caught, but he dropped his flaccid dick and held his fingers out to me.

I leaned in to glide my tongue upward in a lazy taste of his tangy cum off first one, then another finger. "Delicious," I murmured and dove back in for more, sucking each one clean.

Eyeing the wetness on his cock, I considered—hesitated.

A quick glance up, and I knew what Kellen wanted by the lust in his eyes. I dove in, sucking his soft shaft into my mouth, slowly licking him free of spunk.

He hissed a curse, and pre-cum leaked from my slit.

I slowly made my way up his torso, taking extra care to not miss a single droplet from his heated flesh.

I nipped his left pec. Bit his right nipple.

Kellen cursed again but didn't move.

My nose hit his T-shirt still tucked up tight beneath his chin, and I finally lifted my focus to his face mere inches away.

"I'm going home tomorrow. Getting through that damned court case and sitting Alex down, whether he's ready to hear it or not, and telling him that it's time we went our separate ways."

Kellen believed me. I could see it in his eyes.

Fuck, did I want to lose myself in him. Nut so far up his ass my cum would drip from him for days. And vice versa.

Instead, I reluctantly tore myself away and returned to the couch and the beer I'd left behind. Hand shaking from adrenaline and desire, I guzzled it down, eyeing Kellen as he slowly put himself together.

"What are you doing for the holiday?" I asked, keeping him on his toes so he wouldn't get too in his head over what I'd just done or what I'd promised.

"I'll be at my parents, same as always." Kellen picked his beer back up and took a swig. "You?"

"I usually spend the day with Alex and his family, but that won't be happening this year—or ever again. I'll probably get takeout." I shrugged when the thought made me feel anything but nonchalant. "Spend the day all by my lonesome."

He nodded to let me know he'd heard my answer.

I waited, hoping he would extend an invite for me to come back up to be with him and his family for the holiday, but he didn't. The truth I had nowhere else to go, no family of my own without Alex's threatened to drag a shroud of darkness over my thoughts, but I pushed it back, needing to stay in the present with the man I hoped to make mine.

Our conversation moved on to what needed to be finished in the bathroom the next day, Kellen's gaze dropping to my still hard cock more than a dozen times.

I trailed a thumb down my length once, enjoying how he nibbled on his lower lip while watching me.

But I bid him goodnight without initiating anything and disappeared back into the bedroom. I was sure to keep the door open—for the heat of the fireplace, I told myself.

He didn't take me up on my silent invite to join me in bed, and I didn't pass out nearly as quickly as I'd done the night before. I felt as though I'd made progress in the way I wanted things to go, but when it came down to it, Kellen held the cards.

I would have to take whatever hand he dealt me.
No matter what though, I wouldn't fold on him.

Chapter 27

Kellen

JJ took extra-long in the shower the next morning, probably emptying his balls. I hadn't heard a hint of him taking care of himself the night before. If he'd been waiting for me to go into the bedroom and climb aboard after we'd said goodnight, he'd been disappointed.

It was bad enough I'd allowed him to use his tongue to clean my spunk off my body. Sly fucker. I'd been half-blissed out, relaxing in the euphoric feeling that made me never want to move. He'd taken advantage of that fact and helped himself to a little taste. Actually, a big taste. I hadn't jerked off in a few days and had built up a nice supply.

He swallowed it all except for the one shot that had cooled on my chin.

I'm not sure why he hadn't gone after that bit too. Had he hoped I would make the next move to bring our mouths closer together?

But then he'd shifted away and did a one-eighty with the conversation, asking about Thanksgiving. Had he been fishing for an invite after telling me he would be all alone this year since he wouldn't be going to his...whatever Alex still was to him?

Because he *was* something in JJ's life. Even if JJ thought shit was over with Alex, he had yet to set the man straight. Wasn't yet free to pursue someone else.

JJ exited the bathroom wrapped only in a towel, and I groaned, quickly looking away. My hand trembled as I poured myself another cup of coffee. We'd already eaten breakfast and were ready to head upstairs to finish the bathroom. He'd stated he needed a hot shower first to ease his aching muscles from the physical labor I'd put him through the day before.

I hardly classified helping me carry a toilet and vanity up the stairs as hard.

Smirking, I headed up to the second floor bathroom, knowing he would join me once he dressed.

We worked in relative peace with only a little bit of sexual energy between us until around three. I made us an early dinner while he showered again and got his shit together so he could hit the road after we ate.

Our meal together proved a quieter affair. I didn't know what to say to him, and he seemed to feel the same.

But there was nothing to discuss as far as I was concerned. JJ hadn't stated anything about his heart no longer being owned by Alex, only that it was time for them to go their separate ways. Did that mean his love or at least part of what he had available to give would remain his ex-best friend's? He'd claimed he would always care about him, but would he continue to love the man?

I wasn't sure I could live with that.

I needed one hundred and ten percent. No more of this partial shit that allowed room for others to weasel their way into a relationship of mine.

We washed up the dinner things side by side, our shoulders brushing. Every soft touch zinged need straight to my groin, and my entire body ached to be held. I managed to keep my hands to myself. Thank fuck he did the same, or I would have caved for sure.

He picked up his bag and eyed me after pulling his boots on from where he'd left them by the front door. "I'll be seeing you, Kellen Roberts. And I'll be in touch once I have things settled—I promise."

Not a goodbye.

I nodded, and he turned, leaving me with the snick of the latch ringing in my ears.

The stillness, the lack of...*him* all up in my space proved too much after the sound of his car faded away on the gravel road. I grabbed a change of clothes, turned the heat on a low setting to ensure the pipes wouldn't freeze once the fire burned out, and hopped in my SUV.

Mom was thrilled to see me when I walked into the farmhouse unannounced a short while later. She hugged me tight in the exact way I'd been needing but hadn't allowed myself with JJ.

I flopped onto the couch beside her, Dad in his chair across from us.

"Well?" Mom turned slightly, her full attention on me.

"Well what?" I asked even though I was fully aware of what she wanted to hear.

She waited, and her brow started to furrow. I chuckled, knowing right where her mind went.

"I haven't decided yet if I'm happy you told JJ where to find me or not."

"Well?" she pushed.

"He arrived. Apologized."

"And?"

"He left for Boston about an hour ago."

Mom threw her hands up. "Damn him!"

I laughed at mom's idea of a swear, feeling lighter than I had in a while. "He had to go back for work. But things are... okay between us, I guess. There's no clear definition." I shrugged, hating I had no control over the situation or how my heart longed for a man I didn't want to share. "I'm not sure if there ever will be. He's got this friend..."

Mom raised an eyebrow, so I spilled everything that had happened since I'd met JJ. Other than the hottest sex of my life, I shared it all. How I'd reached out to him after learning about Xavier and Teddy and had fallen in deep. The real interest JJ had shown in me, the words he'd said that made me sure we had more than lust between us.

"What do you think I should do?" I asked once I finished up telling them about the two days together up at the camp—without the part about how he'd used his tongue to clean up my cum.

"That's not our call, son," Dad answered first. "We love having you close to home, but if your heart is pushing to offer that man a chance, then give it a shot. What can it hurt?"

I'd experienced enough *hurt* for a lifetime thank you very much, but I understood what Dad was saying.

"Mom?" I turned to find her studying me intently. "What?" I asked, suddenly feeling like I'd been caught doing something I wasn't supposed to.

"You're already in love with him."

Fuck, I hated how she stated shit that I hadn't yet figured out was true. I didn't argue but considered her suggestion. Fallen, definitely. But in love? I wasn't so sure I'd allowed my walls down enough for him to burrow in that deeply.

"You won't know if you don't try," she stated her usual encouragement. "One step at a time." Mom patted my hand, reminding me JJ said similar words to me more than once.

Such a methodical man. Nosey as fuck. Annoyingly gorgeous.

"You're quitting Elite regardless, I'm assuming?" Mom asked, and I nodded.

"Yeah—I'll call Sean in a bit."

"I think you should do what Dad suggested. Head south. Be patient with JJ while he catches up with work and sets things straight with Alex. Then give him a chance when he does finally get in touch with you.

"Go back to Boston for good," she continued, "or move home and attempt a long-distance relationship...it's your decision. You have to do what is right for *you* this time around, baby boy, not what you feel others want or need from you."

Mom hugged me again, and I held onto her until she patted my back. "I'm going to bed, little love," she murmured and kissed my hair.

Dad got up and squeezed my shoulder before following her, and a minute later, I sat alone.

Memories flooded my mind of the living room packed with Roberts. The clan sitting around Christmas trees and singing carols while sipping on hot chocolate with an abundance of marshmallows.

Watching football after stuffing ourselves with turkey and pumpkin pie.

Celebrating birthdays together, even after we'd all grown up and moved out of the house.

We'd always found ways to come home and be together.

JJ didn't have that—hadn't for a few years.

I suddenly understood his hesitancy in giving up Alex's family. After hearing how he'd talked about his friend's boys and how he'd been a part of their lives since birth, I recognized the connection and his empathy for them.

Didn't make me like it though.

One step at a time...

Releasing a heavy exhale, I pulled out my cell and called my boss.

"Not surprised, honestly," Sean said in response to my official resignation when I'd expected a bratty, teasing tone.

"I'm sorry to leave without a proper notice."

"Micah and I have appreciated your professionalism and easygoing nature the past two years, Kellen. That's what's important. You'll be missed, but I'm excited for you." I could hear the smile in Sean's voice—and I wondered who the fuck I spoke to. I guessed the kid had another side to him when it came to his work life. "I still expect you to get your ass to my brother's place on Sundays at least once a month like the other retired Elites. Don't disappear on us, okay? You're family even if you aren't on the payroll anymore."

"I won't—promise."

"Did you receive the invitation my sister-in-law Jasmine mailed out?" he asked.

"I've been up north for a few weeks. Still am, so I haven't gotten any mail."

"She and Micah are having an after Thanksgiving party at their house, and all of Elite and its retirees are invited."

"I'm planning on spending the day with my family."

"Party isn't until later, so feel free to drop in if you can. You know me—we'll be up well past midnight driving my brother insane."

Chuckling at the appearance of the Sean I was used to,

I pushed up to my feet. "We eat early so all the married kids can head to the in-laws for the afternoon, so maybe I will stop by."

I hung up feeling relieved to have taken that first step toward a resolution.

Now, I had to wait on JJ.

Chapter 28

JJ

The court case dragged ass. While the prosecution stated fact after fact without bullshitting, the defense attempted to nitpick every goddamned thing each witness said. Then they shuffled in character witnesses for Joseph, wasting everyone's time on trying to portray him as a fine upstanding citizen from one of Boston's greatest families.

Even the jury seemed tired of the bull, yawning along with everyone else in the court room.

Two fucking weeks...and the jury was finally allowed to go behind closed doors on a Thursday morning, the DA sure the promise of the weekend would have them coming to a verdict quickly.

No such luck.

They prolonged deliberation into Friday, then left us hanging over the weekend. I started to question what I'd thought would be a slam dunk case. I wondered how the fuck Delaney's dad had gotten to some of the jurors to plant seeds of doubt because there was no other reasoning they hadn't come to a quick conclusion regarding Joseph's guilt.

Who could possibly refute fucking video evidence, never mind the DNA, the fingerprints, and the visible results of Joseph's knife work?

On Monday afternoon, the jury returned to the courtroom and declared Joseph Delaney III guilty on all charges. It was the first I felt as though I could breathe freely in months.

I'd been after Alex to meet up for the discussion we needed to have, but he'd blown me off time and again. After the second week of court, I'd stopped trying, too overwhelmed in my head to deal with him.

But with Mason's rapist behind bars for good, I was ready to check the next goddamned thing off my list.

I put through a call to Alex while driving home from the courthouse for a much deserved break—and a nap. Surprisingly, he answered.

"JJ," he greeted, thankfully not sounding high when I'd last gotten in touch with him.

"Busy?" I asked, needing to get to the point.

"Uh...yeah. At the office until later tonight."

"Can you swing by after work? We need to talk."

"I'll try. Shit is crazy here right now, and I have a few things I need to take care of. I'll give you a call when I'm done."

Sure he would. Same as he'd promised the last time I almost tied him down to a meeting.

"Sounds good," I lied, hanging up after he insisted he had to go.

How could a guy in finance be swamped to the point he worked up to twelve-hour days according to Teresa? Sometimes late into the night?

I didn't doubt his addiction getting its claws into him

again. Avoidance had been his MO the first time around, and blaring sirens rang in my head, pointing neon signs at the word *USING!* in my head.

Maybe I needed to just say shit over the phone or text and not bother giving him another minute of my life. He'd been stringing me on too goddamned long as it was already.

If he hadn't been my friend since middle school, I would have chosen that route, making myself available only to Teresa and the boys. But even though he'd taken advantage of my loyalty, I still felt I owed him a face-to-face breakup of whatever we were.

Or had been, rather.

Once home, I sprawled out on my couch regardless of the afternoon hour and closed my eyes, gladly giving in to the need to sleep.

When I finally woke up to find evening had crept in, I sat in my living room in the dark. My thoughts went to Kellen as they did every night when loneliness settled in. We had texted a few times when he'd been at his parents since I'd visited, but nothing serious. More catching up and checking in with each other than deep conversations.

There were no late night FaceTimes for mutual jerking sessions. No sexting. Not even an *I miss you too* in response to the text I'd sent him almost a week ago. I assumed he'd been up at camp and hadn't yet received the message.

Thanksgiving was in three days. He would be surrounded by family, being loved. Appreciated. Wanted.

I would be alone with none of those good feels since I'd turned down Teresa's usual offer to spend the day with them in the hopes I would be with Kellen.

He hadn't initiated an invite when I'd hinted that I wouldn't have any place to go that day, and it shouldn't have hurt as much as it had. Did he not trust me, or was he really that afraid of his desire for me?

Maybe he hadn't caught my obvious as fuck hint...or maybe he believed that I would back out and end up spending the holiday with Alex and his family as I'd been doing for years.

I checked my cell. Other than the few short check-ins I'd had with Teresa, no one had called or texted.

No response from Kellen.

Nothing from Alex either, but I wasn't surprised after his promises to get back to me and never doing so over the previous couple of weeks. Teresa couldn't say one way or the other if he was on drugs, but my stomach twisted, annoyance furrowing my brow over how little all of our years together meant to him.

Alex had done nothing but take advantage of my kindness. My loyalty. And he gave nothing in return.

I was finished sacrificing myself for him.

Fuck that face-to-face I felt I owed to my soon-to-be ex-best friend. He'd proven he didn't have time for me, so I was done making it for him.

I'd already figured out the gist of what I wanted to say to Alex in person, so the explanation came easily as I typed it on screen. Without mincing words, I let him know that I was done—with his lies, his manipulations, with him dragging me along behind him while he spiraled. Our physical relationship had already been over for going on two months. I told him that I would watch over his family the best I could because I saw them as partly mine but was no longer available for him to call in his time of need.

That was it.

End of.

I set aside my cell as a heavy weight seemed to slip off

my shoulders. Once more, I sagged onto the couch, reflecting on my decision. It had been the right one, my gut told me. While it hurt having to cut someone from my life, I didn't mind the pain. For years, I'd been nothing but a convenience for him, but someone had turned me in a new direction and had officially taken me off the market.

He just didn't know it yet.

With Kellen, texting wouldn't do to catch him up to date on where my—*our*—lives headed.

What sounded like sleet pinged against my house, and I climbed off the couch to check the weather. Dark hung over the sky, the streetlights barely holding back the inky shadows. Rain and sleet slashed sideways in the weak light, and a shiver slid over me at the chill from being so close to the windows being pelted with ice.

I needed to get replacements soon.

Flicking on my outside lights, I got a good look at my driveway. The sleet had started to stick, creating what appeared to be a slick surface. Driving conditions would suck due to the nor'easter barreling in, but even if I wanted to head north to get my man, I wouldn't be able to.

I pressed the switch back down, leaving my front yard to the brewing storm, and turned away.

Even though I'd passed out on my couch earlier, my bed called my name.

After work on Tuesday, if the weather allowed and Kellen still hadn't gotten back to me, I would take a trip north. I would invite myself for Thanksgiving and show up bearing gifts, so Sharon wouldn't turn me away even if Kellen wished to.

Then, I would weasel into his heart one way or another. Prove to him that he was it for me.

Alex didn't respond to the novel I'd texted him, but I

wasn't surprised as I climbed into bed, my next three steps settled in my mind.

Telling Siri to turn on *Do Not Disturb* on my cell, I pulled my comforter up beneath my chin and closed my eyes. The storm raged outside, but for the first time in months, calm rested in my soul in knowing the path I planned for the future would bring the contentment I'd been wishing for most of my adult life.

The storm had cleared during the night, leaving less of a mess than predicted by the weathermen. But New England had a saying...if you don't like the weather, wait a minute.

While the early news droned in the background, I poured myself a cup of coffee, feeling fully rested and ready for the workday to be over so I could drive the long journey to get in Kellen's face. I planned to tell him he was mine and I was his, and he wasn't ridding himself of me.

Elation bubbled in my gut from playing the scene over in my head but also left me with a semi too. I couldn't wait to hold him, to breathe in his citrus scent. Feel his warm skin on mine, his heart beating against my chest. I wanted his taste coating my lips, the flavor of his cum on my tongue.

"Jesus," I hissed, pressing down on my fully awake dick.

"*...drug raid last night that left one officer in critical condition.*"

The news anchor's voice made me turn toward my TV, and I immediately recognized the area where she stood.

Lynn.

Big surprise considering she reported about a drug bust.

But anytime an officer got hurt in the line of duty, my ears perked up, and I paid attention. He wasn't being named, as the family hadn't yet been notified, but the live feed cut to an earlier recorded video. Miserable weather from the night before smeared the camera's lens as they'd caught the live action, but I sipped my coffee and watched as a handful of men were led from an apartment building near where I'd found Alex beaten half to death.

Alex.

I choked on my coffee and set aside my cup, hurrying into the living room to get a better look at the screen.

"Oh fuck." I swallowed hard at the sight of my ex-lover in cuffs. He had his head down, but there was no mistaking the man I'd known most of my life.

The reporter stated six men had been arrested, naming each and every one. Alex was the final listed, but I hadn't held out hope my eyes played tricks on me.

Muttering curses, I rubbed my hand over my face then stood with my fists propped on my hips as the rest of the story she'd managed to gather attempted to filter through the buzzing in my ears.

A fucking meth lab. Thousands of dollars' worth of drugs seized. A shoot-out that had left one policeman fighting for his life.

I glanced at the clock in the TV's lefthand corner beside scrolling top stories. Two minutes until my cell's *Do Not Disturb* shut off. Hurrying into the bedroom, I located my phone on the bed stand.

Teresa had texted me late the night before, looking for Alex, but I hadn't received the notification.

I put through a call immediately, shuffling back into the living room. The story on the TV had ended.

"JJ—did you see the news?" Teresa said by way of greeting, her voice broken.

I slumped onto the edge of my couch, swallowing hard. "Yeah."

She sobbed in my ear, and I couldn't even find the words to offer comfort.

Chapter 29

Kellen

Waiting sucked ass.

JJ and I kept in touch in the time after he'd left me alone at the cabin, but no long phone conversations or video chats occurred. Considering I spent most of the time up at the camp with no cell service, I couldn't complain about our lack of communication.

The only thing I wanted and looked for was that he'd left the message I yearned to read. That he'd ended shit with Alex. That he was coming up to see me. Be with me—be mine fully once the jury decided Joseph's fate.

The last text JJ had sent while I'd been in the sticks without service gave me hope when I'd first seen it after parking at the farm.

I miss you.

While my chest ached over similar feelings, I was torn. He'd sent the words almost a week earlier and nothing since.

He'd had more than enough time since that message to talk to Alex about going their separate ways—whatever the fuck that truly meant. Weeks, actually, since JJ had claimed that was his plan.

But he hadn't.

My fingers itched to reply that I missed him too, but goddamnit, I had to remain firm. JJ needed to prove himself before I started slinging around sayings like *I miss you too* that revealed my vulnerability and broke down my walls even further.

I couldn't allow myself to get to that point until I knew without question that JJ was fully on board—alone—with no Alex clinging to the back of his mind or still holding a piece of his heart.

A forecasted storm threatened to move in on the jury's third day deliberating the Delaney case, and I'd grown agitated enough with the silence from JJ that I decided I was done sitting on my hands and doing nothing. Being passive never gained a man anything.

My parents had told me I needed to do what was best for me, and that meant being proactive and getting answers so I could figure out the rest of my life and enjoy Thanksgiving without the emotional turmoil of not knowing where JJ and I stood. After a lunch with my parents of leftovers from dinner the night before, I planned on heading out from the farm for Boston.

I'd winterized the cabin then drove to Nodhead Falls the afternoon I'd left since I wasn't sure when I would be back. It all depended on JJ and what he'd done—or *not* done. I just needed to get out ahead of the storm before it swooped in and hit New England.

But the daytime show Mom had playing on the TV in the background cut out with a breaking story about one of Boston's most prominent families that had made national news.

Joseph Delaney III had been found guilty on all accounts.

I shot off a text to Mason, a **Fuck yes!** I knew he had to be feeling. For the first time in days, I actually grinned. I also looked forward to catching up with him, seeing first-hand the weight that had to have dropped off his shoulders. Mason had been a mere shell of his usual easygoing self since spring and the incident with the Delaney kid, but I'd seen hints of the old Mason thanks to his boyfriend Jasper and the new job. But finally being free of the stalking and fear for good? I would have my friend back, the calm and confident man I'd known for five years.

Excitement for him made me feel the best I had in days, and I wanted to get on the road.

Mom had other ideas, needing to pack up some food for my trip. Make me a fresh batch of cookies to take along. When I hopped on 95 South, the overcast evening had dissolved into black. I didn't need to see the threatening clouds in the night sky—I could feel the storm hovering low, and instinct demanded I hurry.

Rain started falling before I crossed into Massachusetts. Sleet smacked my windshield as I hit the 495 intersection. Roads quickly growing slick, I slowed along with the rest of the brave souls on the highway.

A four-car pileup stalled my progress for over an hour between exits, and I was stuck waiting for the road to be cleared. At least the snow the weathermen had called for never swept in. A dozen smaller accidents littered the roads and berms before I made it to Everett. I got there in one piece, exhausted from the tension of driving in shitty weather and the late hour.

The following morning was Tuesday, so I knew I wouldn't be catching up with JJ until later in the afternoon after he got off of work. Yes, I wanted to see him and get our talk over with, but I wasn't about to call him at midnight and drag him from his bed. He had to be exhausted from the case he'd been working on most of the summer.

I had daydreams about him telling me he'd finished with court, had spoken with Alex, and still had nowhere to go for Thanksgiving. That he would agree to join me and my family when I asked.

I hoped.

A pile of mail lay on my table thanks to the neighbor I'd had checking on my apartment, but I ignored it, dropped my two bags, kicked off my wet shoes on the mat, and headed straight to bed.

I slept in, waking peacefully in knowing I'd made the right decision in taking matters into my own hands. But while lazing around, shuffling through my mail over a second cup of coffee, the local news replay caught my attention from the TV I had on low.

Alex Berset, I heard the reporter say in a list of others being placed under arrest.

A unique name, I'd thought when JJ had first told me about him, so it had stuck in my brain.

I turned up the volume, standing in front of my TV with steaming mug in hand, but only caught the tail end of the earlier-recorded report about a drug raid in Lynn. Remembering I could rewind live TV, I quickly rewound to the beginning of the story.

One of the men in cuffs and being shoved into the back of a cop car was blond and looked a lot like the guy who'd been with JJ at the dance club months earlier.

The reporter listed the arrested men's names again— Alex Berset being the last one mentioned.

No fucking way there were two assholes with that name in the Boston area with the same height, build, and haircut.

Was that the reason JJ hadn't called or texted in close to a week? He'd been busy with court until the day before, but obviously shit wasn't going well on the best friend and his family front.

A knot formed in my gut, all the dreaming I'd been doing fading away to leave an emptiness behind. Alex's arrest would mean JJ's plans to go their separate ways would be set aside yet again.

I wanted to call JJ immediately, find out where the fuck we stood—but fear continued to creep in along the edges of my thoughts. I needed to protect myself.

JJ had recounted his connection with Alex directly to me. He'd shared a shit ton about their relationship, how he'd been manipulated for years, his loyalty being taken advantage of. Even if he hadn't yet broken things off with Alex yet, Teresa and the kids would need JJ's support to see them through the upcoming days.

Alex had been arrested and would probably face charges since with his background there was no way he was simply an innocent bystander who got caught up in the bust.

Whatever JJ thought he might want with me would be set aside yet again for others he saw as a responsibility above me.

Thanksgiving together sure as fuck wouldn't be happening.

Coming back was a mistake.

All the good feelings I'd been having since the day before melted away like the ice with the sunrise earlier that morning.

I was done with not being a priority and being second choice.

I would spend the day in Boston, maybe have lunch with Mason and Jasper if they were available to celebrate the guilty verdict. Rent a trailer to haul with my SUV and pack up all my shit. On Wednesday, I would do some early Christmas shopping, since Nodhead Falls didn't have the kinds of stores in town like the bigger city malls, and then I would return to Maine for good.

There was nothing worth staying for in a city that didn't feel like home. If JJ ever got his head out of his ass and was serious about pursuing something real with me, with Alex nothing but smoke in his life's rearview, he knew where to find me.

But I was done waiting, putting my life on hold for him to make up his goddamned mind and communicate.

I had to choose for *myself*—and that was heading to the woods where I belonged. With people who would have my back, be there when they promised. My family made me feel as though my existence in their life had true meaning, and they would be enough.

Chapter 30

JJ

I went to work at Teresa's insistence on Tuesday. There was nothing else I could do, and I fucking hated the helpless feeling. My hands were as tied as hers. I did, however, offer her the name of a defense attorney since Alex was definitely going to need one. I told her to get in touch with him and explain what had happened.

And if Alex didn't have money in the bank to afford the guy—which I suspected—I promised to help with the lawyer's costs.

But not for Alex.

I was done with his ass even if he'd never gotten my text from the night before while he'd been cooking up meth or bagging that shit up to sell.

What I'd offered, how I would sacrifice yet again, was only for those boys who were going to be without a father for a while. The empathy was almost unbearable. My chest fucking ached for those two innocent munchkins who didn't deserve the kind of childhood I'd endured.

A call came through my cell while I sat buried in work

at my desk but unable to concentrate. It was a number I didn't recognize, but as a detective, I always answered.

"Detective Jenner."

"JJ." The relief in Alex's voice sagged my shoulders.

There was no way he'd been released already—his arraignment was set for two that afternoon.

"I have one call," he said, his voice shaky with wry laughter, "so I figured I'd better get in touch with the only man I know I can count on to help me out."

Fuck.

I pinched the bridge of my nose. "I'm not a lawyer, Alex."

"But you'll take care of everything until they realize I didn't do anything. I'm innocent!"

As if I would believe that considering how shady he'd been, the same behavior I'd seen before years earlier.

"I gave Teresa the name and number of a lawyer, but I'm done."

"What..." An incredulous gasp stilted his question. "What the hell is that supposed to mean?"

"I've been holding your hand for years," I stated, my heart breaking even though I needed to finally let him go and move on. "And you've taken advantage of me—"

"I have not!"

"—manipulated me. You have!" I insisted. "Time and again, I've laid down my life for you and your family. I never even got a thank you. Repaying that kind of self-sacrifice with blow jobs and sex isn't enough anymore. You can't give me what I need, what I've wanted the last ten years, and I was a fool to stick around as long as I did."

"What are you saying, JJ?" he asked, his tone low.

"That I've loved you for too long, but I've found

someone new who treats me better than you ever did. I'm done being your fuck buddy, the man you've strung along. It was unfair for me to never tell you the truth about my feelings for you, but I thought it would be enough to just be near you—a part of your life. But it's not anymore. I can't trust you—I *don't* trust you to make the right decision for me, your family, or even yourself. You've fucked up again, but this time you're going to have the pay the consequences on your own."

"You can't do this to me, JJ!"

"You did this to yourself." I struggled to get the words out.

"Some fucking friend you are," he snipped, and remembering the tirades he'd spewed when going through withdrawal, I pulled the cell from my ear and pressed the end button, cutting his rising voice off mid-sentence.

It was done for real. Saved by the fact he was behind bars and wouldn't be able to nag me into helping him find answers to his problems.

I'd expected relief, but only grief pressed on my chest. How long would I mourn the friend I'd lost with bitter parting words? I hadn't considered Alex to be my lover for months. That title belonged to another man who'd been incredibly patient, not even nagging me for an update.

And I would see him soon.

Once I was able to leave the office that evening, I headed to Alex's to meet with Teresa to help get them settled first before I left for the holiday weekend.

Alex's arraignment had taken place, and he wasn't going anywhere before his court date, which was set for mid-December, a few weeks away. Until then, he would remain behind bars without bail due to the amount of drugs found, illegal gun possession, and the fact a police officer still lay in critical condition without a way of knowing which of the six men arrested had fired the shots.

Teresa let me in, but rather than appearing teary-eyed like I'd expected, her face was a pale rock. I could tell by the look in her eyes that she was finished with Alex's bullshit, same as me. She adored her boys, and they would come first.

"I'm going to my parents in Jersey," she said the second I shut the door behind me.

Alex hated her family and had always looked for excuses to get out of going to see them.

"What can I do to help?" I asked, blowing an exhale into my cupped hands to warm them as we stood in the entryway. The temperatures had dropped drastically with the sunset.

"Nothing." She gathered her cardigan around her center but didn't move from the doorway where the cold lingered from her having opened the door to let me in.

I took that as a clear indication she didn't want me coming into her house and possibly upsetting the quiet still-ness that seemed to hover beneath the roof.

"Wesley and Aaron are in bed?"

"Just now, yes—Janie is upstairs too."

"Sorry if I interrupted."

Teresa shook her head. "She's packing bags for the boys. I'm pulling them from school early for Thanksgiving. I'll decide after the holiday what I'm going to do."

I nodded. "What can I do to make this easier for you? The boys? Anything—I'll have your back. Always."

"I appreciate everything you've done for us, JJ, but it's time for you to walk away. Emotionally, at least."

I raised an eyebrow, shoving my hands into my pants

pockets as she wrapped her sweater tighter around her core. "What are you say, Teresa?" I asked, my insides beginning to twist.

"Loving Alex hasn't done either of us any favors, but at least you can start over," she said. "I have the boys to think of, and while I don't like the idea of them losing their dad, he's toxic. Unhealthy to their mental and emotional health at their young ages."

Either of us...

"How long have you known?" I asked, my voice ragged as her words echoed in my head.

A sad smile lifted her lips. "You're a detective, JJ, but in this you've been as obvious as a book with its pages spread open, demanding to be read. He only ever saw you as a means of release when you would have laid down your life fifty times over to keep him safe. Honestly, I'm surprised you stuck around as long as you did."

I rubbed a weary hand over my face. "My staying used to be for him, but you must know how much I care about you and the boys."

"I do." She offered a pained smile. "And this is going to hurt, but you need to move on, JJ." Her tone adamant knifed at my chest. "Live the life *you* want. Let us go—for now at least. When things settle down, when some healing takes place, maybe we can get together again. But I promise we'll be fine. I have family in Jersey who will look after us."

But *I* didn't have anyone to call mine. Not yet, at least.

"This is a rash decision, but I'm cutting all ties with Alex," Teresa continued. "Janie is going to pay my lawyer fees to file for divorce."

I studied Teresa's face, the dark circles beneath her eyes, and the weariness in the lines I hadn't noticed before.

While I'd been involved in their lives, I wondered over how much I didn't know—how much she'd kept hidden from me. With how her girlfriend Janie hated Alex, I expected she'd been aware of what went on in their home more than I had.

I didn't trust Alex.

But I believe his soon-to-be ex-wife would care for their boys with a protective nature I'd seen more than once. They would be in good hands, especially with her loving parents helping out.

We said goodbye—*for now* as she'd suggested—with tears on both of our faces. She promised to give the boys my love and find a way to explain that Uncle JJ wouldn't be able to visit them in Jersey for a while. She would end up moving there after the divorce regardless of the results of Alex's day in court.

My chest felt heavy, but I focused on slugging forward, same as she did until better times allowed us to see each other again.

When I got home, I checked my phone. Again.

Kellen hadn't responded to the text I'd sent telling him I missed him, which meant he was still up at the camp.

Excitement came to life in my veins knowing I had off until the following Monday and that I finally felt free enough to pursue something real, long-lasting with him. It would be late before I got up to his family's cabin, but he would be happy to see me. I could feel that truth deep in my bones, same as I knew Alex was gone from my life. Whether he escaped jail or not, our intertwined lives had unraveled. My one-time lover lay in my past, and I had zero interest in dragging any of his shit into my future.

I didn't doubt Teresa would get full custody of their boys, and I looked forward to one day being reunited in a healthier atmosphere where they flourished.

After a long talk with Kellen, a full explanation of what had gone down since I'd seen him last, I planned on telling him how hard I'd fallen and how much I wanted him by my side.

Hope finally overshadowed the turmoil, and I couldn't get on the road fast enough.

Chapter 31

Kellen

I took Tuesday to pack, talk to my landlord, and meet up with Mason and Jasper for a late dinner. They were headed to some tropical island on Black Friday, and it was cold enough with the sunset that I envied them.

I also envied their love. The emotion in their eyes when they looked at each other. While happy for them, I left their house feeling even more despondent than when I'd arrived.

Wednesday morning, I headed to the mall as soon as it opened to play Santa for the nieces and nephews who always had high expectations from their childless uncle. Even though Thanksgiving hadn't yet arrived, red and green decorations made the mall festive. Jolly. Christmas carols played on speakers in some of the stores I visited, buoying my mood regardless of my lack of a love life.

Bags quickly loaded down my arms, but I stopped at the coffee shop for a pick-me-up since I hadn't slept well the night before and had a long drive ahead of me.

I stood in line five-people deep, too needy for caffeine to walk away.

The warm scent of a cologne I recognized flooded my

senses, and I swallowed hard, forcing the image of Xavier from my mind. Lots of men wore the same—

"Kellen?"

Oh fuck.

Teeth gritted, I glanced over my shoulder.

A nightmare come to life greeted my eyes. My ex along with his fiancé stood directly behind me, all cozied up in each other's personal space like when I'd last seen them together—but with clothes this time.

They were not the fucking people I needed to see when I'd just started to feel good about shit.

Ignoring them, I turned back around as if I didn't recognize them.

"Rude," Xavier muttered, his voice as petulant as I remembered.

I hesitated a second to inhale deeply, but my anger, the bitterness I'd been holding inside for too many years erupted inside me. I didn't love the man anymore, didn't pine for him, but the hurt still festered.

Spinning, I allowed my eyes to blaze with the heat of a thousand suns, ready to take the opportunity to cut him off at the ankles and leave him floundering as he'd done to me.

"What's *rude*," I hissed, leaning toward him, "was cheating on me right before our wedding and leaving me without a backward glance to pick up the pieces on my own."

His brow furrowed, and his little lover Teddy squirmed, glancing around as though my quiet outburst had made him uncomfortable. Good. Maybe he'd feel half as shitty as I had once I was done saying my piece.

"It wasn't what you thought," Xavier murmured, his face flushed.

I barked a laugh at that fucking line he'd spewed at me

that day before I'd turned around to gather myself—the same fucking words JJ had stated to me while up at camp. But I wasn't an idiot.

"There was no mistaking what I saw, Xavier," I stated, "but what was even worse? You took off the second I gave you privacy to untangle yourself from your little boy toy so we could work things out. But you ghosted me without an explanation. Blocked my number, blocked me on social media too. And when I went to your parents for answers, they wouldn't even talk to me through the door."

Xavier didn't speak—big fucking surprise because he had no fucking argument for what he'd chosen over the potential he'd made me believe we'd had.

"You ignored me as though I'd been nothing but a blip on your life's radar," I continued. "Never mind our years together, the dreams we'd shared, the debt we accrued creating the perfect wedding you wanted." My voice raised, but I didn't give a shit. Xavier had cost me a lot more than just a shit ton of cash that had taken me months to pay off.

On my own.

Because he couldn't be bothered to communicate whatever he'd obviously felt had been lacking between us.

"Then you spread your legs for this...*twink* who looks nothing like the man you claimed was the one of your dreams."

Xavier and I stood almost nose to nose, his height slightly less than mine but his gym-rat shoulders wider. Pecs thicker. He looked like a pure top, a dominant alpha—exactly as he'd been with me.

"Had *everything* been a lie?" I asked, straightening and peering down my nose while glancing over him, remembering how he'd given up his ass to someone completely my opposite.

He vibrated with tension. "It isn't what you're thinking," he repeated his bullshit.

Yet another laugh burst from me, full of sarcasm and vinegar, and I didn't bother keeping down my voice any longer. "I walked in on you letting this kid *fuck you*, Xavier. There wasn't much *thinking* involved considering you were moaning like a whore while he railed your ass."

Teddy squeaked, pressing in closer to Xavier, the little twerp.

My ex sputtered, his face going red from my outburst that the entire cafe had to have heard. But he deserved to feel shame and embarrassment over what he'd done to me. I didn't give a flying fuck who listened in on the drama or what people thought of him. Hopefully the worst, because that was exactly what he'd been for me.

A waste of my motherfucking time, and I was done. Beyond having a capacity for any relationship. Dating. Hell, even fucking.

"I put you first. *Always*," I emphasized. "Date nights? Your choice. Wedding plans? All yours, regardless of my opinion. We rarely made it back to the farm for holidays because you had to go wherever your family was. I followed you down here when you refused to consider moving to Maine. I agreed to leave my home and loved ones for you, and how did you show your devotion in return?

"By being unfaithful to the man who self-sacrificed nonstop to make you happy. You were the one person I thought I could trust with every part of me—how wrong I was. But guess what?" I leaned in close, causing them both to flinch back, my tone hard. "I'm thankful you cheated, that I got to see the real you before I committed my life to you."

Done with a stunned speechless Xavier, I turned toward Teddy.

Big blue eyes peered at me full of fear.

"Once a cheater, always a cheater," I assured him. "If you were smart, you would get out before Xavier gets bored with you and leaves you with a shit ton of bills that will ruin your credit. But the broken heart? It'll heal. I can promise you that too."

Taking my own advice, I walked away, my steps lighter than they had been minutes earlier.

Xavier had never been a big talker, more on the quieter side, but for the first time, I'd never been more thankful he never shared his inner thoughts. That part of him used to bug me, but his close-lipped nature had allowed me to make a spectacle of him, exactly as he'd done to me that weekend our wedding had ended in devastation.

Head high, I walked out of the mall, glad to have the closure he'd never allowed me before. But no grin stretched my lips. No exuberance made my chest feel like Pop Rocks going off beneath my skin.

While I hadn't been nearly in as deep with JJ as I had with Xavier, his similar silence, his lack of communication with me over the whole Alex affair, fucking hurt like hell.

Almost...worse somehow.

But.

I stopped in the middle of the parking lot and inhaled the freezing cold air filling my lungs. It was time to count my motherfucking blessings.

I'd learned my lesson about men who wouldn't put me first like I did with them. I'd finally gotten some closure, even last words with my ex. I also only had a few hours before I could leave Boston behind for good.

My loving family waited for me, my nieces and nephews especially excited for my arrival.

Focusing on those truths, I stowed the shopping bags in my SUV and climbed in, heading for the U-Haul waiting to be hitched up and packed with the few things still left in my apartment.

My brother called me as I pulled onto the highway. A smile cracked my face as I thought about the upcoming holiday.

"What's up, Jacob?" I asked on speaker phone.

"Damn. You sound happy compared to when we last spoke."

I could hear the smile in his voice, and mine stretched wider. "Damn right. You'll never guess who I just saw."

"Who?"

I told my brother about the run-in with Xavier and Teddy, and he laughed, wishing he'd been there to see the short confrontation that had finally put that part of my life to rest.

"That moment was sweeter revenge than my two years of fucking randoms to get back at him," I said, my grin fading as my mind returned to JJ and what I'd hoped for with him.

"Mom said you quit."

I shoved thoughts of the detective down deep. "Yep— the other night before coming here. Gonna miss the guys from Elite, but I'm finally ready to move on ."

"What's going on with JJ?"

Shit.

So much for my plan to avoid going there and dragging my heart down too.

I filled Jacob in on what I'd seen on the news and the lack of communication on JJ's part. I knew where his priorities lay, why he hadn't gotten in touch with me, and I would eventually get over him, same as I had with Xavier.

Jacob told me he was sorry for me but once more changed the topic, thank fuck. "So you're coming home?"

"For good," I stated. "Like you've told me time and again, there's nothing here for me. I'm almost all packed up and ready to roll, itching to get my ass north. I should make it to the farm later tonight."

"We're heading to Mom and Dad's in a few minutes, but I have some news that I didn't want to wait to share. I'm especially glad for it now, since it'll give you something else to think on while traveling rather than shitty men who don't appreciate your awesomeness."

I chuckled, taking an exit off the highway. "What's the news?"

"Remember the hunting cabins we used to go to with Dad and Uncle when we were teens?"

"Yeah." I grinned, imagining the small one-room lodges we'd crammed into the night before the first day of doe season at the old run-down campground northwest of the cabin. The last time we'd gone had been when I was fourteen. So much shit had happened in my life since that I'd forgotten about the place.

"The property is for sale, and you should see how much the campground has expanded since we were kids. They've added more cabins. Full hookups for campers. They even built three heated bathrooms. The roads are paved, and the house acting as the office was partially renovated a couple of years ago—it's a fucking gold mine."

He went on to remind me of how deep in the woods the place was even though it lay in perfect proximity to Big Bear Lake, a tourist attraction that brought hundreds of people to Maine all year long. Boating in the summer, hunting in the fall, ice fishing in winter... How much there would be to tinker with, to keep a man busy while making other people comfortable. Something I'd always enjoyed doing.

Owning such a business would also provide income for whoever wished to live a lifestyle more in tune with nature rather than a big city.

"Tell me more," I demanded, my mind already back in the deep woods, even though I had a few hours' worth of driving ahead of me. And with the day before Thanksgiving traffic, I knew I'd be lucky to get to the farm before dinnertime.

"The owner hasn't put the place on the market yet."

"How'd you learn about it?" I pulled into my parking spot at the apartment complex and shut off the engine. Cold immediately began to creep through the glass and metal which sheltered me from the cold wind slamming into my SUV.

"Amy's cousin is best friends with the owner's daughter. She told Amy that her dad was ready to sell and was hoping to get someone they knew or a friend of a friend buyer they could trust to take care of the property and love it in the same way he has since he bought it twenty or so years ago."

"Any idea how much he wants for it?"

"Not nearly what it's worth in this market—but only if it's not to some stranger. Otherwise, he's going to ask for top dollar."

We discussed my finances briefly before moving back into our memories from the campground and the surrounding woods. It had been my first weekend of hunting with the "men". I'd chickened out when it had come time to pull the trigger though.

None of the guys with us that first year had made fun of

me for refusing to kill an animal—even if it would help feed my family through the winter—and I hadn't realized until later how accepting they'd been. They'd allowed me to be comfortable with my limits.

Jacob had taken that shot but hadn't ever rubbed it in my face in all the years since. He'd always had my back, even when I'd come out to him as bi when I'd been in high school.

Talk about unconditional love.

I'm making the right choice, I told myself again when I climbed back into my SUV a few hours later, the sun disappearing on my left as I hauled the trailer containing all of my meager belongings northward.

I'd texted Mom earlier that morning before hitting the mall, letting her know I was returning home. She'd simply sent a heart emoji and promised to have dinner on the table for me. I would end up arriving later than I'd planned or had even told Jacob, but being the loving mom she was, she wouldn't care about my tardiness.

She would be happy just to have me be with the rest of them because my presence held worth in the other Roberts' minds. Especially the kids who would be climbing off the walls after eating all the candy I'd bought for them.

Boston faded in the rearview mirror, and although the sting of leaving JJ behind still made my chest ache with emotion I would at some point have to face, the path before me was the right one.

Absence made the heart grow fonder, but in my circumstance, distance would bring healing.

Eventually, I hoped.

Chapter 32

JJ

When I got to the cabin around ten on Tuesday night, I knew immediately that Kellen wasn't there. No SUV sat out front. No welcoming light from the living room window. No lazy smoke crawling into the sky like the time I'd been there before.

Sitting in my idling car, gaze on the silent house sitting in the cold dark, I chewed over the predicament I found myself in.

If Kellen wasn't in the sticks, he'd gone to his parents, which meant he had cell service. Why hadn't he texted back telling me he missed me too? I knew he did—there was no fucking way the emotions painted on his face the night I had left him weren't real.

I'd been waiting for him to respond but had figured he couldn't.

So why the fuck *hadn't* he?

Stomach tight and chest aching, I turned around and drove back the way I'd come. With Thanksgiving two days away, I could guess where he'd gone. Cell service came through a good twenty minutes later, but rather than calling him, I headed into Nodhead Falls, wanting a face-to-face conversation for everything I had to say to that man.

I pulled into the Roberts' driveway, my car's headlights flashing over bright white siding that looked cold as ice in the frigid air.

Kellen's SUV wasn't sitting out front.

My heart dropped, and I cursed a blue streak.

Putting my car into park, I decided I didn't have a choice on the whole talking in person plan. I grabbed my cell from the dash's holder, ready to swipe it to life, but the house's front porch light flicked on.

The window covering moved, revealing a gray-haired woman.

Kellen's mom, most likely.

"Fuck." I rubbed my hand over my mouth. No way I could sit there, a stranger in someone's driveway, having a phone conversation that wouldn't be short.

I turned off my car, climbed out, and hurried toward the house, cursing the cold air biting at uncovered skin.

I'd expected Kellen's mom to answer to my knock, but an older man with wide shoulders pulled it open, and I couldn't help my grin. He was the image of what Kellen would be in thirty-some years with the same eyes, his dark hair and scruff more than peppered with sexy silver. Bring. It. On.

"James Jenner," I introduced myself, and the door suddenly flung inward.

Kellen's mom had grasped it from her husband's hold and yanked, revealing herself from where she'd been behind the door. "You." Her gaze narrowed enough that I lifted my hands.

At least she didn't hold a shotgun—things couldn't be as bad as I had started to assume.

"I'm looking for Kellen."

She huffed and glanced up at her husband. They shared a silent moment, then both stepped back as though of one mind.

"Come on in," Mr. Roberts stated gruffly, eyeing me before glancing past my shoulder to my car. "No bag?"

"Is that an invite to stick around?" I joked, only half serious in my usual pushiness.

"Depends on what you have to say for yourself," he stated sternly, the papa bear to Kellen's momma.

"Fair enough." I nodded, moving off to the side so he could shut the door and keep the cold out.

"You just caught us," Sharon said, motioning toward the living room on the left. "We were about to head upstairs to go to bed. Big day of meal prep and pie-making tomorrow."

"Where's your son?" I asked, not having any patience for small talk.

"He's in Boston."

My breath kicked from my lungs at Kellen's mom's answer. "What?" I rasped, my shoulders sagging.

"He went down there—for you." Lips tight, she sat on the couch. Her husband took the recliner, and I remained standing, my mind racing a mile a minute.

"When?"

"He drove through the storm on Monday night. He told me over the phone earlier today that he'd planned to talk to you tonight after you got off work—but then he saw the news."

Alex's arrest.

He figured I hadn't gotten in touch with him because I'd gone to Alex's side once again. In his mind, I'd chosen someone else.

Goddamnit all to fucking hell!

I pulled at my hair, barely suppressing the scream wanting to rip from my lips.

"Since you're here and looking miserable, I'm guessing you finally got your head screwed on straight but didn't bother to let him know."

"Shit." I fisted my hands and clenched my eyes shut. "I—I thought he was at the cabin without service," I said, knowing the words were fucking lame. "I figured I would surprise him—*show* him I'd put him first rather than tell him over the phone."

Huffing out an annoyed as fuck sigh, I opened my eyes to find Sharon's welling with tears.

"You love him," she said quietly, and I considered the fact she didn't ask me a question.

My annoyance dissolved in a blink, my eyes stinging. *So much*, I wanted to whisper. *More than anything.*

But Kellen needed to hear it first.

"Is he still coming home for Thanksgiving?" I asked, my voice unsteady.

"Yes, and we had hoped that you would be with him," Sharon said, still eyeing me with unshed tears.

Curses rang in my head, and I clenched my teeth as I got annoyed once again. "I need to call him."

"No."

My gaze tore off the scratched hardwood floor for Kellen's dad. "What? Why not?" I shot out, my forehead furrowing deeply.

"Because he *will* be home sometime tomorrow, and you were right. Seeing the evidence of your feelings for him will mean more than mere words or promises he's heard before."

Well fuck. The steam leaked out of me, leaving me sagging on my feet. It had been one hell of an emotional roller coaster of a day.

"Okay," I whispered, ready to fall over and sleep for twenty-four hours straight.

"You're staying here tonight," Sharon said, getting up from the couch, her tone no-nonsense as though she'd set her mind, and that was the way it was going to be. "Tomorrow, you can help me in the kitchen and tell me all about yourself—what kind of man my son has fallen in love with this time. But I'll warn you right now." Her brown eyes pinned me in place. "You hurt him..."

"Shoot, shovel, and a deep woods burial," I said, biting back a smirk. "Got it."

She chuckled and ordered me to go get my bag.

I did as told, and a few minutes later, she showed me into the finished basement and the pullout couch Kellen got assigned to when the entire family came back to the farm for the holidays.

"I put on an extra thick mattress pad to make it comfortable, but I'm sure you two will be happy to share a bed regardless of where it's located."

I choked on a dry laugh, praying like fuck he wasn't so pissed off with me for my radio silence that he didn't give me a chance to explain myself.

But moms always knew best, right? And I wanted to believe Sharon had her son's interest at heart—same as I did.

The next morning, Kellen texted his mom with the news that he would be home around dinnertime. She didn't tell him I was there, and that I was anxious as fuck to land eyes on him and apologize for assuming shit like an asshole.

We spent the next few hours exactly as Sharon had said.

In the kitchen with me doing most of the talking and a lot of the prep work. None of what I'd had the pleasure of helping with before.

I learned how to make stuffing from scratch. I helped to cut up sweet potatoes. Rolled out dough for pies. Peeled and sliced apples. Shoved my hand into the cavity of a raw, huge turkey. Memories imprinted in my mind to savor and enjoy in the years ahead with my newfound family.

I hoped.

The others in the Roberts' clan began to arrive. Kellen's oldest sister Sarah had four kids, the younger twins redheaded like their dad, Fred. The oldest, Brian, was the star quarterback I'd heard all about, and it didn't take long before we were discussing stats.

The youngest Roberts' sibling showed up next, and the glare shot my way at introductions made me fear for my life. I'd thought Sharon was a momma bear, but Kellen's baby sister Suzi was a goddamned grizzly. Add in the fact she had an infant in her arms and her husband Donnie carried the two toddler terrors Kellen had told me about, and I expected to walk on eggshells until he arrived and we got shit set straight between us.

"So you're JJ." Suzi eyed me rather than offering a greeting in return to mine. "You hurt him..."

Her dad chuckled, and Donnie rolled his eyes while handing over one of the squirmy boys to their grandpa.

"Let me guess," I said, biting back a smile. "You know how to use a shotgun?"

"Damn right, I do," she muttered, a hint of a smirk lighting her hazel eyes. "Since you're here and *comfortable* rather than hung out to dry by Mom, I'm sure there's a reason. But I want the whole story. In detail. Got it?"

"Yes, ma'am—but not until I talk to Kellen first."

She huffed, lips pursed, and moved farther into the house to get her young brood straightened out.

Kellen's sister-in-law came in next with her three kids, but her husband Jacob pulled up short at seeing me along with everyone gathered to greet the last family to arrive.

His dark eyebrows dipped inward, and he gave me an assessing look. "I must have missed something between my call with Kellen an hour ago and now," he said once all the kids ran off to the playroom attached to the garage.

I held out my hand. "James Jenner."

"Yeah, I figured that. Kellen doesn't know you're here." He eyed my hand rather than taking it, his voice gruff. "*What* are you doing here?"

Arm falling to my side, I glanced around at the eight adults and two teenaged boys still in the vicinity staring at me with a million questions in their eyes. More than one appeared a little perturbed by my presence. Fucking hell, it sucked being the one on the other end of an interrogation— even if it hadn't really started yet.

My gaze flicked between Kellen's three siblings, nerves twisting my stomach even while jealousy rose to tighten my throat. "He's lucky as hell to have you all watching out for him, but let me talk to him before the guns start getting pulled out, okay? Give me a chance to explain myself to him before filling me with lead."

No one spoke, but it was Jacob's gaze I held as he continued to deliberate in his head over my presence and suggestions.

"You hurt him..." He finally spoke, his voice trailing off.

Jesus Christ.

I choked on a laugh. The Roberts were a bunch of bloodthirsty hillbillies. And I fucking adored them. Still grinning, I shook my head. "Please don't make me tell you the words Kellen needs to hear first."

Smiles lit up around the room, chatter breaking into the tenseness as though I hadn't had my life threatened twice within a matter of minutes.

Jacob shoved out his hand, and I shook it firmly. "He has more power to hurt me than I could ever do to him," I shared what I could.

Nodding, Jacob clasped my shoulder. "Want a beer?"

Fuck yeah, I did.

Two hours later, it was as though I'd been a part of the Roberts family for decades. The siblings included me in their ribbing, especially focusing on the fact I'd been allowed in Mom's domain, something even their dad wasn't. Two of the grandkids sat on my feet, demanding I walk around and give them a lift. Even Suzi decided I was all right after learning I'd unwillingly stuffed the turkey, gagging over the process for their family.

"You're ten times the man that asshole ex of Kellen's had been," she said with a snort. Lifting her shirt like she wasn't in the middle of a packed living room, she set on nursing her youngest son.

I quickly looked away, never having witnessed such... freedom in a family before.

"Kellen said he had a nice little run-in with Xavier earlier today, but I'll let him tell the story."

"Tease!" Suzi lobbed a spit cloth at Jacob's face while cradling the baby with her other arm.

Jacob laughed and avoided the missile.

Kellen had spoken with Xavier.

I swallowed hard, the chatter in the room growing dim in my ears. He'd told me how his ex had ghosted him after breaking his heart, and while I didn't fear Xavier ever gaining Kellen's forgiveness or a second chance at love, I wondered over Kellen's emotional state.

Would the reminder of the hurt he'd experienced make him even more closed off to what I planned to beg him for?

The hope I'd been clinging to since the day before grew thin.

I glanced around the room, taking in the laughter, the acceptance and love that lay thick as a warm, snuggly blanket in wintertime.

Fuck, did I long for what Kellen had. Even more so, I wanted *him*.

But would he allow himself to be vulnerable yet again?

Chapter 33

Kellen

I had to pull around the side of the barn to park since too many cars had hogged the driveway. It was *well* past dinnertime—going on ten. I expected everyone to be in bed except for Mom, who had promised to wait up for me when I'd texted at six saying I was barely crawling in traffic trying to escape Boston.

But lights blazed from all of the downstairs windows. Warmth rushed through me regardless of the cold air making my exhales fog in front of my face as I hurried toward the house with the only bag I would need until the morning. Everyone—or at least the adults—had stayed awake to greet me.

Throat tight, I took the porch stairs in two hopping strides and pushed in the front door.

The heat and the scent of baking rushed over my face as I dropped my bag to the floor, and I grinned like a damned dork—until I realized my family jammed unmoving in the entryway rather than surging forward to hug me like usual.

JJ stood front and center, a soft smile on his face, but his eyes held uncertainty.

My breath left in a rush as usual at the sight of him, and I swallowed hard. He was supposed to be with Alex. "What the fu—"

"Language," Mom murmured, cutting me off.

"Hey," JJ greeted me quietly but stayed put. That magnetic current between us hadn't faded one iota. Every cell in my body tensed to move all up in his space in the electric silence hovering in the atmosphere.

Suzi huffed and shoved JJ aside, breaking the dam that had held my family back. She hugged me tight. "Hear him out, or so help me God..." she whispered in my ear, and I shot my attention toward JJ.

He hadn't moved, hands shoved in his pockets, the mere presence of him pulling my focus to him time and again off everyone who wrapped their arms around me. Why was he here?

"Give him a chance," Jacob murmured before patting my shoulder.

"He's the perfect book boyfriend!" Amy squeezed me with a little squeal, her words a lot louder than the others'.

JJ's face flamed.

Everyone else kept quiet, Dad and Mom included, even though Mom gave me a watery smile and nod of encouragement after releasing her hold on me.

Somehow, someway, JJ had gotten my entire family's approval. He'd been invited in and accepted regardless of my not being there for introductions or otherwise.

My loved ones slowly trickled away, calling goodnight and leaving me alone with the only non-relative in the house.

JJ still hadn't moved, but neither had I, my feet rooted on the mat right inside the front door.

"I have some explaining to do," he said, his voice quiet.

Knowing more than one person lingered at the top of the stairs trying to listen in, I picked up my bag and started toward the kitchen, a million questions in my mind. "Not here," I murmured.

JJ stepped back to let me pass.

I breathed the arousing yet comforting sandalwood scent of him deep into my lungs while slipping around him. I wanted to stay strong, but him showing up at the farm when Alex doubtless needed him...

Fucking hope swelled up inside me, choking me. Making my eyes water. Heading down into the basement, I swallowed hard, trying to get ahold of myself. Mom had already made up the pullout for me, and a duffle I recognized sat beside the bed that had already been slept in. JJ had arrived yesterday, I realized. Spent the day with my family. But he hadn't reached out to me.

I dropped my bag on the other side and inhaled until it hurt.

"Kellen."

I finally turned, rubbing my palms down my jeans.

JJ allowed me a half-dozen feet of space, no more. He still had his hands deep in his pockets, but even nervous, he was fucking fine. Dark hair all mussed up like the younger kids had made him their horsey like they did with me whenever I visited. His T-shirt was stained and a bit rumpled as though he'd been carting around a toddler or two with sticky fingers.

But his jeans fit him just right, hugging his thick thighs and a bulge that made my mouth water.

Fuck.

I slowly returned my attention to his face.

Some of the uncertainty had faded from his dark eyes.

"You're supposed to be with Alex," I heard myself say, my tone nothing but gravel.

"No—I'm *supposed* to be here with you." JJ heaved a heavy exhale and perched on the edge of the pullout. He patted the mattress beside him.

I sat, keeping a little space between us when I'd rather have climbed onto his lap and devoured his mouth.

"He'd been giving me the runaround again after I got back to Boston, but that is no excuse for dragging shit out while you were waiting. I'm sorry for not putting you first, Kellen."

I licked my lower lip but didn't speak. No man had ever done so—why would JJ be any different?

"I'd made plans with him Monday night to sit and break things off in person," JJ continued, "but once again he didn't show. You saw the news on Tuesday?"

"Yeah," I rasped.

JJ nodded as though he'd assumed as much. "You thought I would sprint to his side, be there for him, same as always."

I nodded.

"Understandable—but I didn't. He wasted his one call on me, and I took the opportunity to tell him what I should have explained months ago. That I was done, that our relationship, his manipulating and using me, was finished.

"I finally turned my back on Alex," JJ murmured without a hint of regret in his voice, "and it was the smartest decision I've ever made. I told him that I've found someone, and you've come to mean more to me in a short time than he ever did."

"JJ," I choked out his name, my body buzzing with the need to lean into him.

"I thought you were up at the camp and that was why

you didn't reply to my text that I missed you. I came up here to show you where my heart wanted to be rather than putting the words on a screen or telling you over the phone. That wasn't the smartest decision I've made, but I'm here with you now, Kellen." JJ reached over and threaded his fingers through mine, squeezing tight.

Electrical currents rushed up my arm, causing goose bumps to rise along my skin and the hairs straighten on my neck. I held on tight to his hand, unable to form words past the lump in my throat.

JJ had chosen me over Alex.

"I want to be with you," he said again, shifting so our knees brushed. "But if I'm not what *you* want, if I'm not enough—" He voice cut out with a harsh swallow.

Fucking hell.

"You're *more* than enough," I whispered and claimed his mouth.

Hunger clawed through my core, making me desperate for him. His breath in my lungs. His hands on my body. Our tongues stroked into each other's mouths, deep with longing.

I tore at his shirt, releasing his mouth to pull it off overhead.

He literally ripped my button-down open, and our mouths stayed fused while I shoved it from my arms.

Pushing him back, I followed along as he lay down.

"No more hiding away from me," he gasped and kicked off his shoes, two quiet thumps joining in our heavy breaths.

I yanked at his jeans and boxer briefs, freeing his thick cock and leaving him naked all but for his socks. "No more silence between us. We gotta talk shit out." I set my own limit while shoving the rest of my clothes to the floor with his.

"Get your fine ass down here," JJ growled, grasping my wrist and yanking.

I fell on top of him, our bodies perfectly aligned. We rutted and writhed together, our mouths once more fused, our scruff doubtless leaving beard burn behind.

JJ flipped me onto my back, the pullout shuddering beneath the half-violent action.

Not giving a shit if the damn thing collapsed beneath us, I wrapped my legs around his waist and groaned as his leaking cock rubbed over mine. My balls tightened, and I moaned against JJ's mouth.

"You're gonna make me come," I whispered, grabbing hold of his ass and squeezing hard enough to bruise.

"Jesus," he hissed, and another quick flip landed me face-first on the mattress, my ass up—and his mouth buried between my cheeks.

"Oh fuck!" I shoved my face into a pillow and let the curses flow as he lapped and shoved saliva deep inside me with every thrust of his tongue. He wrapped his hand around my length and pulled downward, sending me spiraling. "Gonna come," I gasped, and he released me with a harsh swat to my ass cheek, sitting back on his haunches.

"Look at that ass. Goddamn." He smacked the other side then squeezed both tight, his fingertips bruising with a delicious sting.

I hoped I would have those marks on me for days.

He spat on my hole—spat again but that time not on me.

"Fuck," he muttered, thumbing over my ass and pressing the saliva in.

I arched, moaning as he fucked my hole with squelching noises.

"So hot. Jesus, I can't wait to be inside you."

"Do it," I demanded.

JJ cursed, the sound of his desperation and wet schlicking like music to my ringing ears.

"Put that dick in me, JJ," I ordered, reaching back to spread my cheeks.

"Jesus fuck." He hissed the words through gritted teeth and pressed the head of his dick against my hole.

I bore down, and he pushed inside. Fighting to keep from clenching, I exhaled slowly, allowing his cock to stretch me. The slight sting of not being fully ready for him sent lust burning through me, and I once more stuffed my face into a pillow to keep from waking the whole house.

"Oh fuck yeah, baby." JJ grabbed my hips tight and worked in a little deeper. "Your ass is so hungry for me. Fuck."

His deep guttural groan sent shivers racing over my skin as his groin rested against my ass. He filled me completely—but my heart too. Joy swelled inside me like a tsunami, wiping away all the past hurt, the disappointment.

He'd chosen *me*.

"JJ," I gasped, needing...so much fucking *need* I couldn't think past the delicious thickness in my ass, the rightness of him being one with me. I wanted him to live inside me forever. Never leave me.

He stretched over my back and pressed his weight on me, giving me everything. I sank onto the mattress so my aching cock had something to rub against. A slow gyration of his hips promised he planned to drive me fucking insane with a slow fuck rather than the harsh pounding I'd have preferred.

"You like having my bare cock inside your body, baby?" He bit my neck, without a doubt leaving a mark.

A shudder ripped through me. "Fuck yeah."

"Want me to fill you with my cum?"

"Christ, JJ—yes. Fuck, yes," I begged.

"Mmm," he moaned against my ear, his breath hot as his chest plastered to my back. He gripped one on my waist and slid his other hand up my side until he reached my face, covering my mouth with his palm.

"You said you wanna talk shit out" he said, his words hot against my ear, "but I've got something to say that's non-negotiable."

His hips worked with slow, steady thrusts, pegging my prostate with every deep stroke and making me moan with delirious desire.

My eyes rolled back into my head as I fought off the need to detonate from my dick gliding over the blanket.

We were going to make a mess on Mom's quilt, but in that moment, I didn't give a flying fuck about anything other than JJ loving on my body and the words pouring from his lips.

"You're *mine*, Kellen Roberts, end of. Somehow I knew it the second I first saw you. The draw to you...can't fucking resist."

My eyes stung, and I moved beneath him, clenching around his girth each time he dragged from my body.

"You're going to come first, then I'll fill your ass," he continued, the heat and strength of him pressing me into the mattress. "We'll catch our breath, and I'm going to tell you how hard I've fallen for you. Won't say I love you while I'm balls deep in this lush, hot ass of yours—I'll save that for later—but for now I'll show you. Prove it to you."

Fucking hell, this man.

I moaned against his palm, needing to hear it. Had to have those damned words spoken aloud to heal every last hurt in my heart.

"There's no place I'd rather be than here with you, Kell.

Understand?" JJ shoved in a little harder, making me choke on a groan at how deeply he stabbed into my guts. "I want to be with you. *You*—no one else, baby. Not ever."

Tears slid from my eyes, and I swallowed back a sob. That declaration? Fucking perfect...exactly what I'd been longing to hear from his lips since the day I'd fallen for the man.

"That's it." JJ stilled, soothing his hands along my sides. "Let it out. I got you."

He shifted, pulling me onto my side, and spooned me, his arms tightly wrapped around my chest. Dick still lodged deep inside me, he held me while my emotions ruled me.

"Feel...the same," I gasped out, reaching back for his ass, clutching him tightly against me where he was meant to be.

His cock stayed hard. Mine continued to leak regardless of the swell of feelings rising up inside me as he slowly stroked in and out of my ass.

"Choose *yourself* right now, Kell," JJ whispered, his hand over my heart. "Take what *you* want for a change."

Tears still rolling down my face, I started moving my hips, fucking myself on his dick.

"Fuck yeah," he murmured, and the age-old dance of two bodies in sync began. His pre-cum slickened my insides, making for a more sensual glide between our bodies —but as my emotions settled, I was ready for more.

"Give me your hand," I said, my tone firmer than I'd expected after tears, and he listened like a good boy. I licked up his palm, making him wet. "Get me off."

"Fuck, I love when you tell me what you want." JJ grabbed my cock and set to work in time with his faster thrusts.

I got lost in sensation, feelings coursing through not just my groin but my entire body. I longed to dive deeper, to fall fully into everything JJ poured through my soul as thick as the arousal leaking from my slit.

Tingles came to life in my balls, the brewing of an orgasm that would make me black out.

"Jesus, baby," JJ moaned against my ear as though he knew I was ready to come. "You feel goddamned good. Mine—so fucking mine."

"And you're *mine*." I gasped as he stroked me just right. "Next time, I'm owning your ass. Gonna wreck you. Fill you up."

"Fuck yeah."

"JJ—" My voice broke off at the force of the tremor that ripped through my taint, up through my balls, and into my shaft. I groaned a curse as cum shot all the fuck over the quilt. Long, white ropes coaxed by JJ's thick cock milking my prostate.

"You're choking my dick, Kell—Jesus. Gonna...gonna come in your ass."

"Yes," I gasped as he shoved in deep. "Give me *every-thing*, JJ."

His cock bucked, shooting wet heat inside me.

I shuddered, drinking in his groans, gasping as dribbles continued to leak from my slit with every thrust of his hips.

So much cum.

Such a fucking mess.

But I wouldn't change a goddamned thing about how my night had ended.

With a sensual fuck on the pullout couch in my parents' basement with the man who'd put me first.

Chapter 34

JJ

I came awake slowly, immediately aware I wasn't alone. A heavy thigh lay atop mine, warm exhales ghosting over my neck.

My Kellen.

Groaning, I squeezed him tight, smiling and completely happy. He snuggled the hell out of me even in sleep, the clingy bastard.

I fucking loved it.

Loved *him*.

Humming from the overflowing joy inside my chest, I rolled into his embrace so we pressed together from chest to toes.

He blinked sleepy hazel eyes at me, a slow smile curving his luscious lips as he came awake.

"I love you," I whispered while running my hand up his back to clutch at his shoulder. "More than anything— *anyone*, ever. Even when we aren't fucking around, you fill my heart up to the point it aches. Oh...and sorry about the morning breath." I smacked a smooch on his lips.

He pinched my ass, and I yelped, jerking my head back. "Love you too," he stated with a smirk, his eyes twinkling.

"Fuck, you're so damn fine." I studied his face. The flush on his cheeks, the sleep line across his temple. The scruff lining his jaw.

"Mmm," he hummed, grabbing my ass cheek to hold me tighter against his morning wood. "You too."

We shared unhurried kisses, grinding our cocks together until pre-cum oozed from us both and breaths grew heavy.

"I wanna make another mess," he murmured against my mouth.

"You first," I told him—and he gave me what I wanted, the heat of his spurting spunk and moans taking me with him into euphoric bliss.

That entire day, I was treated like a member of the Roberts' family. I sat beside my lover at the dinner table, our hands on each other's thighs whenever possible. Couldn't keep from touching my man with the thankfulness that flooded my heart.

Friday, the entire clan went to a tree farm and cut down Christmas trees. The grandkids helped Kellen's parents decorate theirs while the rest of us drank hot chocolate and gorged on leftover turkey, all the sides, and pumpkin pies.

Saturday, I heard the family stories. Thumbed through the picture albums. Finally memorized everyone's names. We spent the afternoon playing football in the backyard, our breath fogging, fingers freezing, and noses running. Even the younger kids got involved. We used old dish towels as our flags rather than tackling one another on the frozen ground. Brian acted as quarterback for both teams, so we ended in a tie.

I'd never smiled so much in my goddamned life.

By the time Sunday afternoon rolled around, the grand-kids called me uncle when saying goodbye to us.

No one corrected them, and they all drove away, faces pressed to windows, hands still waving at me, Kellen, Gram, and Grandpa.

Hearing that honorary title stung twofold—being accepted as part of the family, and the reminder of the two boys I wondered when I would see again. Would they remember me? Would the memories we'd made together eventually fade from their little minds?

I'd texted Teresa on Thanksgiving day, and it had taken her until Sunday afternoon to reply. She'd included a picture of the boys sitting with their grandparents, their laughter captured in bright color.

While the truth they were happy at least for that day had settled me somewhat, I still thought of them. Hoped the best for them.

Leaving my lover early the next morning physically hurt—like an aching chest that had my hand pressing on it while driving back to Boston in the pre-dawn hours kind of hurt.

I hadn't been able to tear myself away from Kellen on Sunday, so I had stayed the night. We both set our phone alarms to get me up long before the sun, so I would make it into headquarters by eight.

The wicked early morning drive meant no traffic, but the hours dragged by without being in Kellen's presence. Days slid past even more slowly, but Kellen drove into town from the cabin he'd gone back to every other day so we could talk on the phone.

He went to look at the property northwest of the farm that Jacob had told him about and quickly closed the deal, investing his hard-earned money—pun intended—on over fifty acres, half of which had been turned into a campground I couldn't wait to see.

After our holiday weekend together, every night spent messing up the sheets we laundered daily at his parents', I urged him to do what his heart dictated.

"I want to love you," he'd responded.

"You can do that with some distance between us while you move forward with the purchase," I'd assured him.

Trust would be an issue without being together every day, but I promised him I loved him every time we spoke on the phone. If he had questions about Alex and his family, I didn't have answers because I didn't seek them out.

Other than the one text, I didn't hear from Teresa and didn't expect to for quite some time.

Eventually, she would feel confident in reaching out. Her boys would be settled enough that a reminder of their past—*me*—wouldn't hinder their growth in learning to live without their dad.

It was a couple of weeks before I was able to travel to Maine again, and I only had two days, but Kellen and I made the most of it.

I toured the campground with its new owner—they had cell service, thank fuck. Internet too. I also fucked Kellen into the mattress of his king-sized bed in the office/home-owner's residence master bedroom in celebration of his closing on the property three days before my arrival.

Snow fell that night, leaving the land, trees, and cabins covered in pristine white. There were no people staying at the campground until spring due to the property sale, so we had the place to ourselves.

The two days passed too quickly, and I once more found myself back in the city, strangely uncomfortable in the noise and bustle that used to feel like home.

We spent Christmas with my new family, the ones who had welcomed me with open arms for loving their Kellen. He and I had a blast shopping for the nieces and nephews on the weekend he'd spent with me in Boston prior to the holiday.

I'd never been so...content. Peaceful.

But the distance ate at my patience throughout January, and even though Alex had ended up getting ten years in prison, I knew worry still sometimes lay heavy on Kellen's mind about where my loyalties rested.

Winter seemed to last forever, and once March arrived, I was fucking done with the constant travel on weekends, the two short days off work we got to spend together.

It was March third when I sat scowling at my office wall, wishing it were Friday instead of Tuesday. I wanted my man, goddamnit. Needed him like crazy.

Me: **Miss you.**

My Kell: **Miss you more.**

I grinned at his immediate response. **Not possible**, I shot back. **My bed is cold. The shirt I stole from you doesn't smell like bergamot and citrus anymore.**

My Kell: **My cock is lonely.**

A chuckle left me, and I shifted on my squeaky office chair as my own twitched.

Me: **That delicious dick of yours just had a thorough make out session with my ass two nights ago.**

My Kell: **Tell him that.**

Me: **FaceTime me, and I will.**

The fucker actually called. Face flushed, Kellen smirked at me from my cell's too-small screen.

"Are you a gorgeous shade of pink because you were you outside in the cold, or are you turned on and ready to fuck your fist and come for me?"

"Goddamnit, JJ," he growled, the color on his cheeks darkening. "I was outside, but now I want to strip down and give you what you want."

I hopped up, locked my office door, and settled back in my chair. "Get yourself off for me, baby. Make my day."

He did—but our hot five minutes of phone sex didn't cause the waiting to see him in person again to pass any faster.

Friday afternoon, I got a call on my cell while sitting in the same chair, thinking about how my lover had shot spunk clear up to his chin then had licked it off. That sight had been in my spank bank every night since.

"Detective Jenner," I answered, setting aside thoughts of my sexy man and how badly I ached for him.

The gentleman on the phone introduced himself—and promptly etched a grin onto my face as a shot of adrenaline raced through my system. The second I hung up, I went to see my commanding officer to have a little chat.

But it was Kellen I looked forward to talking to.

Even though the last time I'd waited to tell him something important face-to-face almost backfired, I decided to hold off because the news would cause an immediately and necessary celebratory fuck.

I pulled into his garage's second stall, thankful Kellen's new place had plenty of space for me. At least the snow was melted, and there was none in the forecast. But that whole *wait a minute* thing for New England's weather promised we very well might not be done with the white stuff just yet.

Kellen entered the garage from the kitchen door before I climbed from my car, a tall, sexy drink of water dressed in black from head to toe as usual. Same as always, the sight of him stole my damned breath and made my heart race.

"Fuck, did I miss you," I told him, wrapping him up in my arms and lifting him off the ground.

He laughed, grabbed ahold of my face, and planted his lips on mine while I spun us in a circle.

Groaning, I squeezed him tighter, licking into his mouth, so damn needy for his nearness.

"Want your dick on my tongue," Kellen said, biting at my lower lip while I set him on his feet. "Then you're going to paint the inside of my ass with your cum."

My dick thickened at his suggestion, but I stepped back. "Let me at least get my bag out of the car and into the warm house."

He yanked open my car's back door, grabbed my duffle, and dragged me by the forearm with his free hand toward the kitchen door he'd left open.

Snickering, I allowed myself to be led, but when he shut us inside and spun toward me, I held my palm to his chest once. "Wait."

He glowered. "Talking can wait."

"This time it can't—I have something to tell you that I didn't want to text you or explain over the phone."

Kellen straightened, his pupil-blown irises going wary.

"I was offered a position in Nodhead Fall's police department," I stated bluntly rather than prolonging.

It took a few seconds for my words to register through the worry that had leaked into his brain. A grin split his face, and it was his turn to throw his arms around me and lift me off the floor.

Laughing against his mouth, I tried to tell him I'd given

my two weeks' notice and that I'd already put my house on the market.

"Two weeks," he whispered, kissing me over and over with soft peppered presses of his lips.

"And I'm all yours."

"Fucking hell, that's too long," he groaned, tipping his forehead against mine.

"*Well*," I said, drawing the word out as though deep in thought, "we could spend the next two days in bed making memories to reminisce over during our alone hours."

"Yes." A simple-worded answer, and Kellen grabbed hold of my hand and started toward the stairs. "I'm going to start by sucking your dick, then I'm going to ride you until we both come. Then you're going to be the little spoon until I'm hard again and can slide inside your ass."

Goddamn, honest communication was sexy as fuck.

"Need to suck some new hickeys on your neck," I noted while following him up the stairs. "Those ones I left so Suzi would make fun of you disappeared."

Kellen snorted. "She's a pain in my ass."

"And you love her."

"Unconditionally." Kellen turned toward me once we made it into our room, draping his arms over my shoulders, his fingers rubbing over my freshly shaven hair at the back of my head. "But I love you more than any of my family members, all of them combined. With every piece of me. Every breath, every heartbeat is yours, JJ."

"Fuck, baby." I rested my forehead on his, taking his exhales deep into my lungs, his words flooding me with happiness like I'd never known.

Epilogue

Kellen

On a beautiful, hot August afternoon, Elite Escort retiree Jarod finally married his flame-haired goddess down the Cape at some fancy resort right on the water. They'd spent one hell of a pretty penny to throw a wedding the likes I'd never seen.

But the lavish event, and especially the reception afterward, was well worth it.

They'd invited everyone. Family. Friends. Ex co-workers. Almost all of EE and EEMM enjoyed the flowing champagne and hors d'oeuvres while mingling. The newly married couple were brave having an open bar, considering their guests.

JJ and I stood hand in hand with a small group from the gay branch of Elite, bullshitting and getting caught up with each other, since JJ and I only got down to Boston every other month or so to hang out with our friends.

Most often, we stayed with Mason and Jasper, and the four of us went to Micah's on Sunday afternoons for a smorgasbord of good food and beer. The few weekends I'd visited JJ over the winter before he'd moved to Maine with me had been spent in his bed. We'd rarely even escaped his house, let alone mingled with acquaintances.

He'd sold the place within days of it going up on the market and bought himself a brand new SUV along with a snowmobile for the winter and ATV to toy around with at the campground, now run by a manager I'd hired to care for the daily grind while I was away.

The rest JJ put into a joint savings for a rainy day since I'd only ended up mortgaging about a third of the campground property and didn't need help to pay the bills.

He'd also sent some money to Teresa and her boys who were thriving in Jersey. We'd made plans at Teresa's invitation to visit with them in a few weeks before school started. She'd specifically asked for me to come as well so she could meet the man JJ had found love with.

She and Janie were still together, living in a small bungalow home perfect for the four of them.

Life, she'd claimed when we'd spoken with her last, had been good to them. The move from Boston a perfect new beginning—same as it had been for me and JJ.

"I'm going to grab more beers," Sean said, breaking into my thoughts. "Don't miss me too hard."

Snorting, I turned to Drake, ready to take advantage of the opportunity to talk to him without Sean being all up in our business. I'd been dying to find out if anything had happened with Preston but wasn't sure how to pry without raising any flags. I'd been quiet about it around Sean because the guy was nosey as hell and wasn't good at keeping his mouth shut.

"How's work?" I asked, enjoying the fuck out of being with my old "family" again. It had been almost two months since I'd seen the guys.

Drake shrugged, his vivid blue eyes scanning the dance

floor. "Not too bad. I'm not nearly as busy as you were, but I can't complain about the pay."

"The last client I had...Mason was his favorite...cute little redhead—five-foot-ten-ish," I said, watching his face closely. "You booked with him at all?"

"No redheads yet for me. Good thing too. They're my kryptonite. I'd probably fall head over heels for the first ginger I escorted then have to quit because I'd want to marry them and have their babies."

So no Preston. I wondered if he'd been booking with anyone else at EEMM.

I glanced over at Mason and Jasper all wrapped up with each other on the dance floor, but none of the usual jealousy slid through me at the sight of them. Squeezing JJ's hand a little tighter, I leaned against his shoulder.

He was my rock, something Xavier had never aspired to be. My best friend. My sounding board in business and life. He'd found a family in mine, and I couldn't have been happier with how seamlessly we fit together. Sure, we'd had arguments, but when two people in love chose to consider the other's feelings in all things, relationships were easier. More fulfilling. Fucking fantastic.

Mason smiled at something his husband said, his face lighting up at the younger man who'd helped save him from a serious spiral.

Like me and JJ, they shared something special, something worth fighting for.

"Mason's a different man than when he was escorting," Drake said, and I turned to find him watching the two of them as well.

"He's become who he was always meant to be," I tacked on.

Drake's lips thinned for a second, but then he nodded and finished off the beer in his hand.

"I heard Sean's going back to college," I said, ready for the next bit of gossip. "Think he's going to be able to focus enough to pass classes this time around?"

He'd attempted college right out of high school, but claims he quit to save his parent's money since he hadn't known what he wanted to do for the rest of his life.

A soft huff escaped Drake. "He's dead set on trying. Wants to prove to his dad that he's not just a partying playboy—that he can be just as smart and successful as Micah."

He'd already done the latter with how he's built up EEMM. "What's he going for?"

"MBA. It'll be two years of hell for him, that's for sure."

I grimaced, doubtful he would make it even though the kid was stubborn as hell.

Speaking of the devil, the fuck boy sidled up, a half-dozen amber bottles in his hands and a wide grin on his face. "I come bearing gifts!" He handed them out, including Zack Briggs, who I'd met at Micah's the year before, and the new guy, Jimmy, who'd been chatting with JJ beside me.

The six of us clinked our drinks together.

Sean glanced over my man like I caught him doing every time we got together, but I didn't care. Police officer James Jenner was hot as fuck and worth a second or third look.

"JJ's got a bulge worth drooling over, but don't you miss the variety?" Sean asked me, and I about snorted my beer through my nose.

"Jesus, Sean." I laughed. "You have zero filter."

He grinned, his blue eyes twinkling.

"Someone needs their ass spanked," JJ stated, teasing in his tone even though he radiated dominant daddy in the moment. The stern alpha-ness turned my blood to lava and satisfied my cravings to be put in my place on occasion—including the marks he left behind.

Sean huffed. "I don't need a goddamned *daddy.*"

"So maybe just a sexy older man to tell you what a good boy you are? Assure you how much they adore your sassy ass and tight little hole?" JJ asked, and I bit my tongue to keep from laughing.

Sean blinked at him, his eyes shining with more than just lust at JJ's words.

"Hmm. That's what I thought." JJ cocked his head to the side, studying Sean's face with his detective intuition. "I do believe this naughty boy has a praise kink, gentlemen."

Sean sputtered, and laughing, I tugged my lover toward the dance floor, leaving the others to listen to his craziness.

We settled in beside Mason and Jasper, and I wrapped one arm around JJ's neck, the other hand still holding my beer.

"Looking good, kid," I said to Jasper, and he shot a fake glare at me.

"Not a *kid.*"

Oh, I knew that for a fact, but I'd picked up on the Boston use of that word for anyone younger than me. "Seriously though, I love your pink blouse. Looks great on you. And those heeled boot things on your feet? Fuck, you're brave." I shook my head. "I'd faceplant if I wore shoes like that."

Jasper flushed, and Mason leaned down to nuzzle his neck.

"You're beautiful," my friend murmured to his husband, and my heart warmed over their shared affection.

Turning back toward my man, I grinned. "So. You left Sean a panting puddle of need," I said, not jealous in the least. "Better be careful with him—he might steal up to the campground and try to weasel his way into our bed."

"That boy does nothing for me," JJ said, leaning in to plant his lips on mine for a hard kiss. "The little brat just needs some affirmation and a firm hand."

"Speaking of...those bruises you left on my ass cheeks last week are fading. Think you can give me some more tonight? That king-sized bed waiting for us in our room upstairs is attached to the wall and looks sturdy as fuck. I wouldn't mind being tossed around a little bit."

JJ grabbed hold of my backside, bringing his groin tight against mine as we moved with the slow, sensual song that had enticed a lot of couples onto the dance floor. "You have to know by now that I'll give you whatever the fuck you want, baby."

A shiver raised the hairs on my arms. Oh, I did. JJ's pleasure over making my day—and night—still amazed me.

"Choke me?" I whispered.

"Fuck yeah."

"Do I get to come first?" I teased, grinding my semi against his.

He groaned through gritted teeth. "Jesus fuck...are you trying to get me to take you right here where everyone can watch?"

Exhibition wasn't my thing, but I loved turning JJ on at inopportune times since he tended to lose his cool with me in the best way possible behind closed doors.

"So do I get to come first?" I repeated and thrust, loving how his dark eyes filled with adoration and lust.

JJ cupped my cheek softly, but the rest of him was hard against me. "Always with me, Kell—fucking love you, baby."

"Love you too," I murmured against his lips then sealed our mouths together.

THE END

262

About the Author

Spicy romance author Lynn Burke believes everyone deserves healing and a happily ever after. She loves writing hot, inclusive stories of various pairings or triplings and creates characters who will steal your heart.

She is a USA Today Bestselling author, a wrangler of her three spawn, and a farmer's daughter who grows organic food. To escape reality, she hides in a quiet corner with her nose in a book.

You can find more about Lynn at her website: www.authorlynnburke.com

Also By Lynn Burke

Abel's Obsession

Divulging Secrets

Healing Storms

In Between

Reluctant Lumberjack

Resisting his Mate

Billion Dollar Love Anthology

Blood Born Series

Bonds of Worship Series

Dark Leopards MC

Darkest Desires Series

Devil's Outlaws MC

Elite Escort Series

Elite Escorts MM Series

Fallen Gliders MC

Forbidden Obsession Duet

Found by Fate Series

Midnight Sun Series

Missing Link Series

Pippen Creek Series

Risso Family Series

Sandy Ridge Series

Sinful Nature Series

Vicious Vipers MC